Praise for Jo!

"This is writing and literature a
combined with maybe Cormac McCarthy and a bit of Edgar Allan
Poe tossed in" Bestebookreviews.blogspot.co.uk

"Beautifully written…compelling…literary fiction/tartan noir/ thriller/zany black comedy…Logan dances on a literary knife edge…blazing talent" Linda Gillard, author of *A Lifetime Burning*

"A gripping thriller…a brilliant creation… mystery and symbolic depth…compelling stuff…it has been wildly successful" *Northwords Now*

"An award-winning author weaves a striking, beautifully written tale of a car-crash survivor desperate to identify the driver, and the deadly forces standing in his way – a harrowing story of corruption, redemption, and intertwining destinies" Bookbub.com

"Wonderful characters who have haunted me throughout the reading, even to the point that one invaded my dreams" Goodreads.com

"A blistering, tough book, tempered with tenderness and mystery" Alan Warner, author of *The Stars In The Bright Sky*

"A thrilling page-turner, a quite extraordinary book…brilliant" Amazon.com

"The literary survival of author John A. A. Logan" *The Northern Times*

"New chapter for thriller man" *Highland News*

"City author's e-book breaks into Top 100" *The Inverness Courier*

"Bold" *Scotland On Sunday*

"New talent" *The Hindustan Times*

"Writerly prowess" *The Spectator*

"Logan writes in very original terms" *Scottish Studies Review*

Now available for the first time in paperback,
the award-winning ebook bestseller

200,000 downloads on Amazon Kindle

Special Award Winner in the
Best of the Independent Ebook Awards

Goodreads Book of the Month

Alliance of Independent Authors Book of the Month

The Survival Of
THOMAS FORD

Other books by John A. A. Logan

Storm Damage

Agency Woman

Starnegin's Camp

The Major

Rocks In The Head

The Survival Of THOMAS FORD

John A. A. Logan

Copyright © 2011 John A. A. Logan

WHITE BUTTERFLY PRESS

This edition printed 2015

The right of John A. A. Logan to be identified as the author of this work has been asserted by him in accordance with the Copyright, Designs and Patents Act, 1988.

This is a work of fiction. Names, characters, brands, media and incidents are either the product of the author's imagination or are used fictitiously. Any resemblance to real persons, living or dead, is purely coincidental.

This book is sold subject to the condition that it shall not, by way of trade or otherwise, be lent, resold, hired out, or otherwise circulated without the author's prior consent in any form of binding or cover other than that in which it is published and without a similar condition being imposed on the subsequent purchaser.

ISBN 978-1-5115271-4-9

Book design: Dean Fetzer, www.gunboss.com

With thanks to Deborah L. Logan, who helped in many ways to get this book ready for publication.

This book is dedicated to my Mother, Agnes Dench Logan.

Chapter One

There was an old road that had no name and very few people ever walked on it. Littered and abandoned at the sides of this road were many vehicles. Tractors with high, rusted metal, moulded seats. Vans that had been depended on to deliver fish or groceries. All left here now, to countless seasons of rain and snow. Frozen vehicles on an old road where no-one went any more. Birds would land on the metal surfaces, stand and sing, then fly off to somewhere more attractive. Sunlight would sparkle on chrome and steel, though there was nobody to see it. The weight of the vehicles, over decades, had compressed the earth below. Metal wheel rims had punctured rotted rubber tyres, then the wheel rims had shoved deeper and deeper into the beleaguered ground's surface.

And from that brown surface, it seemed now to Thomas as he stared, something old and unhappy with the situation could almost be seen to seep out of the earth's guts, like a barely visible gas emission. He assumed it was a trick of the light, or his own faulty and tired perception, but the air really did seem to shimmer just beside where the metal wheel rim broke the ground. Thomas sniffed and walked over to the wheel. He kneeled down and sniffed again, thinking if this really was some gas coming up from the earth he would smell it surely. But there was nothing to smell. He reached forward and positioned his hand hesitantly at the centre of the shimmering area. He felt a quick smile come to his mouth as the air danced coldly, just at the edge of his fingertips. At that moment he heard a whirring at his right ear, then a large white butterfly flew straight at Thomas' twitching fingers. The butterfly's wings kissed the side of Thomas' index finger. Its white form passed through the shimmering air, then lifted suddenly, gained height. Thomas looked up to follow it. It rose higher and higher above him, then he couldn't see it any more. He was staring up now at the bronze and copper leaves growing from the thick outreaching branch of a tree overhead.

"Thomas! Come on! I'm cold."

Thomas looked back at where he had seen the gas coming up from the earth. There was none there now. He bit his lip and stood up straight, taking a deep breath. He turned and jogged along the road's rough and broken surface, until he caught up with Lea and took her hand.

"What were you doing?" she said.

"I thought I saw something."

"What?"

"Nothing."

They drove back to the city on that car-packed road beside the water. Lea was quiet. Twice Thomas thought she had fallen asleep she was so quiet, but when he looked over her eyes were open, focused out the window, on the rippled water.

After the second time he looked over, when his eyes returned to the road, he saw the next corner closer than he had realised. He slowed down and went into the left turn, but he knew he wasn't quite in control, felt the car's weight shift to the right. Half-way through the turn Thomas saw, just ahead, a

The Survival of Thomas Ford

lorry and a car, abreast, filling the road. Thomas could see the young male faces above the car's red bonnet, understood instantly the gamble that driver had made, overtaking just before the bend. The nose of the car ahead was exactly even with the nose of the lorry's huge, broad truck bed. Again Thomas stared at the two male heads above the car's red bonnet. The driver had a bird-like hooked nose and something hawkish about his eyebrows. The passenger had a straight black fringe and the jaw of a heavyweight boxer. Thomas saw their heads float above their car's red bonnet like white eggs on a red dish and he thought *you've killed us.*

Thomas didn't have time to look at the lorry driver above the truck's thick grille. Instinct told Thomas there was no time for either himself or the bird-faced car driver to brake. There was nowhere for either car to go to Thomas' left, it was just a high embankment of thick trees there, tight to the road. Thomas couldn't believe he was doing it as he raised his left wrist sharply on the steering wheel. He turned into the lorry's path, accelerating, bursting through a short stone dyke with the Toyota's nose. Thomas heard Lea scream at the same moment the lorry struck the rear left wheel of the Toyota, turning the car's long dive towards the water below into a spinning and twisting which made Thomas' gut whirl. He had time to blink jerkily and open his mouth while the car fell. He meant to turn to Lea, look at her, but his neck was frozen. Instead, between each blink, Thomas saw the white butterfly again, its wings fluttering as it ascended. The car hit the water with a sound that had nothing wet about it. Weightlessness, like a sorcerer's spell, ended. Thomas only knew that the seat-belt had stopped his head being battered against the Toyota's roof. Thomas heard himself breathe out. He turned to look at Lea. She was staring at him, unseeing, eyes bloodshot, her hands shaking and darting around. Thomas saw she was trying to undo her seatbelt. He nodded and reached across, but her hands were in the way. He wanted to slap them out of the way, but there was some restraint stopping him. Then it seemed something enormous and merciless was sucking air out of the car. Thomas looked ahead, up, out the windscreen which was starred with the pattern of broken glass, but still intact. The windscreen was like a portal into the real world, a circle of sky and cloud and sunlight at the centre. But encroaching at the edges, the black water. Then the circle of sky vanished. Thomas felt the car sinking. All light was gone. He felt Lea's hand strike his face, heard her scream. He tried to lean toward her again, find the seatbelt release. Her hands again, flailing. He batted them out of the way. The car was sinking and twisting in the deep water, already several metres down by the time Thomas gave up on Lea's seatbelt, brought his hands back to the side of his own waist, easily found the seatbelt release there. Thomas heard the Toyota's frame screech with the pressure, then the windscreen burst in and Thomas could not tell how much of what hit his face was glass and how much was cold water.

The lorry had gone round the blind corner and travelled far along the next section of straight road before its driver could stop. He saw the red Volvo that had caused the crash flash past on the right and shoot ahead. The lorry driver had a clear view of the Volvo driver's profiled, bird-like nose and the passenger's square jaw. He stared at the rear window of the Volvo to see if their heads would turn and look back. They did not. The lorry driver tried to focus on their license plate and even said the number aloud to himself once, but it instantly vanished from his mind. He could feel the wash of

The Survival of Thomas Ford

fresh sweat across his back and hips. There was a dull heavy pain in his left arm and the temple by the side of his left eye. He thought to reach for his phone. The hand he raised towards it was shaking violently. He swallowed, checked the mirror. Nothing coming from behind. He opened the driver's side door, stepped down, the pain shifting from his arm to his chest now. He heard himself wheezing as he started to walk back in the direction of the corner, that car, the man and woman whose faces he had seen clearly as the car crossed his path and headed for the drop to the water.

"*Aaaa!*"

He heard himself make the sound, hadn't realised it was about to come out of him. He sucked in air twice and stopped walking. He remembered that he had left the phone in the lorry cab. He turned on the road, fell to one knee, hissed in air, slid to the rough tarmac unconscious already. A light rain came then, sprinkling gently on the road, the lorry, and the sprawled man who had been left behind to die here by the bird-faced Volvo driver.

Already far along the dampening road from the carnage he had left behind himself, the bird-faced driver of the red Volvo noted the new fall of rain, stretched a long arm forward, and flicked on his windscreen wipers. The black-haired, square-jawed passenger turned to stare at the driver's hawk-nosed profile. The driver's eyes were wide like an excited child's as he bit his lower lip.

"That was *mental*!" shouted the driver. "They're all fucked back there, man. Fucked!"

The passenger turned away and looked forward, into the new rain. He shook his head. In contrast to the vivacious eyes of the driver the passenger's eyes were solemn, almost numb.

"Did you see the woman, she wasn't bad eh?" said the driver.

"Do you think they'll get out alright?"

The driver sniffed, long and hard.

"Not a fucking chance, Robert. No after hitting the water from that height. Uh uh."

The passenger looked covertly at the speedometer. Jimmy was doing 80.

"Better slow down eh Jimmy? Don't want the cops stopping us after that."

Jimmy sniffed again, eased his foot up a few degrees. The rain was washing away at the leaves of the silver birches up on the right, stacked across the high embankment. Jimmy sat up stiff and straight suddenly in the seat, his lean frame quivering with tension.

"I am the *Gandolfini*! *I* am the Gandolfini!" he screamed. "Jesus! Did you see that? Fuck, that guy just drove right through the stone wall eh? That took nerve, man. He knew it was his only chance. Either hit us head on or try for the water. So he took the water. Fuck. He reacted fast or we'd be dead with him."

The square-jawed passenger flinched.

"Slow down a bit more before we get to the village eh Jimmy? I can't handle it if the cops stop us and get us for this, man."

"What do you mean, get us? You did fuck all!" Jimmy shouted as he stared ahead into the rain.

"No, Jimmy, they'd have me questioned for hours man, then Court, no, I'm no well enough for that."

Jimmy bared his teeth and shook his head. He was thinking of the hair and eyes on the head of that woman in the Toyota. He only needed to see a woman for a second to

The Survival of Thomas Ford

know if he liked her. He had liked that one. And now she was dead in the water. He let his foot raise off the throttle another few degrees. Ahead, the last corner before the village was coming up. Robert was right. They should do their best to be invisible for a while. He followed the slow banking left turn into the village, then indicated to turn right. Robert was surprised when Jimmy flicked the indicator.

"Where are we going?"

Jimmy said nothing. Robert turned to look at Jimmy's grinning profile. He knew the grin didn't signify anything in particular. It was the default expression for Jimmy's strange soul. A kind of primeval, skull-like repose for a restless spirit. A mask. Robert watched his friend's mask-face for a few more seconds. The Volvo was accelerating now, along a narrow road Robert had never been on before. He looked out the windscreen, past the working wipers and the drizzled glass. They were heading straight for the foot of the brooding hill of dark trees that overlooked the village and the water. It was high and incongruous, like some Rwandan rain forest, gorilla-rich, looming above. The car followed the road through a sharp turn near the edge of the hill. The rear wheels skidded, very slightly, as the Volvo came out of the turn. They drove along a little further until Robert saw a parking area and a sign saying Chalet Reception. Robert was surprised when Jimmy braked abruptly, flung an elbow up on the back of his seat, stared into the driver's mirror sharply, then spun his neck to look out the rear window. The Volvo started to reverse as though Jimmy intended to ram the chalet reception building. Then Robert saw that Jimmy was aiming the car for a rough track, just to the right of the reception building. The Volvo's rear wheels dug hard into the ground. Robert saw dirt spray up all around the car's boot. The nose of the Volvo dipped heavily as the car started to struggle its way up a steep rough track, overgrown with grass and vegetation.

Jimmy hooted and slapped the back of his seat, his mask-grin intent on the rear of the car as it attacked the steep hill. Robert looked ahead, at the chalet reception that grew smaller below them, then disappeared behind trees.

"Aye," said Jimmy. "Imagine going in the water like that, man. The falling. Jesus. Beautiful woman like that."

Jimmy sniffed.

"Hey," he said, "check it out, they've covered this hill with chalets. Well, they're spaced out, but they're all over the hill. One family owns the ones on the bottom half of the hill, another totally different one has the chalets on the top. But up this track, man, no-one comes here. Even if that lorry driver can describe us, like, no-one will look here."

The Volvo was labouring now, starting to fail. There was a turn to the left coming up, Robert could see it as he strained his neck to look behind. The engine screamed until Robert thought something in it would give right there. But then Jimmy was using a shallow bank at the track's edge, ploughing against it with the Volvo's rear end. It gave him enough room to turn round again, face the windscreen, throw the car into first gear. Jimmy's well-trained forearms swelled and popped below rolled-up shirt sleeves as he brutally screwed the steering column all the way to the right. Then he let the clutch out gently, slowly, and the Volvo just missed the track's opposite edge, made the turn and started to push its nose up this steep hill. Even in first gear it was a battle to drive the car on.

They started to pass abandoned vehicles that evidently had failed long ago to manage this climb. There was an ancient rusted tractor with a high seat that Robert stared out at. Then

The Survival of Thomas Ford

an old van, most of its bodywork rotted away and unrecognisable. The Volvo's engine was involved in that high, unnatural, terrifying metallic scream again, as though its soul and metal were being torn apart in a final rupturing surge of power. Another tractor came up on the right. Robert stared at it past Jimmy's grinning gargoyle profile. Robert didn't feel well enough for any of this. The rain was clearing up now and, just beside the tractor's rotted tyre, burst through by a rusted metal rim, Robert thought for a second he saw some kind of steam or gas rising up from the ground, just there, by the tractor's broken wheel as he stared. Then a clank came from the Volvo's engine, beneath the bonnet right in front of Robert. He stared ahead at the frightening, dead sound. It was followed by a whining screech from the engine. Jimmy hooted again, then jammed the brakes on. He pulled the handbrake up hard, turned the engine off. Suddenly they were sitting there, in silence, at an absurd tilted angle, like astronauts on a launch pad, waiting for countdown.

Jimmy flung his door open and got out. Robert fumbled with the handle on his side and stepped onto the steeply angled thick grass.

"We're the first car up here for years, Robert. Maybe the first vehicle to ever get this high up here without exploding eh?"

Robert stared over at Jimmy. From this angle Jimmy's face had that bird-like essence. Robert often looked at Jimmy and saw in the combed-up black hair and long nose the impression of something parrot or budgie-like. Now Jimmy was walking back down the rough hill, to the rear of the Volvo. He opened the back of the car and raised it. Robert stayed where he was until Jimmy's face popped round the edge of the car, grinning. Jimmy didn't speak, he just gestured with a flick of his head, for Robert to come down to him. Robert arrived beside Jimmy and looked into the back of the car at what Jimmy wanted to show him. It was a big pair of thigh-length leather boots, lying there, violent-looking five-inch heels coming to sharp dagger points. Robert looked at Jimmy. Jimmy just nodded at the boots, twice, not looking at Robert. Jimmy's eyes were screwed down to tiny slits of mirth, his white teeth gleamed in the refreshed sunlight that was following the short fall of rain. Robert looked back at the boots.

"Aye," said Jimmy, "they're Lorna's."

"Why's Lorna let you have them?"

"No man, she doesn't know I've got them. Sound boots eh?"

Jimmy reached into the back of the car, grabbed each boot by the thigh-end of the leather. He withdrew them from the car and dangled them like they were animals he had just caught. The toes and heels swung in the sunlight.

"Lorna's a big girl," said Robert.

"Aye."

Jimmy held out the boots to Robert.

"Want a shot?" said Jimmy.

"Eh?"

"You could lick them or put them on or something. I won't tell her."

Robert shook his head. Jimmy sniffed, put the boots back in the car, slammed down the rear door.

"Come on," Jimmy said.

He started walking up the rough track, past the Volvo. Robert wondered if he should try walking up here without his medication. He needed to get home, eat something,

The Survival of Thomas Ford

sleep, but he knew better than to suggest that to Jimmy yet. Robert imagined that man and woman in their car, falling through the air, hitting the water, sinking. He felt sick suddenly. But he started walking up the hill, fast, to catch up with Jimmy.

"Aye," said Jimmy, "no-one comes up here. My dad bought the two acres up here in 1988, well, his dad gave him the money. When I was a boy we lived up here, for two years, in an old fucked-up caravan. But it was alright man. My dad was going to build a house here for us, it just never worked out that way. But he put bricks under the caravan, all round the bottom, and he left a space there, and that's where our cats lived man, under there, under the caravan. Insulated us through the winter, a whole big gang of cats, breeding and purring under us."

Robert's heart was pounding with the effort to keep walking up the steep, rough ground. Now he was seeing Lorna, wearing those boots, her big feline face looking back at him from darkness. They turned another corner, passing the low ruins of an ancient building on the right. Robert could hear the rushing flow of some stream near-by. All around, the trees were thickly packed, high and silver. The huge hill of forest stretched up ahead of them, seemingly limitless.

"Aye," said Jimmy, "there's the caravan, see? A wreck now, like, but still here."

Through the trees Robert saw some white and blue form, in the rear of an area that had once been cleared and levelled. They walked past trees, over rough clumps of earth, then Jimmy reached out with a long-fingered hand. He touched the rotted aluminium shell of the caravan.

"Two years we lived in there," said Jimmy.

He spat on the grass and leaf-covered earth. Robert looked down, saw the bricks carefully laid beneath the caravan, and the gap there like Jimmy had said, for cats to go in and out. Jimmy sniffed.

"They might be looking for the Volvo," he said. "That lorry driver might have seen the license plate clear, or maybe not. But there's lots of red Volvos on the road eh?"

Robert looked at Jimmy, then back at the caravan.

"We better stay here tonight," said Jimmy.

"No Jimmy, I'm no well enough man."

"Not in the caravan," said Jimmy. "No, the car. We'll be alright. I've got some cans of Coke and Mars Bars and that. I'll get you home in the morning. No too early, but half eight or something, when folk are headed for work."

"I need my medication, Jimmy."

"Fuck, you'll last 'til morning."

Jimmy walked away, back towards the car. Robert felt hollow, very light, as he stood alone in the clearing by the wrecked caravan. None of it felt real. Not since that man and woman went into the water. The doctor had told Robert to avoid stress. Robert's mother had told him to avoid Jimmy. But it was boring, at the house, just watching TV or on the computer. Robert put his hands deep in his coat pockets, started walking down the hill behind Jimmy.

They sat together silently in the car, facing the wrong way, their backs to the stunning view of the water below. Robert chewed a Mars Bar and watched the surface of the loch, reflected in Jimmy's driver's mirror. He tried not to picture the blue car, the man and the woman who Jimmy said must be dead now at the bottom of the water. Jimmy sipped Coke and watched Robert out of an eye's sly edge.

The Survival of Thomas Ford

"Aye," said Jimmy, "there was a programme on about the loch the other day, on Freeview eh? You no see it? *The Loch Ness Monster and the Aliens* it was called. Going on about how Nessie might not be a dinosaur, but some creature left behind like, by aliens, to guard a space ship at the bottom of the loch eh? Maybe those two in the Toyota will get rescued by aliens like, at the bottom of the loch see? So no need to worry."

Jimmy gripped a Mars Bar in his hands, ripped the wrapper open, broke it in half, put the half in his mouth. Robert looked away from the mirror as Jimmy said, "Aye, or maybe the car just went right down Nessie's throat at the bottom of the fall eh? Maybe the cunts never even hit the water…just…*gulp!*"

Robert watched Jimmy's mouth open wide, the teeth and tongue all coated in Mars Bar nougat and chocolate. Then Jimmy snapped his jaws shut, chewed mightily once, swallowed. Robert looked away, out the windscreen. He sipped Coke.

Robert's eyes opened on absolute darkness. He heard his shivering breathing. He was cold. He clenched his thighs and buttocks tight, trying to calm himself. He did not understand where he was or why his body was tilted at an angle. Then he remembered he was in the car on the steep hillside, with Jimmy. He understood that he must have fallen asleep and now it was late, it was night.

"Jimmy?" said Robert.

But he had already known somehow that he was alone in the car. He heard a rustling from somewhere ahead, up the hill, in the trees maybe. His heart started to pump hard. The breath was thin in his throat now. Everything was utter blackness, the most complete darkness that Robert could remember experiencing. It must be the trees that were doing it. No starlight, no moonlight, no light reaching this hill track from the village at the car's back. Robert knew he was cut off from everything here, except Jimmy, but where was Jimmy? A twig or branch snapped loud, from ahead, up the hill. Jimmy must be out there. Now the real fear hit Robert, somewhere in the guts, a wave of chemical wizardry that cleared his brain in an instant. He reached out with his right hand, leaned over, fumbled with the console by the steering wheel, flicked a switch. He heard the windscreen wipers start up, making a dry, abrasive sweep of the glass. He flicked that switch back, felt to the left, found the headlight switch, pressed it up to full-beam.

The effect was instant and incredible. Unnatural white light flooded the rough hillside above the Volvo. There was Jimmy's black hair and eyes, his parrot features, ten metres up the hill from the car. Robert blinked. Jimmy did not react to the sudden bath of light. He just kept on doing the circular dance he had been doing. Perhaps he had entered some deep trance where he did not even know he was illuminated by the Volvo headlights.

Robert stared up the hill. Jimmy was entirely naked apart from the thigh-high leather boots that were just a little too big for him, he didn't have Lorna's breadth of thigh. Jimmy raised each booted leg alternately, as he danced. The long, thin heels dug holes in the rough hillside as each leg came down. Robert saw Jimmy's dart-like erection and looked away.

Just at that moment a white butterfly flashed through the air, half-way between the car headlights and Jimmy. Robert tried to follow it as it made its own dance through the air and light. It went up high, circled, dived at the grass, whirled and

The Survival of Thomas Ford

hovered, then flew directly at the Volvo's right headlight. The butterfly swerved just before the headlamp, veered up crazily, skimmed the bonnet and pressed itself to the windscreen, inches from Robert's staring eyes. It stayed there for a few heartbeats, wings splayed. Robert felt that it was watching him. Then it shifted, flew upwards and vanished.

Chapter Two

"I thought he was awake earlier. Just after rounds. He did that thing where his eyes opened, you know?"

"Aye."

"But I think he was just dry, so I gave him a suck on the lollipop. Then he was quiet."

"Can you reach over to the bin with this, Jill?"

Thomas Ford heard a loud crashing sound near his head.

"Thanks. Well, you can never be sure, Jill. It's the human body. Nothing is predictable."

Thomas Ford opened his eyes on bright light, closed them again. The pain. Deep in his eyes. He couldn't feel himself properly. Something disconnected.

"No, look, there's his hand twitching. He hasn't done it like that before."

Thomas Ford felt a presence at his side, a soap-smell.

"Thomas. Thomas, are you awake? Can you hear me?"

Thomas Ford tried to speak. Nothing happened. He stuck his tongue out and licked at his lips.

"See?"

"Aye. Keep talking to him. I'll get a doctor."

Thomas Ford learned that he'd been unconscious in the Intensive Therapy Unit for six weeks and four days. The first few days he had done no breathing for himself, only the

The Survival of Thomas Ford

ventilator kept him alive. Dr Lennox told him that he'd started breathing on the morning of the fifth day, just before they would have had to send him to surgery for a tracheostomy, a tube from the ventilator into his neck, to replace the tube that had gone down his throat. Then there had been the problem of Thomas not waking up, not for six weeks, but he was awake now as Dr Lennox tested Thomas' reflexes, asked him questions which Thomas could nod or shake his head to.

"Do you remember the accident Thomas? Would you rather I call you Mr Ford? Or Tom? Or is Thomas fine? Thomas? Alright then. Do you remember the accident Thomas?"

There was a nurse standing at the other side of the bed and Thomas felt her eyes on him. He looked up at her. She smiled. It was a warm expression, involving her eyes and mouth and cheeks. Her cheeks seemed to perk and redden with the smile. Thomas swallowed and looked back at the doctor. He blinked again and saw the windscreen shattered like a coating of frost. Thomas already knew that Lea must be dead or she would be here, or at least they would have told him she was alright. He was trying to remember what had happened after the windscreen shattered and the cold water had come in. But his memory was frozen, as though by the water itself. He had no idea why he was alive here, how he had survived if Lea had not. Thomas opened his mouth wide, meaning to speak. He shook his head. With the doctor and the nurse staring at him, Thomas felt the hot tears come out of his eyes, pressure shoving them out and now they wouldn't stop. He felt the doctor's hand on his shoulder.

"It's alright Thomas."

The heavy metal clang near his head woke him up. It was the bin. His bed was beside the bin and the nurses would lift the lid, drop something in, and then let the lid go so it landed hard and woke Thomas regularly through the night. Night and day were indistinguishable under the fluorescent lighting in the ITU. No, it was night. The young red-haired man was on duty and he would sit on a high chair and read sometimes at night. Thomas had tried to read the cover of the book, the title, but it was too far away or else his eyesight had gone. It was night and he was alive and Lea was dead and none of them would ask outright how she had died and he had lived. He knew that it was perhaps the seatbelt. She had not undone her belt. She had slapped his hands away when he had tried to lean over and undo it for her. Then he had sat back, like a stupid bastard thinking he had all the time in the world, and he had undone his own belt just as the water had rushed in to prove that there was no time left at all. No time for Lea anyway.

When the doctor finally told Thomas formally that Lea was dead, the doctor seemed uneasy as Thomas only stared back, saying nothing, showing nothing.

The next morning the police arrived with questions. Thomas was surprised that Lea's parents had not come here to ask him any. Surely they must have wanted to. Someone must have stopped them. Maybe the police had the right to ask questions first.

"I don't remember leaving the car," said Thomas. "I wouldn't have left her."

"Do you remember what happened just before the accident, Mr Ford?"

It was a detective in a tweed jacket, about forty. There was a younger woman in her thirties, watching and listening carefully.

The Survival of Thomas Ford

"We were coming back from Drumnadrochit. I'd taken Lea to show her this old, abandoned track on the hill there, at Ardlarich. We turned the corner and there was a lorry there, and right beside it a car that was overtaking the lorry. The road was full. I could see the car was too far up to slow in time and get behind the lorry. There was nowhere to go. Except off the road. I steered to the right hard and accelerated and took us off the road."

"Into the loch."

"Aye."

"And that would have been some drop first, before you hit the water?"

"Aye."

"Then you were in the water."

Thomas nodded. The woman was staring at him. Just doing her job, he told himself.

"We didn't sink right away. I could see the sky through the windscreen. Lea, she was panicking. I tried to help her undo her seatbelt but she slapped my hands away."

"She slapped you?"

"My hands. She didn't mean to. She was terrified."

The hot sensation was in Thomas' stomach. His lungs and shoulders felt hot now too, itchy. Like some poisonous plant was stinging him there. Thomas swallowed and shook his head. He looked down.

"Mr Ford," he heard the woman say.

Thomas looked up at her blue eyes.

"What colour was the car, Mr Ford?"

That's right. The colour of the car. Thomas had never thought of that. He remembered the car, the two heads above the bonnet.

"The bonnet was red," said Thomas. "The man in the passenger seat was young, his face sort of square. The driver had black hair I think. The car was red. I can't remember what colour the lorry was."

The man was writing furiously in a black notebook.

"That's alright Mr Ford. We know the lorry colour," said the woman.

The man sniffed and cleared his throat. The woman shifted suddenly, some odd flinch. The man said, "Mr Ford, the fact of the matter is that the lorry driver died at the scene. He had a heart attack and fell by the roadside and died before anyone could reach him with assistance. Now, the problem that this creates for us, and in a way for your late wife's family who have an awful lot of unanswered questions they want us to pursue with you, the problem now is that your account of the accident, the presence of this red car and two occupants, this is uncorroborated."

Thomas leaned back in the bed, stared at the high white ceiling.

"It's not that we in any way doubt your word, Mr Ford. It's just a technical problem, with accounts and evidence. This sort of thing happens with us all the time."

"I don't trust my own memory," said Thomas Ford. "It just seems like a dream. The red car bonnet and the two heads. I only saw them for a second, then we were falling to the water. The head in the passenger seat was sort of square, like a boxer, young. The driver was young too, very black hair and black eyes. Sort of like a bird."

"What Mr Ford?"

It is the woman speaking. Thomas Ford looks at her eyes again.

The Survival of Thomas Ford

"That's what I see when I remember him, a black-eyed guy looking like a bird, driving a red car. It would probably be better if I hadn't told you. It sounds crazy."

"No, Mr Ford," said the man. "Any detail might be important."

Chapter Three

Jimmy was in his bedroom, on his knees in front of the large round mirror above the chest of drawers that had been his grandmother's. He had a smaller mirror in his raised left hand. He was using the smaller mirror to get a view of his profile in the large mirror. There it was. The hooked nose, the birdlike eyebrows, even the texture of his black hair, as though there was something featherlike in its weave. Tears stung Jimmy's eyes as he faced the facts again. Some kind of surgery might be possible, he knew that.

He put the mirror down and walked across to his bed in the room's corner. On the wall, beside his pillow, Jimmy had taped the newspaper article with the colour picture of the woman from the car that had gone into the loch.

Mrs Lea Ford, 35. The article told about how she had been a local chiropractor. Jimmy didn't know what that was. But then the article said that she had recently stopped doing that, to open a small art gallery in the city, concentrating on international folk art. Jimmy had been astonished at this, because not long before the day of the crash he had found himself drawn in off the street, into that gallery, where he had walked around fascinated for an hour by the carvings and statues and paintings on sale there. He had even tried to tell his mother later, about the rough and violent works he'd been looking at, in what used to be a record shop on the corner of a busy street.

The Survival of Thomas Ford

Jimmy lay on his bed and stared up at the woman's luscious brown hair, her green eyes. After six weeks of lying there, ritually absorbed in worship of the dead woman from the car, Jimmy was surprised to still feel the tingle in him. He was just about to undo the button on his jeans and pay tribute to her once again, when he heard his mother's voice call up the stairs, "Jimmy! Robert's here for you."

Jimmy sighed and shook his head. He punched the wall, just beside Mrs Ford's lush hairdo. He heard Robert's heavy, monotonous tread on the old stairs. Jimmy whistled and sat up suddenly on the bed, spinning his hips so he faced the door as Robert's steps stopped. Three polite taps on the wooden door.

"Jimmy, it's Robert."

Jimmy shook his head.

"Come in!" he shouted.

Robert's large frame and square, worried face appeared in the doorway. Robert focused on Jimmy's hard stare, the black eyes, then he looked up, over Jimmy's shoulder, at the newspaper clipping stuck to the wall, the resplendent colour photo of Mrs Lea Ford, gallery owner.

"Jimmy, man, should you no take that down now eh?"

Jimmy sniffed and got up from the bed explosively. He walked over to the window and leaned against the wall. He stared out over the fields at the back of the house.

"It was on the news tonight, Jimmy. That man's woken up in the hospital. Thomas Ford. It said the police had gotten information from him about the crash. It didn't say, Jimmy, but do you think he'll have seen us and the car and described it like? Or did it happen too fast maybe eh?"

Jimmy whistled. He was watching a young rabbit that had just got the courage up to step out of the hedge at the roadside of the field. It was looking all round itself.

"Jimmy, what if he got a really good look at us though? If you see folk, even for a second, you can get a picture of them that sticks in your head for your whole life. He could identify us."

"Maybe."

"You said that wouldn't happen though, Jimmy, you said he'd never wake up. I'm frightened Jimmy. I nearly told my mum last night."

Jimmy blinked and looked away from the rabbit. He walked over to Robert, grinning widely.

"Come on, that man will no remember us. No way! Anyway, if he did, so what? It was just an accident. We overtook at a corner, we didn't stop at the scene of the accident. So what?"

"No, Jimmy, it would be death by reckless driving, and I'm an accessory."

Jimmy laughed.

"Fucking right you're an accessory. You're a fucking tool, so you are. Come on, let's go for a drive."

The red Volvo shoved its headlighted nose through the early evening country lanes leading away from Jimmy's parents' big house.

"Aye," said Jimmy, "we'd better not be out too late man. My dad was cracking up at me for no doing enough work lately. He's starting a new build tomorrow, for some cardiologist, got some architect up from London to design an eco-friendly thing for the side of a hill. My dad says it's going to be some sight from the road. I might as well turn up tomorrow, give a hand. You fancy a day's work Robert?"

"No, Jimmy, my medication isn't working right just now. I have to be careful not to exert myself."

The Survival of Thomas Ford

Jimmy whistled through his teeth, slapped the steering wheel.

"A day's work would probably sort you out fine man," said Jimmy.

Robert blinked, staring directly forward. At the edge of the headlight's beam, on the moor, a deer was illuminated for a moment, its head and antlers and shoulders, then the moor was empty space again, just a border for the Volvo to plough a course through.

"See that?" said Jimmy. "That's dangerous eh? You need a four-by-four like my dad's for out here man. Otherwise one of those things is going to walk in front one night and we'll be written off along with the beast eh?"

Jimmy turned his head to stare at Robert hard.

In the town that was growing faster every year now, desperate to become a real city, they parked on the steep incline down from the castle, behind three Taxis. Jimmy reached into his jacket pocket and took out two Mars Bars. He passed one to Robert and began to unwrap his own. The big grin was on Jimmy's face now, Robert saw, the mask-face that Jimmy always wore in public. Jimmy was leering out of the windscreen, at girls passing on the High Street below, tight-skirted and high-booted.

"Check that out eh?" said Jimmy. "Fuck's sake man. They'll all be going to G's tonight eh? Do you fancy heading there?"

"Can't afford it."

"I'll pay you in. You could work tomorrow eh, pay me back see?"

Robert sniffed, bit into his bar.

"Mrs Lea Ford," said Jimmy. "Dead woman. See how the paper said she had that gallery place? I went in there one day man, some great stuff, from all over the world like. Carvings, statues. Really old things, it looked like."

Robert felt sick. He had forgotten about the woman temporarily. Now the Mars Bar was paste in his mouth. His saliva was gone from fear. He knew he couldn't cope with prison for being an accessory, if that is what they would do with him when they found out. No, he couldn't even cope with a day's work for Jimmy's dad. Robert felt the sting of resentment at Jimmy, for involving him in it all.

"We could go round and visit Lorna eh? See what she's up to," said Jimmy.

Last time Robert had gone there with Jimmy, Jimmy and Lorna had vanished instantly into her bedroom. Robert had been left alone in front of the TV for three hours, hearing sounds coming from the bedroom.

"How about McDonald's?" said Robert. "I wouldn't mind a tea."

They sat at a table by the window. Robert knew that anyone passing was going to notice Jimmy's big grinning birdlike head, right at the glass. He watched passing tourists and drunks. Many of them did a long stare and gazed back at Jimmy as they passed the window. Robert sipped tea and looked around at the other people under the glaring fluorescent lights.

"Fucking Poles everywhere here now," said Jimmy in a low voice. "When I went up to order the tea man, all Poles working here now. Same at my dad's sites, half of them Poles now. What's going on eh?"

Robert had noticed the Poles too. They stood out. If you ordered coffee from one they talked and smiled. Robert had always assumed the people in the town cafes were finding

The Survival of Thomas Ford

him personally objectionable, the way they were miserable when you ordered a drink. Now he realised it hadn't been him necessarily. The new Poles had brought a level of politeness to the town/city or whatever this place was. Same thing when Robert had gone to the dentist's and the Polish dental nurse who collected him from reception had made conversation. The locals had never bothered. Mind you, it had been disconcerting, being expected to make conversation on the way to the dental chair.

"Some of their birds are no bad though," said Jimmy. "I'll give them that."

Jimmy made a face like he was a dog, then he worked his jaws like a bulldog or a Doberman, biting. Robert nodded back politely. Then Jimmy's eyes flitted up over Robert's shoulder. He had spotted something. Probably a woman. Robert didn't bother turning to make sure.

Now Jimmy was laughing and shaking his head. He was staring down at the plastic table's surface.

"What these people don't understand, Robert, is that civilisation is only an idea."

Jimmy looked up quickly at Robert. Robert blinked, but held Jimmy's gaze.

"No," said Jimmy. "It's not even an idea. It's just a fucking word."

Jimmy sniffed

"Anyway," he said, "this man Thomas Ford won't remember us. He won't remember you. He won't remember me. He won't even remember the wife maybe, or who he used to be before he got fucked up in the loch. He'll be in trauma, man. Post-trauma like Stallone in that film where he's back from Viet Nam. Flashbacks and that. Well, trauma and flashbacks are no use in court, son. Thomas Ford eh? Who the fuck do you think he is eh? The fucking bogey man? He's just some posh nonce with a sexy wife who had a wee accident. Thomas Ford's no going to hurt you and he's no going to hurt me, I'll fucking guarantee you that."

Robert wasn't so sure. He felt an area of his heart turn cold as he looked at Jimmy's dark eyes. Then, for some reason, the memory of the white butterfly came into Robert's mind, the image of it on the windscreen, looking in at him through the glass. Something flexed and tensed in Robert's brain, near the back of the skull, and for a moment he felt himself stretched out too tightly, caught between Jimmy's gaze and the butterfly's gaze, understanding neither.

Chapter Four

Thomas Ford was sitting up in the hospital bed.

"I missed her funeral. I've missed two months of my life. I'm not missing any more," he said.

"It's a miracle you survived at all, Thomas," said Finlay. "You've just got to take things slowly for now."

Thomas snorted.

"No," he said. "There's no point to this. I'm going to get out today."

"Come on, man, you're not even steady enough to walk to the toilet alone yet. Give it a few more days."

"The police don't believe me Finlay, you know that? Questions, questions. You know what it is. It's Alan and Jean, telling them that Lea was wanting to leave me. That detective they keep sending in here, McPherson, he just stares at me and asks these shitey questions, nipping and nipping away, with the female cop sitting watching me too, and all they're thinking is the one thing they never say. They're sure I drove that car into the loch on purpose. Eh? Like some final solution to marital breakdown. Fuck."

Finlay frowned.

"You know, that cop McPherson was at the funeral, Tom. The woman was there too."

Thomas stared over at Finlay, surprised.

"They've been talking a lot to Alan and Jean right enough," said Finlay.

"Aye," said Thomas. "I bet Alan and Jean have been talking to a lot of folk."

"They're destroyed by it, Tom. And you've got to give them credit, they've not breathed a word about anything being wrong with you and Lea, to the papers or the TV."

Thomas sat up straighter in the bed. There was that dull pain deep in his side, behind the ribs. He felt sleepy suddenly, like a wave of soporific fog had just rolled in on him, from some humid ocean he had no name for. Finlay smiled.

"Right, Tom. I'm off for now. You're no going anywhere today lad. Just lie back there awhile. I'll come back in tomorrow."

Thomas nodded and closed his eyes. He let his weight back down towards the pillow. He breathed out. In again. Soon, there was the red car bonnet just in front of him. Above it, the two heads, so familiar now. That dark-eyed bird-boy. Beside him the square-jawed passenger. Thomas swallowed as the car left the road. He heard Lea scream. Then the shock of the car striking the loch's surface, that shock seemed worse now than the first time it happened. The impact travelled up Thomas' spine, all down his nerves, to his eyes, the edges of his brain. Looking up now, out the windscreen, at the blue and grey sky. Turning to Lea, trying to help her get her seatbelt unfastened. But she is scratching at his hands, striking his hands with her own hands. He tries to shout at her to stop it, let him help, but his mouth is frozen, numb. Then the car dips in the water, the windscreen glass implodes. In the last instant of sunlight before everything becomes freezing blackness, Thomas stares at Lea as her eyes stare ahead, blind with terror. The terror had killed her just as surely as any of the rest of it.

The Survival of Thomas Ford

"Suzy?"

"Hi Thomas. Here's some apple juice, ok? I'll put it down here on the table by your arm. You've slept a lot today. That's a good sign."

She was gone already, off to take some other invalid their sustenance. Now it was Thomas' back that hurt most, probably just from being laid on so much. He looked over at the apple juice. The colour was nice, a nut brown. But he was asleep again, his eyes were staring at the liquid one moment, then he was asleep the next, air getting breathed out of himself in a long deflating sigh that seemed to be absorbed by the thin, starched pillow material.

His eyes opened and Lea was sitting on the plastic visitor's chair at the side of his bed. She was sitting very upright, her shoulders drawn back as though consciously. She saw Thomas wake and she smiled.

"I've been watching you sleep," she said.

"Lea?"

But he knew it was not her, not exactly. This was Lea from about two years earlier, before the troubles and arguments had begun. As she looked at him there was no shadow in her eyes, nothing withheld.

"Lea, I couldn't undo your seatbelt. You kept knocking my hands away. You were terrified. I couldn't calm you. I was terrified too. There was no time."

She doesn't speak. She nods. Thomas hears a familiar extended creaking sound. He knows it is the bin attached to the wall.

The bin lid is allowed to crash hard, dropped by a busy hand. Thomas' eyes snap wide open. He breathes deep. He lets his eyes swivel to the right without moving his head. It's Lorna, the cleaner.

"Sorry Thomas. I didn't mean to let it drop that time. It's a bad habit. Not much peace in this place."

Thomas tried to smile.

"I was dreaming," he said. "Just dreaming."

"A nice dream?"

Thomas nodded. The girl raised her eyebrows conspiratorially, then turned away, headed to the next bed area. Thomas watched her back, her legs, then let his eyes focus up toward the high ceiling. He tried to see Lea there, but he couldn't.

Chapter Five

Jimmy's father accelerated the Subaru along the narrow track that led from the house to the main road.

"I want a proper day's work out of you, Jimmy, for a change."

Jimmy stared both ways at the road end. His father looked at him quickly and Jimmy nodded that it was safe to move out. His father couldn't see for himself to the left, not with the heavy pine foliage there. Jimmy always enjoyed that moment when his father had to trust him. He knew something twisted in his father's gut at such times. Occasionally it would happen at work too. Maybe when they were on a roof together and Jimmy had to take the weight of something they were both carrying while his father was standing at an awkward, vulnerable angle. At times like that, Jimmy and his father both knew what could happen, in a moment. The father's trust in his son was more out of convention than conviction. Long ago, Jimmy's father had understood that something was very wrong with Jimmy, but understanding had to wage a daily battle against parental hope.

"I'm serious Jimmy. No pissing off at dinner time and not coming back on-site. It's a fucking embarrassment, these Polish lads breaking their backs every day and then they see you treat your own father like that."

Jimmy sneered out his passenger window. He shook his head.

"What are you shaking your head at? Eh?"

His father had him rolling a wheelbarrow all morning, guiding it carefully along narrow planks of wood set up high over the mudded earth. He was taking bricks for the Poles to lay. The Poles just ignored him. Jimmy didn't mind the work. It was a good shoulder workout. He had his tight yellow vest on and he knew the fine striations in his arms would be dancing and twitching under the dull sky as he worked. That's what Robert didn't appreciate. A good day's work would pump some of that medicine shite out of his system. He would feel better. One of the Poles was grinning at Jimmy and saying something.

"Eh?" said Jimmy.

The Pole was waving his hands in the air and staring at Jimmy. Jimmy shook his head and grinned back. He looked all around the group of men laying the brick foundation for this cardiologist's new house.

"What's he on about eh?" said Jimmy.

Most of the men didn't look up. A couple looked at the gesticulating Pole and shrugged. Jimmy laughed loud.

"What you don't know son," he said to the Pole very slowly and loudly, "is that I am the Gandolfini son! You didn't know that, did you? *I am the Gandolfini!*"

Jimmy tipped the last bricks from the wheelbarrow, near the Pole's toes. Three of the bricks chipped as they fell and knocked against each other, ruined. The Pole stopped gesticulating and stared at the broken objects. Jimmy waited for the man to look back at him, then he grinned wide, nodded savagely, ploughed the wheelbarrow hard through the mud, swerved it, and headed back to get more bricks.

The Survival of Thomas Ford

At that precise second, Robert was lying in his bed at his mother's house, staring up at the ceiling. His head didn't feel right, there was a fuzziness. He closed his eyes and concentrated on the fuzziness. He held his breath. But the fuzziness didn't clear, if anything it seemed to intensify. There had been no fuzziness beside the loch that day as Jimmy had brought the red Volvo up alongside the lorry, overtaking just before the blind corner. Then Robert had seen the car appear ahead, the faces behind a windscreen. He had known that one face was a man, and the other a woman, but he knew he hadn't taken a perfect photograph of the scene with his mind, not like Jimmy had done. Robert didn't see why Jimmy had needed to take the picture of the woman from the newspaper and tape it to the wall above his pillow; Robert knew from experience the perfect instrument that Jimmy's memory and imagination could be. He wondered if Jimmy hadn't been trying to dare the universe, or his mum, to take note of the audacity and arrogance represented by the taping of the dead woman's picture to the wall. But few people, or even cosmic forces, challenged Jimmy. It worried Robert, how much Jimmy got away with. Only Jimmy's dad seemed to try to get control of him, and then only on occasions.

Robert laid quietly on the bed and tried to open his nerve-ends, lay them bare to the cosmos. He thought it might be possible for him to sense whether or not he was safe. That is, whether or not some organ or machine of the universe had been set into motion, against Jimmy, because of the woman's death, and therefore against Robert too, as Jimmy's accomplice and ally. Robert believed that it was sometimes possible for the universe to overlook certain misdeeds, even serious ones. He had believed from an early age that the universe made errors, usually errors of omission. He believed, in fact, that Jimmy's very existence was evidence of such an error.

If Jimmy was a vacuum, then Robert had been sucked in.

If Jimmy was fly-paper then Robert was stuck and wriggling hopelessly.

It was just a fact.

On the other side of the city, Lorna was arriving home from her cleaning job at the hospital. She had been too tired to bother with any shopping on the way back. She looked at the date on the bread and frowned. She pulled the first slice out of the packet. It looked alright. The second one had some mould at the edge. She picked the mould off and put the two slices of bread under the grill.

Her eyes were almost closing in front of the TV, as she chewed the cheese on toast. Someone had told her once not to eat the bread when there was any visible mould because there would be other invisible mould inside the bread that would make her ill. Lorna didn't believe it, but she felt a burning sensation in her gut as she ate the toast. She put the plate down and walked out of the living room.

The first thing she saw in her bedroom was her pair of thigh-high leather boots. They were lying on her pillow, carefully positioned, entwined together like lovers, the heels poking out at erect angles.

That bastard Jimmy. She couldn't believe it. The boots had vanished weeks ago. He had denied any knowledge of them and Lorna had known he was lying. Now he had been in the flat during the night, to do this, while she was at the hospital. She'd started a twelve hour shift at 1am because the hospital wanted to get a clean status certificate from the

The Survival of Thomas Ford

government at the next inspection and all wards and theatres were being almost dismantled to scour them. She looked around the bedroom, feeling unsafe at the thought of Jimmy having been here like this.

Tired as she was, Lorna went through every corner and cupboard in the small flat. She looked under the bed, behind every chair. She even found herself, insanely, opening the washing machine door for a moment, gazing in.

Only when she was sure that Jimmy was not hiding somewhere in her home, did Lorna check the snib Yale lock was on, then go to sleep.

Jimmy, of course, was not hiding in Lorna's home. He was three miles away, bringing back a hugely overloaded barrow of bricks for this new, mad Pole guy. His hands were shaking with the weight of the load. Twice, he almost spilled it all in the mud, as he had to manoeuvre a corner. But now he was safely headed towards the gang of bricklayers at the far edge of what would be this fancy doctor's house one day. Jimmy pretended to stumble at the last moment. He lunged the barrow forward and the bricks fell and scattered. Two of the bricks bounced and cracked, then continued on before hitting the man who had been gesticulating at Jimmy. One brick hit his ankle. The other hit his hand. The man rose up immediately, screaming, again in Polish.

Jimmy adopted his largest grin. He pivoted his neck, side to side, and made an audience of the other bricklayers. He shrugged his shoulders, consciously flexing his muscles as he did so, as though asking the gang of men to support him in this ridiculous matter. For a moment the men were a frozen unit, staring back at him. They did not look supportive. Then the men moved, again as a unit. They surrounded the injured man, inspecting him, comforting him, and holding him back as he shifted abruptly in Jimmy's direction.

"Aw, come on eh?" said Jimmy. "Fuck's sake eh? Accidents happen."

The men were all speaking in loud Polish as Jimmy's black eyes sparkled at them. Some of the men were strenuously reminding some of the other men that this was their boss' son.

"What are you?" shouted one of the bricklayers. "Fucking mental boy?"

"He did it deliberately," another man shouted.

Jimmy watched their eyes as though they were all one huge eye now, staring at him. The man with the bleeding wrist jerked his shoulder and freed it from a restraining hand. He limped and lurched across the mud toward Jimmy. Jimmy raised a hand.

"Hey now son. You shouldn't be walking on that ankle eh? Industrial accident eh? My dad will get you up to Casualty to have it looked at, then you can fuck off back to Pole-land and stop draining our economy eh? Cunt."

The injured man swung a punch at Jimmy's head. Jimmy sidestepped it, then drove his boot hard against the man's damaged ankle. A definite cracking sound filled the air. The Polish man screamed and fell in the mud as his leg buckled. Five of the bricklayers moved quickly toward Jimmy as though they were one man. Jimmy hooted and stamped in the mud. He lowered himself into a horse kung fu stance he had learned from a library book. He was thinking what a fucking brilliant day this was turning out to be after all. He had the first Pole's chest targeted for a thumping jump-kick that would send the guy back into his gang of mates like a bowling ball. But then Jimmy heard a few splashes in the mud at his

The Survival of Thomas Ford

back, very rapid. He knew before he felt the arm round his neck that it was his dad. Jimmy's dad nearly broke Jimmy's neck with a violent twist that brought Jimmy's face down six feet and into the mud. He was breathing and eating mud. The feel of his father's forearm round his neck, crushing, was horrible. Jimmy could feel his father's sweat and individual manky hairs. Jimmy's head raised for a moment out of the mud and he heard his father's shouting voice and the bricklayers' shouting voices. There was mud in Jimmy's ears so he couldn't make out the words. Then his father rammed Jimmy's whole head down into the mud again. Jimmy kicked and bucked and screamed into the mud. He tried to grab his father but he couldn't reach and he was weakening. When he stopped trying to scream he suddenly felt the panic of being empty now, of air.

Jimmy's father kept his son's head in the mud for a long time. The man with the injured ankle and hand watched silently from where he lay. The gang of bricklayers went through their phase of shouting and gesticulating at Jimmy's dad as he nodded back at them, the veins in his forehead and neck swollen with the effort to control Jimmy. The bricklayers stopped shouting and became silent under the mild sunshine, as they saw that their boss was not raising his son's head out of the mud. Gradually the situation's meaning inverted, until the Poles, even the injured man, only wanted to see their boss lift the boy's strange parrot-like face out of the mud. They felt the beginning of a killing happening here, on the afternoon site, and they didn't want to be any part of a killing in this new country. Jimmy's arms and legs stopped twitching. His chest heaved high once, nearly bringing his head up into the air. But the father kept the son's head down in the mud.

Some of the watching bricklayers had said silent prayers. Some of them had felt a galvanising impulse to walk forward and get the father off the son. None of them moved. It was Jimmy's father's black eyes that stopped them. The same eyes as the son, burning like twin coals beneath the father's head of thick white hair.

Suddenly the father released his grip. He grabbed his son's shoulders and spun the boy's body. Jimmy's dead weight landed with a slick splash, on its back in the mud. His father stood up and looked down at him. Jimmy's face was covered in thick, dirty mud. His nose and mouth were gummed up and blocked with the stuff. Jimmy's father raised a boot high, stamped down on Jimmy's gut. The boy didn't move or make a sound. His father stamped again. Nothing. On the third stamp the boy's body genuflected into an involuntary sit-up. Jimmy vomited a thread of mud and mucus. He fell back to the earth, his body racked with spasmic coughs. One cough a second came out of Jimmy, each one seeming to rip his body apart.

Jimmy's father reached in a pocket, found the Subaru keys. He tossed them to a big, fair-haired man.

"Get him in the Subaru, in the back. I'll drive him up to Casualty. He'll be alright."

Three of the bricklayers started to walk towards Jimmy.

"Not him!" shouted Jimmy's dad.

He shook his head and pointed at the man sitting up in the mud, with the bleeding hand and damaged ankle.

"Your man!" shouted Jimmy's dad. "Him! Get him in the Subaru. In the back. Get a move on! We're losing daylight here. The rest of you get back to work! I want to see half that foundation laid by the time I get back here!"

Jimmy hacked out another cough and rolled onto his side in the mud.

Chapter Six

Lorna was woken out of a deep sleep by violent knocking at her door. She reached up to the bedside drawers and grabbed the pair of dirty foam earplugs. Automatically, she inserted them. Her eyes closed again, but the knocking got louder and broke through. She sighed and shook her head.

At the door, it was Jimmy. He was filthy, covered in thick, caked, dried-in mud it seemed. She was about to shut the door when she saw his eyes staring through the muck.

"Jimmy. I was asleep."

"I'm going to fucking kill him!" said Jimmy, in a sobbing, low voice.

Lorna saw the tears streaming from his eyes. There was snot coming from one nostril in a steady flow. The other nostril was plugged up with dried earth.

"Jimmy, how can I let you in like that eh? You'll ruin my place!"

He stood and stared at her.

"Wait then, until I put newspaper down. You can walk on that to the shower, right? Promise you'll no go in the living room or bedroom like that eh?"

The mudded head nodded.

In her bed, he was clean and seemed light as air as she held his face to her breast, her arm round his neck.

"Your dad shouldn't have done that to you, Jimmy. No matter what. I told you you shouldn't be working together. It's dangerous the way you two are. You shouldn't be living with him either."

"Can I stay here with you then?"

Lorna was stiff, silent for moments. Jimmy sniffed.

"I'm just saying, one of you's going to kill the other eh?" she said.

She felt Jimmy's nose nod against her breast. She could smell the shampoo in his thick, black hair. She kissed his hair, at the crown of his head, and reached around his waist until her fingertips grazed his bottom lightly.

"My guts hurt where my dad stamped on me," said Jimmy.

"He stamped on you? Christ Jimmy."

Lorna felt his arms lift until he had her breasts cupped in his palms.

"Going to wear the boots, Lorna? Put them on eh?"

Lorna shook her head, pulled at Jimmy's arse until he was inside her.

When Lorna woke, the room was in full black darkness. She remembered that Jimmy was there before she heard his breathing or felt his skin against her side. She blinked, then somehow knew beyond doubt that Jimmy was awake. It was as though his mind was sending out some faint, buzzing, restless signal. And the next thing she knew was that Jimmy was sensing her wakefulness too. It frightened her, the speed of these unspoken transmissions that could pass between them, especially after sex.

"I was thinking about atoms," she heard his voice say, and it was as if he addressed, not her, but the darkness itself. As

The Survival of Thomas Ford

though to Jimmy the last thing the darkness could ever be was unpopulated empty space.

"There's more atoms in a glass of water than there are glasses of water in all the oceans of the world, did you know that?" he said.

Lorna sniffed.

"BBC4?" she said.

"Aye. This bald guy was going on about it. It was interesting though. About how Einstein and all the scientists on Einstein's side, they really hated this later wave of scientists, what the later wave of them believed about atoms. But it was this later wave that started the science that led to the atomic bomb. *Pwoooooosssshhhhhhh*. You know, Hiroshima, Nagasaki."

"Aye."

"It's all war eh?" said Jimmy. "The scientists hating the other scientists. The bombs being dropped. Oh, and this bald guy was saying about how the main guy in the new wave of scientists had been on a week's holiday, holed up in a hotel room with an ex-girlfriend, shagging, and it was then that he had the ideas for the new maths and that."

Lorna felt Jimmy's hand on her hip.

"Like shagging gave him the idea, for all the stuff that led to the nuclear bomb eh?" he said.

Jimmy kissed her in the total absence of light.

"All just a big bang eh?" said Jimmy. "Big bangs and fucking accidents."

"Accidents?"

"Aye. Like eh, chaos theory and that. The bald guy on TV, he was saying like, how Einstein just hated the idea of everything being just accidents. But I like it, man. Fucking chaos. Like the universe doing kung fu with itself all day eh?

Fucking bombs going whoosh and cities full of people going to dust, man. Fucking cars falling through the air into water."

"I need to sleep for work, Jimmy, OK?"

"Aye. But that Einstein was talking shite eh? There's nothing wrong with chaos. Accidents happen. So what? There's nothing to be scared of. That's right eh?"

"Let me sleep."

"But you see what I mean? It's not our fault there's accidents, not if everything around us is chaos anyway, man, eh? Like, imagine if cars were atoms eh, rushing around, they'd be bound to get in each others way eh, it wouldn't be any one particular atom or car's fault would it, if there was a crash? No, it'd just be an inevitable consequence eh, of how the whole thing is set up. You see? No-one's fault."

"Aye, I see. Go to sleep."

Jimmy sniffed. He listened to Lorna's breathing deepen as she fell asleep.

"Not my fault," he said, into the darkness.

Chapter Seven

Thomas Ford was dressed early, sitting upright in the chair by the bed. He was regretting that he'd arranged with Finlay to be picked up at the hospital. It would have been better to just get a taxi by himself, back to the house. But then again he knew he was still unsteady on his feet, safer to fall with Finlay there. By the time Thomas saw Finlay's head coming through the double doors at the end of the ward he had been ready to just get up and leave on his own anyway though, fall or not.

As Finlay drove down towards the roundabout, Thomas felt a kind of terror. It was like a sickly sweet insanity, lapping at the edges of his soul in waves of suggestion. Obviously, Thomas told himself, this is what it has to be like, the first time in a car since the Toyota went into the water. He sat stiffly in Finlay's passenger seat, trying not to look crazy. He felt his eyeballs swivelling here and there, trying to see too much, too fast. He felt his throat doing rapid swallowing motions.

"Alright there Thomas?"

Thomas blinked and stared straight ahead. He was surprised to find he couldn't bring himself to turn his neck and look back at Finlay. Something in him was jammed. He could only sniff and nod as Finlay indicated right and took the car into the long, smooth turn.

Soon they were passing through streets full of people, faces, crowds it seemed to Thomas. There had been plenty of people coming and going at the hospital, but this was different. At the hospital everyone had shared a unifying context. Here, outside the car windows, was humanity in the wild. Many of these pairs of eyes would have read about the crash, seen photographs of Lea and himself. Somehow that thought made the crash real in a horrible new way. Thomas thought he recognised a face in the crowd.

"Slow down Finlay," said Thomas suddenly.

"Sorry man. I can't go slower here. We're packed in tight with this traffic."

Thomas twisted his neck, trying to look back. The thick black hair had been the same, even something birdlike in the face. Thomas had only glimpsed the face for a moment, in the crowd. Now it was gone, there was no way to tell from the backs of all those heads there, which one might have been the driver of the red car that killed Lea. Thomas turned to face the road ahead again.

"I thought I saw someone," he said.

"Who?"

"No-one. Just my head playing a trick."

"Yeah?"

"No. Wait. I don't know. Finlay, stop the car."

"I can't stop here."

Thomas punched the dashboard in front of Finlay.

"Stop the fucking car here or I'm jumping out!"

"Alright. Alright."

Thomas was shoving at the door handle. Some part of his brain wouldn't slip into gear, he just kept fumbling at the handle. He saw his hands doing it and realised the gesture was like Lea in the car, twitching uselessly with her hands, neither undoing her seatbelt nor letting Thomas undo it for her. This was the first moment he felt understanding for the way her

The Survival of Thomas Ford

hands had behaved in that sinking car. Thomas sensed rather than saw, that Finlay had managed to stop in the traffic. He heard horns beeping from behind. Then, almost as though by accident, Thomas had the passenger door open. He lurched his weight toward the pavement. It was full of moving bodies and his legs were shaking with the unaccustomed effort. The physiotherapists at the hospital had made him walk up stairs and down, but this was different. There were so many ways his legs had forgotten to work, to support him, move him, balance him.

"Tom!" Finlay shouted once.

But Thomas Ford didn't hear. He was in the crowd now, moving up Academy Street, past the bank. The mad thought flashed through his mind, that he should go in and check his account. Then he remembered why he had left the car. He looked ahead, as far as the traffic lights. He would have to cross over, then get to the corner, before he would be at the place where he had seen that black hair and bird face in the crowd. He bit his lip, realising that, no, he would have to get much further than that, to catch up with the head. The head had been walking, its body had been walking, when he saw it from the car. Thomas' legs just wouldn't move fast enough, to catch up with the man, not unless the man had stopped for some reason, just round the corner. There was a bus-stop just round that corner, and the back entrance to the railway station, and the big shopping centre. Maybe if the man had been going to the bus-stop, that was Thomas' only chance of catching up with him.

Thomas felt his left leg bend too much as he took a step. It was just before the traffic lights. The leg buckled and Thomas fell heavily against a large female thigh, covered in cotton. He made a strange sound, hitting the pavement with his shoulder. Then pain spread out from a point deep in Thomas' chest. It was as though some wild animal had bitten him there and was now chewing. The pain was so intense and relentless that Thomas had to close his eyes and rest his head fully on the pavement. He was oblivious to the pedestrians, the traffic noise, who he was, or where. Only the pain existed now.

Jimmy and Lorna had walked well past the corner by the time Thomas Ford collapsed at the traffic lights behind them. They were not headed for the bus-stop. They were going to the shopping centre. Jimmy liked to stalk its floors and escalators. The observation of the public was both a discipline and a hobby to Jimmy. He enjoyed the feeling of passing anonymously through crowds. His stomach still hurt where his dad had stamped on him. He had to stop and sit for a while on a bench, just inside the shopping centre's large doorway. He leaned forward on the bench, grinning, looking straight ahead, hugging his belly.

"No Jimmy. That's not right. You should go up to the hospital and get it checked. You could come up with me on the bus when I start my shift. OK?"

Jimmy grinned harder and shook his head. He did not look at Lorna. He sighed out air, then sucked in a breath greedily. He blew out quickly twice. He laughed.

"Come on," he said. "I'll get you a coffee up in Starbucks."

Jimmy chose the high seats by the window. Lorna was sipping coffee and watching Jimmy watching the people pass by. It was disconcerting, the attitude he had to the passing crowd, as though he was watching television and these people passing were only half-real to him. Sometimes Lorna would see someone in the crowd notice Jimmy staring. The person would look back at Jimmy but Jimmy would not react, he

The Survival of Thomas Ford

would show no awareness that he was being looked at. He would just continue to grin like an Alsatian dog on a hot day. Lorna looked away from Jimmy, down into her coffee. At that exact moment Jimmy turned his black eyes on her.

"Did you talk to that man again at work?" he said.

"Who?"

"That man you said you'd talked to. The one who had the accident out near Drumnadrochit, at Loch Ness. His wife died in the car eh?"

Lorna frowned.

"Thomas Ford? He'll have gotten out today. Gone home."

"Aye," said Jimmy. "You were saying you got talking to him eh? That he was quite nice."

This was the third time Jimmy had asked, over the weeks since he had found out that Lorna was cleaning in Intensive Care when Thomas Ford was there. The first time had made sense to Lorna, because Jimmy had been reading in the paper about the crash and he had asked her if she had seen the man whose photo was in the paper, at the hospital. But now there was something strange to Lorna, about Jimmy asking, and the tone of his voice when he asked.

"Did he ever say anything to you about his wife?" said Jimmy. "Or about the crash, how it happened?"

Lorna watched Jimmy. He blinked. He grinned. He lifted his mug to take a drink of coffee, but he swallowed before he drank.

"No, Jimmy, of course he didn't."

"I don't know," said Jimmy. "Stressful situation. People will talk about anything, after an accident like that. Bonnie lassie like you, Lorna. Shoulder to cry on."

Lorna shook her head and looked out the window, into the crowd of faces.

Chapter Eight

The Accident and Emergency staff couldn't believe that this was Thomas Ford back again. They recognised him right away. The story of a man escaping from a car that crashed into a freezing loch and sunk didn't come along every day around there. The Indian doctor was asking Thomas about the pain, but Thomas' eyes were darting around the ceiling like twin flying insects.

"Mr Ford? Mr Ford? No, Jill, call ITU and tell them Mr Ford's on the way back up."

By the time the bus arrived at the hospital there was only five minutes left before the start of Lorna's shift. The west theatre was still undergoing its rapid clean and detox, to ready it for the spot-inspection that hospital admin had been forewarned was to happen. Jimmy was curled forward on the seat beside Lorna. Sweat glistened on his forehead. Lorna had an arm round him as they got off the bus. She half-carried him to the reception for Accident and Emergency. Finlay, who was sitting, still waiting for word to come back about Thomas, looked up as the girl and young guy tottered through the double doors. At first, Finlay thought they were drunk, but no, the young man seemed to be in pain, his guts.

Five minutes later, Jimmy found himself lying back on a trolley in a room full of people, looking at the ceiling.

The Survival of Thomas Ford

"Hey," he said, "I don't think I should be here. It was my girlfriend. I just had some pain and she made this big thing of it."

Jimmy's shirt was off. He noticed a nice-looking young nurse and stared at her. He hoped she was impressed by his tight abdomen and healthy pink torso. But she didn't meet his eyes. Then his stomach started that whooshing pain again.

"Whhoooooo!" went Jimmy. "Hey though, I think I'll be fine eh?"

"Mr McCallum, I see you have deep bruising here on your stomach. Mr McCallum, have you been in a recent altercation? I would say that is the imprint of a boot there."

The first thing that came to Jimmy's mind was Lorna's boots.

"Aye, well, maybe playing around a bit with the girlfriend and that eh? She might have eh, stood on me like."

"Stood on you?"

"Aye. She's a sound lassie like. Lorna. Works here eh? Aye, a cleaner like. I better no tell you her name or you'll know who it is eh? Don't want you going up to her like, in her tea-break or that, and asking her to stand on you too eh doc?"

Jimmy let his head fall back on the hard trolley. He laughed up into the harsh overhead lighting.

"Bit like the dentist this eh doc? Eh? You haven't got a pillow have you? Aw, you know, I've changed my mind eh? There's no need for all this. I'll just split eh?"

A nurse was taking Jimmy's pulse. Jimmy moved jerkily, reaching for his shirt which he could see stacked on his jacket near the trolley he was on. The nurse's hand was batted away roughly. She moved back in reaction and knocked a tray of instruments over. They clattered noisily to the floor. The

John A. A. Logan

doctor turned to see what had happened. Another nurse instinctively put a hand on Jimmy's bare shoulder.

"Hey," said Jimmy, "get your paw off! I'm splitting eh? Shouldn't have come. Bloody girlfriend's idea."

"Mr McCallum!" said the doctor. "Calm yourself!"

"I'm calm! Just get your bitch here off me eh, before he loses the hand. I just want my shirt."

The nurse's hand stayed on Jimmy's shoulder.

"Get the fuck off eh!"

"Mr McCallum!"

Jimmy pushed the nurse hard, on the chest. The nurse moved through the air slowly it seemed, until his back hit a large, expensive-looking machine on wheels. The machine tipped over and crashed to the floor. There was an electrical fizz, then a loud explosion and sparks filled the air. Jimmy felt more arms on his shoulders and chest, pushing him back and down. Jimmy saw the doctor's face close to his.

"Control yourself, Mr McCallum!"

"Hey, don't touch me motherfucker...*hey motherfuckers...don't fucking touch me...you'll lose that hand motherfucker...*"

Over the shoulder of the doctor, Jimmy saw a young, pretty nurse filling a syringe from a tiny bottle. He saw her hold the syringe up to the fluorescent lights, as though in a moment of sacrament, and flick it casually with a long finger. He fixed his eyes on hers as she approached him.

"Hey bitch, don't think you're going to stick that fucking needle in me...I'll stick it up you...get your filthy fucking paws off me! Do you know who I am? I could kill all you cunts with one hand! Get the fuck off me!"

When they got the needle into him, nothing happened for a second. Then it felt like a brick was in his arm. The brick

The Survival of Thomas Ford

travelled very slowly up to Jimmy's chest, then his neck. When the brick reached Jimmy's eyeballs his head got heavier and heavier until it flopped back on the trolley and bounced.

As soon as Thomas Ford was back in the bed in Intensive Care his mind seemed to clear. The pain was gone from his chest. Kate, the nurse, was grinning at him.

"Thomas, what have you been up to? We let you go and you just come right back. How's that going to look on our annual statistics? You're not making us look exactly competent."

Thomas blinked at her. Then a tall man appeared at her shoulder in profile. He had a strange sloping look to his face. He murmured something to Kate and she nodded. The man turned to face Thomas.

"Hello Mr Ford. I'm Dr Radthammon. I'm a cardiologist. I hear you collapsed on the street, shortly after discharge this morning, that is correct?"

Thomas nodded.

"I know you have reported pains in your chest area, Mr Ford, which is why I have been asked to consult. I've talked to Dr Timmons and read his notes. Now I'd like to examine you myself, OK? Could you manage to sit up a little? That's good."

Thomas tried to shift on the bed.

"Are you able to speak, Mr Ford?"

"Yes. Actually, I feel a lot better now. The pain is gone."

"I see. Breathe deeply please. Yes. And out again. Good. Is there pain when you breathe?"

"No. Not now."

"But earlier there was?"

"Well, not exactly. The pain was just huge, like something was biting my chest."

"Right, Mr Ford, we'll do some more tests then. We'll talk again when I have the results."

Lorna was thinking about Jimmy as she took the cleaning solutions from the storeroom and began to stack them on the small trolley. How could his own father stamp on his stomach? She had met Mr McCallum, Jimmy's dad, twice. Jimmy had told her so much, about his father being a hard man. Jimmy was proud of his father's status, the respect he had from his employees, but at the same time Jimmy was always arguing and fighting with his father.

She pushed the trolley along the corridor, noticing a damp area on the high yellow wall, near the ceiling. At the left turn towards the theatre, she was able to glance through into Intensive Care by the rear exit. There, framed perfectly by the green-painted walls, she saw Thomas Ford's head, lying on a pillow. That was strange. He should have been discharged. She remembered Jimmy asking about the man again today, in the café, and now, there was the man here still. He must have had some kind of relapse. That could certainly happen, with the pressure to get folk out of ITU and down to High Dependency or the normal wards. Then you saw people in the normal wards getting sent home too soon. Lorna had seen an eighty-year-old woman discharged from the chest ward the day before, against her family's wishes. The old woman's son had made a scene with the Sister, accusing them of only putting his mother out to clear a bed. But the woman had left in the son's car, only to pass out at the first roundabout and have to be brought back. Lorna and another cleaner had watched and listened to it all, as it unfolded, like it was a play.

She pushed the trolley against the theatre doors, and Jimmy came back into her mind again. What was that he had

The Survival of Thomas Ford

been saying last night, about atoms and accidents, cars falling through the air? No-one else ever talked to her about things like that. Lorna laughed. God, she hoped he was alright, but what the hell could he be saying right now, to the A&E doctors and nurses? She leaned on the trolley and let out a long, braying laugh. He could be saying absolutely anything. He'd be lucky to get out of here without being Sectioned. Mr McCallum, we are keeping you here under Article so-and-so of the Mental Health Act. She finished laughing and shook her head. No, really, he would be lucky to get home without being Sectioned if he said to the staff here half the things she'd heard him going on about lately.

She blinked and pushed the trolley again.

Shit, and he would blame her, for making him come here.

Chapter Nine

Thomas Ford woke up suddenly, surprised that he had been asleep. He looked to his right and saw the face of Dr Radthammon, who was sitting in the chair by the bed.

"Hello again, Mr Ford. Well, I have good news for you. There is nothing organically wrong with your thoracic area. Your heart and lungs are in admirable condition. Therefore, and very understandably Mr Ford, given your personal circumstances, I am sure that the pains you experienced were phantom in nature. Pains of the mind, as it were. How do you feel just now?"

Thomas swallowed.

"Alright I think."

"No pain?"

Thomas shook his head.

"No."

"Good, good. Well, Mr Ford, your friend, Mr Johnson, is still here. He is waiting to drive you home, for the second time today!"

Dr Radthammon laughed. He wanted to get away quickly from ITU, to go to have a look at the house site. Radthammon wanted to see whether McCallum was personally on site, or was he leaving all the responsibility to his foreman. Radthammon looked at his Rolex Yachtmaster watch.

The Survival of Thomas Ford

"Now, Mr Ford, just before I go, I have contacted a colleague, Dr Nissen. I would like you to see Dr Nissen in a few days, especially if you have any recurrence of these pains. Alright? Good day Mr Ford! The nurse will give you Dr Nissen's contact details."

Dr Radthammon jogged away from Thomas Ford's bed.

Five floors above Thomas and the Intensive Therapy Unit, Jimmy woke slowly to find himself in a bed with thin, starched white sheets. He had never woken so slowly in his life. There was something very wrong. All the wild cells in Jimmy's body were screaming out. This was capture of some kind, his instinct knew it. Jimmy tried to blink, but his eyes were gummed up. He couldn't open the right eye.

"Christ eh?" he shouted. "Eh? Christ! Who the *fuck*!"

Jimmy coughed, sniffed. He heard the clipping of a woman's short heels on a hard floor.

"Now just stay calm, Mr McCallum!" he heard a female voice say.

Jimmy moved to get up. His arms and thighs were strapped tight to the bed.

"Whooooaaa! Hey to *fuck*!" Jimmy screamed. "Do you cunts know who I *am*?"

A large, round, girl's face appeared above him.

"Calm down, Mr McCallum! Now, you were acting like this in A&E and you had to be sedated. Do you remember that, Mr McCallum? Do you understand what I'm saying Mr McCallum?"

Jimmy raised his head as far as he could. His neck flexed and strained. Veins bulged above his eyebrows and all the way up to his thick black hair. Black bird eyes blazed beneath the hospital's fluorescent lighting.

"*Woo woo woo!*" he said. "You'd better untie me. I'm just telling you a fact. You'd best untie me right now. If you're no going to untie me you better kill me eh? Just don't ever let me up off this bed unless you do it right now eh? Make sure you can keep me down here forever eh? Otherwise make sure you're no on planet Earth when I do ever get up eh? Understand?"

Jimmy said the last words very quietly. Some of them went into the young girl's brain. She retreated from the bed and went to get Dr Nissen.

Jimmy's dad, Jack McCallum, was in the double garage at the side of his house, in the Subaru, in the back seat, where Jimmy's mum, Cathy, would never come to look for him. He was masturbating and looking at the crumpled colour photograph of Farrah Fawcett Majors that he had kept loyally in his wallet for the past thirty-one years. He breathed out steadily, watching her blue eyes and the flick of her famous hair.

The phone went.

"Fuck," said Jack.

He kept stroking, but the phone kept ringing.

Eventually he sighed and took the call.

"Hello."

"Dad! Fuck's sake eh! They've got me up at the hospital man. They've drugged me! I'm tied in a bed. There's a nurse holding the phone for me eh!"

"Jimmy?"

"Aye! Dad! Going to talk to them eh, get me out of here!"

Jack heard shuffling sounds and deduced that the phone was being taken by someone new.

A deep voice came on the line.

"Hello. Mr McCallum?"

The Survival of Thomas Ford

Jack placed the photo of Farrah face down on the top edge of the driver's seat in front of himself.

"Yes. Who is this?"

"I'm Dr Nissen, Mr McCallum. I'm afraid your son was admitted to the psychiatric ward here this afternoon, after having some kind of episode. The situation is, Mr McCallum, that I would very much like to keep him here for evaluation and observation. I have to be honest with you and let you know that I am currently in the process of obtaining a second signature from the doctor in A&E who was very disturbed by your son's behaviour, so that we can hold him under the terms of the Mental Health Act Scotland."

Jack heard Jimmy's voice in the background.

Jack rolled his eyes to the beige roof of the four-by-four. He noticed a greasy spot there and wondered what had caused it. He reached up with his finger and shoved at the area but it was dry.

"Dr Nissen, did you say? Well, Dr Nissen, do you mind if I call back in ten minutes? Sorry, but I have to take care of some business. Please delay your plans until I call you back in ten minutes, alright Dr Nissen? Thank you."

Jack terminated the call without waiting for the doctor's reply.

He sniffed and reached for the photo of Farrah. He looked at her blue eyes again, longingly. He leaned forward, his gut getting in the way as he tried to reach the dashboard. He pulsed his weight forward twice, then gripped his wallet, put the photo away safe.

Jack entered the house by the door from the garage, walked through the hall, turned right into his study/office.

On the desk, he grabbed the array of contact cards in their plastic green case.

He flipped through, looking for R.

When he saw Radthammon's address and number, he dialled.

The phone rang four times then Dr Radthammon answered.

"It's McCallum here. Listen…"

"No, Mr McCallum, you listen! Do you know where I am? This is a great coincidence sir, because I am at the site of my house you are building for me. But you, sir, you are not here evidently. You are never here when I come, are you Mr McCallum?"

Jack sighed.

"Don't worry about the build, Doctor. It's perfectly under control. My foreman, Lanski, has it fully in hand, and I'm there very regularly, I assure you."

"Well…"

"Anyway, Dr Radthammon, I called because I need you to do me a favour, at the hospital."

"The hospital?"

"Yes. There's been some sort of scene there with my boy, Jimmy. Do you know a Dr Nissen?"

"Yes. He is a psychiatrist."

"Well, Dr Radthammon, that silly wee bugger Jimmy must have gotten up to something there today. I just had a call from Nissen and he is all set on getting Jimmy Sectioned right now. I told him I'd call back in ten minutes. He said he won't proceed until then."

"Well, Mr McCallum, I cannot interfere with the clinical findings of a man like Dr Nissen. In fact…"

"Radthammon, I'm going to build you a good house. You'll be able to rely on the work being done well and on schedule."

The Survival of Thomas Ford

"I appreciate that, Mr McCallum."

"No, I don't think you do, Dr Radthammon. I've got your deposit. My boys have laid the foundations for a fine house. I know what you earn and what the plot already cost you, doctor. Even on your salary, I know you're stretched now. You can't afford any big problems with this house, Dr Radthammon."

"Mr McCallum, are you threatening me?"

Jack didn't answer. He let the silence build up on the line. When the doctor spoke again, it was in a new tone.

"McCallum, in my country Radthammon is a name to be feared. My family are not spoken to in this way, not anywhere, not by anyone. I will take you to Court for my deposit and I will transfer the work to another building firm by noon on Friday of this week. Good-day..."

Jack licked his lips.

"Radthammon, you don't understand the position you're in. You don't know who I am and you don't know how this city works. I can have you blacklisted in this city. No builder, no labourer, no architect will touch your house. Now, get my boy home for his supper, before his mum knows where he's been, or I'll have those Poles pour fucking battery acid, toxic waste, atomic fuel rod leftovers, oil, piss, paraffin, all over the foundations of your beautiful house, doctor, and the land around it. Then no-one will be able to build a house there for a hundred years, Radthammon, whether your name is to be feared or not, ok doc? Cheers."

Jack cut the call off and sat down in the big leather chair. He tapped his fingers against his forehead, rhythmically. Cathy appeared in the doorway.

"Who was that on the phone?" she said.

"That Dr Radthammon. He's worried about his house."

"That's a beautiful spot he got for it, Jack. That view."
"Aye."
"I'm worried about Jimmy," said Cathy.
"He'll be alright," said Jack.

The ten minutes had elapsed and Mr McCallum had not phoned back. Dr Nissen tilted his neck to one side. It wasn't often that he felt such urgency about a case. He did not often make snap decisions. But he had to admit, when he first encountered Jimmy, the bird-like face, the black eyes, the things the boy was shouting, only moments had passed before Dr Nissen was going through a mental list of possible colleagues to bring in for the second signature needed. Dr Nissen had lied to McCallum on the phone. Jimmy's admitting A&E doctor had gone off duty so it was too late to use him now.

Dr Nissen sat in his small office, bit his lip, then decided on Ray Mellor. Ray was a sensitive man. He would pick up on the Satanic vibe coming off this lad right away and be happy to sign off on it.

Dr Nissen couldn't see the bed where Jimmy was restrained, not from his chair in the office. The boy would keep there for a while longer though. He wasn't going anywhere, and Karen had an eye on him.

Karen, the young nurse, was standing at the side of Jimmy's bed, an expression of suppressed fascination on her face and in her eyes. Jimmy was raising his head high off the pillow now, to stare at her. He was grinning.

"Come on now eh?" he was saying, very quietly. "What's your name? Hey, don't worry about me, I'm cool. My girlfriend's a cleaner in this hospital eh? Working a shift right now. We came up on the bus together. I had sore guts, that's all, and she says I had to go to A&E. Then I wake up here! Go

The Survival of Thomas Ford

and ask her. Do you know her? Lorna Stewart. She says she's cleaning the theatre today, getting ready for some big inspection you're having here."

"Lorna the cleaner?"

"Aye. Young lassie like you. Bonnie like you. You know her? Go and tell her what's happened eh?"

The wide double doors of the ward slammed open. Karen looked over, startled, to see Dr Radthammon running in. He was sweating and wheezing. His eyes glared.

"Where is Dr Nissen?" he shouted at Karen.

"He's in the office, Dr Radthammon."

Radthammon's eyes swivelled, almost involuntarily, toward Jimmy on the bed. Radthammon saw the same birdlike features as McCallum the builder. The same black eyes. Instead of thick white hair, there was thick black hair. Radthammon turned away and headed for Nissen's office.

"This place is mental eh?" said Jimmy from the bed. "What's your name?"

She looked at the black eyes.

"Karen."

"Karen. Do you go out much in the city Karen?"

"Aye. A bit."

She felt herself smiling.

"Going to scratch my neck, Karen? I'm awful itchy there."

The girl sighed. She swallowed. She walked to the bedside, glancing back at Nissen's office door. Loud voices could be heard from the office, muffled emissions, like baby elephants senselessly trumpeting. Karen felt herself blush as she reached toward Jimmy's neck. At the last moment she looked up at the hungry black eyes and pulled her hand back.

"How about going out tomorrow night eh Karen? You off then?"

"No, I'm working tomorrow night."

"Night after then?"

"I'm working then too."

"Just one wee scratch eh Karen?"

She reached toward his neck again. Before her hand could touch his skin he darted forward with his head and enveloped her index finger in his mouth, the whole finger. He sucked like a greedy calf. She pulled her finger away and stepped back from the bed. Jimmy grinned at her.

Dr Nissen's office door opened. Dr Nissen and Dr Radthammon walked jerkily across the hard floor, their expensive shoe heels clipping.

"We're very sorry about this misunderstanding, Mr McCallum. We'll arrange for a taxi to take you home right away. Karen, please undo Mr McCallum's restraints," said Nissen.

Karen looked strangely at the doctors. Both their faces were red, their eyes bloodshot. Karen had never seen them like that. She turned towards Jimmy. He was grinning hard now, at all of them.

"Doctors eh?" said Jimmy. "You'll be educated men eh? I'm an educated man too, like, self-educated, at the library and on the internet and BBC4 and that. An autodidact, in the Scottish tradition eh? But my old man wouldn't let me stay on at school like. He wanted me on the building sites."

Jimmy stared at Dr Radthammon.

"Aye aye, Dr Radthammon, how's your house coming on? I was there yesterday, man, carrying bricks for you, helping those Poles!"

Dr Nissen stared at Dr Radthammon sharply. Karen was undoing the strap on Jimmy's left ankle.

"Oh, Karen, give a wee scratch there eh? I think I'm getting some skin condition or something, itchy everywhere.

The Survival of Thomas Ford

Funny thing though, my guts feel better. Hey docs, what do you think of all that physics eh? Atoms and particles eh? Hey, what do you think about those quarks? Those up and down quarks, and charm quarks? It's great eh? Fucking chaos eh? Man, I should have stayed in school. Karen! No go on, a wee scratch eh?"

When Jimmy and Dr Radthammon were gone from his ward, Dr Nissen walked into his small office, sat in his chair, and held his head in his hands. There was a strange feeling in him. It took him fifteen minutes to recognise it from the summer holiday the year before, with Anna, to Florida. They'd chartered a boat and gone out into the deep fishing waters. It had all gone well until Dr Nissen got something heavy on the line. After what seemed hours, with raw hands despite the hide gloves, Dr Nissen had eventually pulled a long silver-finned shark half out of the water. The boat's captain had come running over and cut the line. He had explained to Dr Nissen and Anna that the law protected this rare shark in those waters, even though the shark could be a decimation machine, consuming and disturbing the rest of the fish population there. But the law was the law.

So the shark had to be released. Just as it had vanished back into the water, Dr Nissen's brain had taken a clear and indelible mental photograph of its gaping mouth, the snaggled teeth, and above, the blank, black eyes.

Nissen rubbed at the skin by the edge of his forehead. Maybe he should have resisted Radthammon. There was the feeling in the belly, like acid working in there, the knowledge that this boy had been released back into the world.

Just before Karen had undone the first wrist strap she had looked at Dr Nissen for confirmation. The girl had known what they were doing was wrong. Nissen could have acted then, told her, no, don't undo it, let's get him tied up again.

He could have helped her with it.

Instead, he had done nothing. He had let Radthammon bully him and now something terrible that could have been contained has not been.

It wasn't what the boy said, or what he did.

It was the dead, blank, black eyes that watched you, waiting.

The Survival of Thomas Ford

Chapter Ten

Thomas Ford has been alone at his house for three hours now. Finlay had offered to stay longer, but Thomas told him he wanted to sleep. He had not slept though. He just stared ahead, alone for the first time since the accident. The house no longer made sense. It had only made sense with Lea there. For a while, Thomas tortured himself, expertly and creatively, staring for minutes at the space above a chair or cushion, imagining Lea sitting there, drinking tea from a mug, or looking back at him, or watching television with sleepy, hooded eyes. Then he learned not to imagine her; instead, he went through a series of memories, snapshots of Lea in time and space in this room, stored images Thomas had never been aware of until now. He saw her by the living room door, her back to him, a black satin dress hugging close to her waist and hips. He was remembering the night of the launch of her gallery. They had argued that night. The tension in her at the culmination of the new project that had absorbed her for months, it had brimmed over that night, just before they left the house.

Thomas sniffed and looked down at the carpet, a safer place, no memories of her on that spot of carpet.

Had that really been him on the street, the driver of the red car, with the birdlike features? Thomas smiled and bit his lip. No, he couldn't trust his judgements now. He had to accept that this whole situation rendered him a very poorly calibrated instrument indeed.

Thomas got up stiffly, walked into the kitchen, filled a pint glass with water. He returned to the sofa and started drinking. He looked to his left and realised he was sitting there to leave space for Lea to join him. He looked over at the thick brown chairs, three of them, used by guests. Lea and himself, even when they argued, had stayed together on this sofa, a couple.

Thomas sighed and reached over for the slip of paper on the table. Dr Nissen's contact details. Psychiatric Department. Radthammon had been sly, never stating that the doctor he was referring Thomas to about those chest pains was a psychiatrist. Radthammon thought the pains were all in his head. Thomas blinked. No, they had been in his chest. And maybe he shouldn't underestimate the instinct that had made him get out of the car and try to follow that man in the crowd.

Thomas leaned back, positioned his neck and head against the sofa, closed his eyes. He tried to imagine that a seatbelt held him securely in the sofa. He raised his hands and imagined fumbling with them, in a panic, to release the seatbelt. He moved his hands faster and faster, jerkily, trying to duplicate the movements Lea had made while he had tried to get past her hands and undo her belt in the car. Thomas tried to clench his fists tight and small, like Lea's hands. He tried to imagine what it had felt like for her, as her hands had knocked his own hands out of the way that day. He knocked his right hand against the left, as though the right hand was Lea's panicking hand and the left was his own hand, trying to reach her seatbelt release button. Why had it been so hard, so impossible, to reach one red plastic button?

The Survival of Thomas Ford

Thomas tried to remember the size of the button. He wasn't sure.

And there was a feeling that it was not himself, or Lea, he was remembering in the car at all. As though everything personal to himself or Lea had vanished the moment the car fell to the water. After that, they had become something impersonal, to themselves, to each other. They had become one with every dying thing that had ever wanted badly to live. Their personalities had been put aside so that something more fundamental could step in and take over. In Lea's case, this had taken the form of panic, and it had killed her. In Thomas something else must have happened, but he had no memory of it. All he had was the memory of the police and doctors and nurses' eyes that had looked at him after the accident, the way their eyes had been when they asked him how he had escaped the car and he had only been able to answer that he couldn't remember.

The eyes had looked at Thomas as they came to an unspoken conclusion.

Thomas opened his own eyes and looked at the ceiling, as though he was trying to read there the formula of this conclusion everyone was coming to about what to them was only a story: man and woman and car enter water, only man comes out.

Man remembers nothing, except red car no-one else has ever seen, bird-faced driver, square-jawed passenger.

It was an off-balance equation that couldn't be made to add up.

Einstein or Newton might have fashioned it into something workable, but unfortunately it only left Thomas Ford drained and flopped on the over-large sofa, eyes to the ceiling, Dr Nissen's contact details beginning to crumble already in his sweaty grip.

Chapter Eleven

Robert was making Jimmy a cup of coffee in his mother's kitchen. Robert's mother had gone to her room in the far end of the bungalow. She wasn't comfortable with Jimmy.

"They had me tied down to a fucking bed eh? Couldn't believe it man! If it wasn't for my dad I think I'd still be there now. This country, man! Liberties are just an illusion eh?"

"Do you want sugar?" asked Robert.

It was difficult making coffee for Jimmy. He always wanted it made a different way every time.

"Eh? Aye man. Five please."

Robert dropped the lumps of sugar in Jimmy's mug, one at a time, making five plops in the hot liquid. Jimmy grabbed the mug. Robert watched him, knowing that Jimmy would drink it fast, not caring if his mouth burned, as he tried to catch a whole coffee-infused cube to eat before it melted. It was a game of Jimmy's. Most of Jimmy's games, Robert noted, had their penalties and rewards clearly delineated in that way.

"Aye," said Jimmy, "I only went up because I had sore guts eh? After my dad stamping on me at the site. Lorna talked me into it. I went up to the hospital with her on the bus."

"Was she there when they tied you up?"

Jimmy stuck his tongue out, grinning. There was a brown sugar cube on the tongue. Jimmy shook his head.

The Survival of Thomas Ford

"No man, she'd gone off to start her shift. So they had me alone eh, tied down. But there was this nice young nurse man. I asked her out, but she didn't go for it. Where's your mum?"

"I think she's in her room."

"How's she getting on? I've not seen your mum for a while."

"Aye, she's ok."

"Will I go and say hello to her just now, see how she's doing?"

"She might be sleeping I think."

Jimmy sniffed. He sipped coffee. Jimmy twisted his neck to one side and grinned quickly.

"I'll just pop along to the end of the corridor and do a knock at her door eh? See how she is."

Jimmy walked out of the kitchen. Robert blinked and listened to Jimmy's footsteps on the wooden hall floor. He heard three sharp knocks on his mother's door.

"Mrs Ferguson!" Jimmy shouted. "It's me eh? Jimmy!"

Jimmy was standing with his nose an inch from the door, grinning. He waited a few moments, then he gave three more hard raps.

A quiet, muffled reply came through the door, "I'm sleeping Jimmy."

Jimmy opened the door and walked in to Mrs Ferguson's bedroom. The window was open and Jimmy felt a fresh texture to the room's atmosphere. Mrs Ferguson was a long lump beneath a blue duvet. At the pillow end, Jimmy saw her thick and luxurious black hair.

"Aye aye, Mrs Ferguson! Just grabbing some Zs eh? Aye, I know how you feel! I'm just out of the hospital myself eh! Had me tied to a bed up there so they did. But my dad sorted it out."

Jimmy's reptilian grin remained engaged, although Mrs Ferguson's face made no appearance above the duvet. She did not reply.

"That's a nice blue duvet cover, Mrs Ferguson. Did you get that from Argos?"

"Jimmy, I really need to get some sleep just now, ok love? I might get up later and see you then if you're still here."

Jimmy grinned. After several seconds he stepped back and closed the door. He walked along the hall to the kitchen.

"Aye," he said to Robert, "your mum's getting some kip."

Robert nodded. He crunched his square jaws against a digestive biscuit.

"But your stomach's better now?" he said.

Jimmy placed a flat palm to his belly. He nodded.

"Aye, it's fine now. That's the weird thing. It was hurting like fuck until they drugged me up and tied me in that bed."

"Maybe you needed the rest," said Robert.

Jimmy nodded. The grin was gone.

"Hey Jimmy, you don't think it had anything to do with the crash do you?"

"What?"

"Them drugging you and tying you up."

"How could it be to do with the crash?"

Jimmy's face showed an exaggerated incredulity as he stared at Robert. Robert shrugged.

"I don't know. I just thought of it there. Like, maybe they know. Maybe you said something."

"I've not said anything. How, have you said anything?"

"No."

"Have you said anything to your mum?"

Robert swallowed. He shook his head.

"Eh?" said Jimmy. "Have you?"

The Survival of Thomas Ford

"No Jimmy."

Jimmy sniffed.

"But maybe you shouldn't have that woman's picture up on your bedroom wall at home, Jimmy."

"How no?"

"I don't know. It's sort of...disrespectful."

Jimmy raised his eyebrows. He nodded his head slowly.

At 8 o'clock that evening, Jack McCallum was in the office at his house, reading a newspaper, when he heard the front door slam. Jack was out of his chair and half-running to the hall before Jimmy had reached the living room.

"Hi Dad," said Jimmy.

Jack grabbed the collar of Jimmy's jacket and pulled it until Jimmy was bent double. Jack started walking fast back to the office. When he had Jimmy inside he turned to push the door shut. Jack jerked hard at the neck of Jimmy's jacket, then put a large palm to Jimmy's chest, shoved his son against a high bookcase in the corner of the room.

"Aye," said Jack. "Hi to you too."

Jack pulled his big fist back, tight to his right shoulder. He watched Jimmy's eyes glare at him, then Jack released the punch like a heavy spring-bolt had just been let go. Jack saw his fist go through the glass panel beside Jimmy's face. The glass in Jack's hand bit like some big wasp had hold of it. Jack continued to look at Jimmy's eyes, dimly aware of a red area spreading across the hand at his vision's periphery.

"You're causing me trouble Jimmy. You're causing me trouble boy."

He expected Jimmy to grin and Jack wasn't sure what would happen next if Jimmy grinned. But the grin didn't come. Instead, Jimmy's body flopped. Jimmy sighed.

"Aye Dad. I know," he said.

Jack's neck relaxed a notch, his head tilted forward, his chin dropped.

"Just go to bed," said Jack.

The next morning, Lorna woke up at her flat, thinking about Jimmy. Halfway through her shift the night before, a nurse she knew called Karen had come up and told Lorna all about Jimmy's trip to Dr Nissen's psychiatric observation ward. Lorna had felt her stomach begin to twist toward a tight knot, as Karen told her the story with a strange light in her eyes. Karen had asked if Jimmy was Lorna's boyfriend. Lorna had somehow dodged the question. She couldn't remember now, how she had managed not to answer. Lorna lay with her head on the pillow. She half-expected to hear a knock on the door at any moment, Jimmy there, blaming her for what had happened at the hospital. Then again, from Karen's description, it sounded like the scenario of Jimmy tied down in the bed and Karen standing over him in neat nurse's uniform must have ticked off several of the boxes on Jimmy's fantasy list.

Lorna got up and made toast. She turned the television on. She raised her eyebrows and bit into the toast, as she heard the local newsreader announce that Thomas Ford, survivor of the tragic car accident which had killed his wife, had left hospital the day before. Lorna could hear the note, or tone, in the announcer's voice, when they used the word *survivor*, or was she only imagining it? At the hospital she had heard the staff talking about the case, sometimes only yards from Thomas Ford's bed. Almost everyone had managed to inflect some tone into their comments that left you half-suspicious too, about how the man had *survived* with his wife

The Survival of Thomas Ford

at the bottom of a loch and no witnesses. Lorna had liked Mr Ford though. It was strange. Yes, he had been due to leave hospital, but she had clearly seen him still there yesterday, after she had left Jimmy at A&E. Maybe the news had got the day wrong.

Thomas Ford was sitting in his living-room, on the lonely chair, also watching the news announcement on TV, about his release from hospital. He heard it too. The way the girl reading the news said *survivor*.

Five minutes later the phone rang. Thomas jumped in the chair, from sudden adrenaline. His heart was pounding. He forced himself to pick up the phone.

"Hello Thomas. It's Alan. I just saw on the news that you were out."

Lea's father.

"Yes Alan. Hello. I was watching it too."

There was a long silence before Alan spoke again.

"Aye, well, you missed the funeral."

"Aye."

"We've not talked to you since…"

"I know."

"Me and Jean were thinking we could maybe come round…"

"Aye, Alan, of course. I'm just sleeping a lot still, off and on. If you give me a time I'll make sure I'm awake for you."

Jimmy hadn't been watching the TV news, but it was on the fifth page of the newspaper. Thomas Ford released from hospital. Jimmy had taken the paper up to his bedroom and now he was carefully cutting out the black-and-white photograph of Thomas Ford. Jimmy peeled off the Sellotape, tore it, folded the tape into double-sided hinges, got two on the back of the photo, stuck it up beside the colour photo of Mrs Ford.

Jimmy laid down on the bed in a foetal position and stared up at this man's face. It had been hard to sleep the night before, as though electricity pulsed through Jimmy's arms and down the back of his head. He knew what it was. It wasn't the drugs they'd knocked him out with, though he could still feel them getting worked out of his system. No, it was being tied up and captured. He couldn't cope with it. It had done something terrible to him, deep within. He couldn't let it happen again. Jimmy blinked. With the woman dying, and him causing it, it would be prison if they caught him. Driving on the wrong side of the road. At that speed. Fair enough if the woman hadn't died, but with her dying that's causing death by dangerous driving. His only chance would have been if this man, Thomas Ford, had died in the water like he should have. But there was the man, at home. Jimmy stared at the eyes in the black-and-white photograph. They looked like they would be blue eyes, in colour.

Survivor. Jimmy had noticed that word in the newspaper articles too.

Jimmy looked down and tried to think. If he was lucky then he would never hear any more about this. But Jimmy remembered Lea Ford's face, and Thomas Ford's face, perfectly embedded in his memory from that single second before the Fords' car had veered off toward the loch.

Jimmy bared his teeth. He looked up at Thomas Ford's eyes.

"If I remember you, then you remember me," Jimmy whispered. "If I was you, Mr Ford, I would remember me. Forever and ever."

The Survival of Thomas Ford

At that moment, Jimmy decided to kill Thomas Ford. It was like something in Jimmy had always been waiting for the decision to kill someone.

Chapter Twelve

Jack McCallum had been on the site of Dr Radthammon's new house since 7am. Only the Polish foreman, Lanski, had been there earlier. Jack sensed that he'd gone too far the day before, with Radthammon. Jack's nerves felt exposed. He had wanted to be out of the house this morning before Jimmy was up. He also wanted to make a point of being sure everything was getting done perfectly here on Radthammon's build. But, of course, with Lanski in charge, as Jack knew, there was nothing to worry about. This was going to be a fine house with a stunning view. A place to fulfil the deepest dreams of this Lebanese cardiologist. Jack understood the fear he must have put into Radthammon, threatening to leave this site like downtown 1982 Beirut on a bad day.

"Mr McCallum," said Lanski, "you don't even need to be here, sir. You know this. I will take care of this build."

Jack sniffed and nodded.

"Don't be too keen to keep me away, Lanski. You'll make me wonder why."

"The why is because I always do the best work for you, and you know this."

"You've checked that tilt in the far corner again?"

"It's nothing," said Lanski.

"But you checked it?"

Lanski laughed. "I checked."

The Survival of Thomas Ford

"I'm sorry about my boy hurting your man, Lanski. Is he alright?"

"He will be two weeks at home watching tv and sleeping."

"I'll see he's alright."

"Yes yes, he knows this Mr McCallum."

"Right then."

"And your son is alright too?"

"He's alright. He's a lazy little turd, but he's alright."

Lanski shrugged, as if to imply that, were it not for lazy little turds like Jimmy, there would be less rich pickings in this country for men like himself.

Jack looked off at the horizon, the trees, the fields, the sporadic houses. He wanted to see McCallum Homes all over that horizon, with not a tree, field, or cow in sight.

"It is a beautiful part of the country, Mr McCallum," said Lanski.

"It could be, Lanski. One day it could be."

Robert's mother was shouting.

"Robert! It's the phone. It's Jimmy McCallum."

Robert didn't feel like moving. He had been lying very still. He bit his lip and got up.

"Have you seen the papers?" said Jimmy. "He's home now. Thomas Ford. They let him out of hospital yesterday. Fucking strange that, man, the day he goes out was the same day I was in."

"Aye?"

"Fucking right aye! We need to find out where he lives. Open the phone-book. Look for Ford, T Ford."

Robert put the phone down and fumbled through the pages of the book. Every few seconds he heard a whistling shriek from the phone. Robert picked up the phone again.

"16 Cromwell Drive," said Robert.

"Write it down," said Jimmy. "I'll be at yours in an hour."

"I was going to go…"

"I'll be there in an hour! You better be too."

The hour went slowly for Robert. His mother left the house to go into town. Robert ate Cornflakes to try to fight the feeling of ominous despair in his stomach. The despair remained and now his stomach gurgled. He had only been a passenger in the car. Now he was an accomplice to death by dangerous driving. No, an *accessory*. Robert opened his mouth. He was sweating. Eight hard raps at the wooden front door. Robert flinched. He walked towards the door and saw, through frosted glass, the silhouette of Jimmy's high, parrot-like hairstyle, framed against the mid-morning sun.

As soon as Robert opened the door, Jimmy stepped past him, nudging Robert's shoulder roughly. Robert closed the door and turned to follow Jimmy along the hall to the kitchen.

"Where's your mum?" said Jimmy.

"She's out shopping. I was going to…"

"We've got to do something about this fucker, Robert. Our freedom is at stake here."

"Do you want tea?"

"Coffee."

Robert turned the kettle on. He felt Jimmy's hand on his arm.

"You've not said anything to your mum though eh?"

Robert shook his head. Jimmy nodded, frowned.

"What was the address?"

"16 Cromwell Drive," said Robert.

"Where's that?"

"I don't know."

The Survival of Thomas Ford

"Is it not out by that park with the tennis courts?"

Robert shrugged. He was looking for the sugar.

"We can get a map off the internet," said Jimmy. "Make sure."

Robert handed Jimmy a mug.

"Ta. Man, this is going to be some trip eh? I am the *Gandolfini* right enough eh? Most people, Robert, they'd just wait around and hope this Thomas Ford man had no memory of our faces, you know? They'd hope and pray and that. But we're no like them. We're going to be pro-active eh? Like the U.S. Marine Corps. Aggressive strategy eh? That's how you win!"

Robert took a sip of tea.

"But there was nothing about us in the papers," said Robert. "Nothing about the car, or us."

Jimmy grinned.

"Aye, that's the cops man, being sly. No, Ford must have remembered the car at least. We saw their heads so they saw our heads, even only unconsciously. And the cops will have been on at Ford, in the hospital like. Either he didn't remember clearly enough, or else he remembered it all clear as fuck, man, and they're looking for cunts matching our description right now. But they're keeping it quiet."

Jimmy gulped coffee, whistled through his teeth, blew out air. He could still feel the hospital drugs in his system, from the day before, some dark substance clotted at the base of his skull. He blinked. He remembered the curve of the breasts on that nurse Karen, under the tight uniform.

"Are you going to work today?" said Robert.

"No, man. No way. No after last time."

"Is your stomach still sore?"

"A wee bit. Anyway, I'm going round to Lorna's for a while. But you be ready for nine tonight, Robert, Ok? I'll be back then. We've a job to do. Don't tell your mum anything."

Lorna heard the distinctive raps on her door and thought of not answering. But then a wave of guilt passed through her, about the outcome of her advising Jimmy to go to the hospital the day before. She should at least face him. She opened the door to a healthy, grinning Jimmy. He leaned in and kissed the side of her mouth, then her cheek. She found herself laughing.

Chapter Thirteen

At exactly 9.30pm, the red nose of the Volvo moved smoothly round the corner at the beginning of Cromwell Drive. Robert felt an itch under his skin, at the forearms and armpits, his medication working its way through his system. He yawned vigorously.

"That's number five there," said Jimmy. "Sixteen must be one of those big houses at the end."

The Volvo continued its slow trawl along the road.

"This is like hunting eh?" said Jimmy. "Like that film, The Deer Hunter. One shot eh? Ha man. Right. That's it. Nice house."

"There's a car there."

"Aye. Her car maybe. They probably had a car each. His car's at the bottom of the loch and that's her car, Mrs Ford's."

"The lights are on in the house."

"Aye, well, where did you think he'd be, out partying eh?"

Jimmy pulled the Volvo in to park against the opposite pavement from 16 Cromwell Drive. When Jimmy turned the engine off, the car was suddenly silent. Robert could hear his own breathing.

"What now?" he said.

"Just sit there a minute. Get comfy. We need to settle in and get a feel for the situation eh?"

"Ok."

Jimmy sniffed loudly. He let his head rest on his seat. He kept his gaze steady on Thomas Ford's living room window. There were blinds, half-closed, and the edges of purple curtains showing too.

"But what are we going to do?" said Robert.

Jimmy shook his head and sniffed again.

On the other side of the living-room window and the purple curtains, where Jimmy couldn't see, Thomas Ford was sitting on the lonely brown chair. Alan and Jean, Lea's parents, were sitting opposite him on the sofa. Mugs of tea sat on coasters, on the glass table between them. Thomas had often forgotten to obey Lea's rule of using those coasters when she was there to watch. Now that she was gone he was following the rule. Thomas looked at Lea's father, Alan. Alan was staring at the glass table. Lea's mother, Jean, was looking straight ahead with watered eyes. Thomas had been explaining to them about Lea's hands knocking away his own hands, as he had tried to undo her seatbelt.

"She panicked," said Thomas. "Then the car just sunk straight down. It was all black, the windscreen gave in, the water came. I don't remember anything after that."

Alan was nodding. Thomas noticed that Alan's hair was longer than he had ever seen it before. He looked at Jean's eyes. They were wet and red, staring at him.

"I don't remember," Thomas repeated. "Not until waking up in the hospital, and that was six weeks later."

Now Alan looked up.

"Mr McPherson has told us that, Thomas. You remember him, the detective who interviewed you?"

"Aye. There was a woman with him."

The Survival of Thomas Ford

"Sergeant Davies," said Jean. "She's been awful nice to us, Thomas."

"Aye," said Alan, "so they told us about the red car and the two young men you told them caused it."

Thomas nodded.

"Aye Alan, the only thing about that though, I'm the only one who saw them. That lorry driver saw them, if he'd lived. But it's just me, and I only remember seeing them for a second, even less, then I had to go across the lorry's path and into the loch."

"What kind of car was it?" said Alan.

"I don't know. Red. All I saw was the bonnet. The driver looked strange."

"McPherson told us you said he looked like a bird," said Alan.

"Aye," said Jean, "that's what they said, Thomas. They said you said the driver looked like a bird. And that the passenger had a big, square jaw. That they were both young, dark-haired."

"Aye Jean, that's what I remember."

Alan swallowed, nodded.

"Aye, McPherson told us the police have kept an eye out since, you know, for a red car and two young guys like that," said Alan.

"Right," said Thomas.

"Are you alright here on your own, Thomas?" said Jean.

Thomas raised his eyebrows.

"Not used to it at all yet. I keep expecting her to come home."

Jean nodded.

"Aye," she said.

"None of it makes any sense to me either," said Thomas. "I'm sorry. I tried to undo her seatbelt. She knocked my hands away."

Jimmy tensed in his seat as the front door of 16 Cromwell Drive opened. Robert felt some wave of energy pass from Jimmy's spine to his own, like electricity had leaped the space between them. Two men and a woman were standing on the doorstep of the house. Robert recognised Thomas Ford's head. The woman hugged Thomas Ford. The man shook Thomas Ford's hand. The couple walked slowly to the car parked in the driveway.

"It wasn't Mrs Ford's car," said Robert.

"That must be his mum and dad eh?" said Jimmy.

The car reversed down the drive and began a sweeping curve that Jimmy saw was about to bring it head on with the Volvo. Robert and himself would be caught sitting there, silhouetted by the headlight beam.

"Down," growled Jimmy.

He reached over and grabbed Robert's thick neck. He pulled savagely until Robert's face was driven hard into his lap. Robert let out a yelp as the Volvo was flooded with halogen high-beam. Then there was a rumble of engine and the car had passed the Volvo.

"Stay down," hissed Jimmy. "Ford's at the doorstep."

Thomas Ford was standing on the doorstep, looking down Cromwell Drive, watching Alan and Jean move off. His feeling was that so much had been left unsaid, both by himself and Lea's parents. Not that talk would change anything. He stayed on the doorstep and looked up at the sky. This was the first time he had been outside, alone, for nearly two months. The last time had been during the day, up that abandoned

The Survival of Thomas Ford

track at Ardlarich, when he had stood and stared at the rusted vehicles. Lea had been there, waiting just down the track. He had seen that weird gas coming up from the earth. Then the butterfly, a white one, Thomas remembered, it had flown straight at his hand, its wings had touched his index finger. He smiled and held up the finger, staring at it.

"What's he doing?" said Robert in the car.

"I don't fucking know. I'm just waiting to hear that door shutting."

"Maybe it's a quiet door."

Thomas clenched his hand into a fist, turned, pulled the heavy door closed behind him.

"That's him in," said Jimmy. "Have a look, Robert. Make sure he's no there."

Robert eased himself up in degrees, until he could see past Jimmy's hooked nose, through the driver's window.

"Aye," said Robert. "He's in."

Thomas was standing in the kitchen, running water into a pint glass from the tap. He took a sip and tasted the chlorine. He ran his tongue round his mouth. It was like licking bleach. Thomas gripped the worktop surface. It was a smooth jade area that Lea had picked out. Two stabbing pains coursed through Thomas' chest. He breathed out and let his knees bend. The glass fell and broke. Thomas felt his right leg getting wet against the spilled water. From the hard floor the kitchen looked unfamiliar, a new set of angles. Beneath the wave of pain Thomas felt the beginning of the panic that had taken over when he collapsed on the pavement. Maybe Radthammon was right. All in the mind. Thomas tried to concentrate on his breathing, instead of either the pain or the panic. Another piercing pain came, but Thomas persisted. He felt himself growing calmer in the stillness. He didn't want to go back to the hospital.

Outside the house, Robert and Jimmy were trying to walk silently on the gravel path leading up to the front door. Stones crunched under their boots. A woman walked down Cromwell Drive, with a dog, behind them. Jimmy turned to stare at her as she passed the house, but the woman did not see them.

Four more steps and Jimmy had disappeared around the side of the house, into darkness. Robert followed, pressing his hand to the stone wall. He couldn't see Jimmy now, except as a shape sometimes, against starlight. They entered the garden at the back of the house. Jimmy saw the brightly lit kitchen. No-one was in it. The other long room with patio doors and two big windows, that must be the living room. Jimmy stared. The living room was dimly lit, atmospheric even from out here. Jimmy couldn't see anyone in there. He stared at Robert and waved an arm at him, meaning that he should stay still until they knew Ford's location. At that moment, Thomas Ford stood up from the kitchen floor. Robert saw Thomas Ford's head and back appear suddenly in the kitchen, only feet from Jimmy. Jimmy's eyes were still on Robert's face. He saw Robert's face freeze as Robert looked through the kitchen window at Thomas Ford's back. Jimmy turned to look at the kitchen.

Thomas was looking down at the broken glass on the wooden floor. He wasn't sure if he could be bothered clearing it up, not tonight anyway. The pain was gone from his chest, but an odd sensation passed through Thomas' neck, like an electric pulse. Thomas found himself turning round, to look into the garden. There was the rockery that Lea had spent so much money on. She had loved the mauve, pink and jade stones out there. So proud of them. In the light from the kitchen, Thomas couldn't appreciate the colours. He would

The Survival of Thomas Ford

go out there and sit by them tomorrow. He walked past the broken glass and turned off the kitchen light.

Jimmy and Robert were squatting low against the kitchen's outer wall, their necks bent. Jimmy's mouth felt dry. He hadn't expected the intense fear that was in him now. He looked over at Robert as though to take some comfort or steadiness from Robert's presence. Robert's face was screwed up, his heavy jaw clenched. Robert's gaze was focused down at the ground. Jimmy bit his lip. At least the kitchen light was off now. The garden was still lit, but relatively dimly. Jimmy was having to face the fact that he wasn't at all sure what to do next. It was as though he had relied on some deep predatorial instinct to kick in once they were this close to Ford. It wasn't happening. Instead, grave doubts were surfacing. Jimmy hadn't expected Ford's back and neck to look that thick. Jimmy blinked and stared at the grass. There was something else wrong too. A new feeling. Jimmy hadn't had time to process it yet and identify it as guilt, the first stirring of guilt for his part in the death of Lea Ford. Robert was staring now, at the silhouette of Jimmy's head seen against the low wall. At this moment Jimmy resembled a cockatoo or a budgerigar. As though the new inner turmoil in Jimmy had taken secret shadowed form as a puffing of head feathers. Robert imagined his friend about to screech under the starlit sky. He felt the faltering and floundering of Jimmy's purpose and realised this had never happened before. Jimmy's inhuman resolve seemed to have deserted him, and if it had deserted Jimmy it had also deserted Robert, leaving them stranded in this foreign garden like broken gnomes.

Inside the house, Thomas Ford was walking up the stairs in stocking feet. He turned on the landing light and opened the bedroom door. There was the pine king-size bed with the purple duvet cover. Thomas had no intention of going anywhere near it. Instead, he turned off the landing light and laid down on the bedroom floor. The thick carpet was enough of a pillow. The slight chill in the air was a pleasant touch of reality after the standardised hospital temperature. It was better without a pillow. The blood seemed to run down from the feet to the chest and then into the head, the brain, the eyes. Thoughts seemed cleaner, lighter, surer. There was the red bonnet of the car and that bird-faced murdering bastard at the wheel. Thomas tried to imagine a voice for him. He had the bird-face speak words to the square-jawed passenger. *What time is it? Are we nearly there?* said the bird-face in Thomas' skull. The voice was shrill, psychotic. No, thought Thomas, I'm stereotyping him, that's a mistake. He let the bird-face speak in a gentler tone, its pronunciation more succinct. *What time is it? Are we nearly there?* And for the square-jawed passenger...a deep bass surely, except no, why not try a falsetto squeak...*It is 4 o'clock...we'll be there by teatime...*

Thomas considered giving them names. No, that would be like admitting they would never really be found and their real names known. Their crime known. Thomas breathed deep. Jean hadn't seemed to hate him. Thomas wasn't sure about Alan. He had never been sure about Alan. Alan had never seemed convinced that Thomas was the right husband for his daughter. Thomas frowned and groaned. Hot tears left the edges of his eyes and ran down the side of his head. He remained still, feeling the stinging heat on his face.

In the garden, Jimmy's internal motor kicked back into gear. He raised his head until he could see into the empty

The Survival of Thomas Ford

living room. The dim light was still on in there. He stared at the long sofa. Robert watched Jimmy's head until it turned toward him and shook. Jimmy squat-walked along the wall, then stopped at the patio doors. He raised a hand and grabbed at the doors' metal frame. He tried to tug the doors apart but they were locked. Jimmy turned and made a shoo-ing gesture at Robert with an arm. Robert started to retrace his steps along the wall. He turned the corner of the house, into the salvation of darkness again.

They reached the Volvo in silence, opened the doors stealthily. When Robert was in his seat, Jimmy slammed the driver's door and turned the ignition, almost in one movement. He gunned the Volvo's engine and, on the bedroom floor, Thomas Ford heard the car's surging, powerful scream. Then, in a burst of acceleration and spinning wheels, leaving rubber on the tarmac surface of Cromwell Drive, Jimmy and Robert were gone.

Chapter Fourteen

Robert had asked Jimmy, on the drive home, what had been the point of it? Jimmy had only said one word. Reconnaissance.

Robert thought the word over. It was a military word. Jimmy must have got it from a war film. Or those old Commando books. So it had been a mission, the trip to Mr Ford's garden. Intelligence had been gathered, Robert presumed, by Jimmy. Robert himself did not feel any better informed by the expedition.

He had seen Mr Ford again, this time from behind, and he had seen the man's house. Robert could imagine that Mr Ford was finding it a very different house now, with the absence of Mrs Ford.

In a way, Robert was relieved. Jimmy had not entered the house, he had not made Mr Ford aware of his presence. He had not done anything crazy or irrevocable. They already had the accident to live with. That had been crazy and irrevocable enough. Robert fell asleep, taking with him into his dreams the image of Thomas Ford standing in the kitchen, a broad back and thick neck, but in Robert's dream Robert is frozen on the spot in the garden, unable to move his legs, as Thomas Ford turns slowly and sees him standing there in his garden. But Thomas Ford's face is not the face Robert has seen in the newspapers, or can remember from the moment of the crash.

The Survival of Thomas Ford

No, in this dream, as sweat spurts from Robert's neck and armpits, Thomas Ford's face is the long, hairy snout of a wolf, teeth gleaming and jaws slavering. Thomas Ford's eyes are enormous yellow orbs and Robert cries out in his sleep twice, waking his mother with the second cry.

At her flat, Lorna is on the verge of sleep when she hears Jimmy's ratatat knock on the door. She swears, then throws off her duvet. She opens the door to a sober-faced Jimmy. His only expression is a raised eyebrow. Then he smiles.

In the bed, afterwards, they lie again in that familiar zone of total blackness, which Lorna thinks now is something that she never experiences when alone in the bedroom. The nebulous vacuum only seems to come with Jimmy's presence, as though some density within him has absorbed the light. She finds herself wishing he was not there, that she had not let him in.

"There's something I want to tell you about," he says, and Lorna wishes he would stop talking. "It's about that man at the hospital, Thomas Ford."

Lorna starts to feel sleepy again.

"He's not at the hospital any more," she says. "He went home."

"Aye. I know. Me and Robert were round at his house just now. We were in his garden eh?"

Lorna frowned.

"How do you mean?"

"Just what I said. We were in his garden."

"What were you doing in his garden? How would you know where his garden is anyway? You're talking shite Jimmy. Let me sleep."

"His garden's at 16 Cromwell Drive," said Jimmy. "That's his house. Nice area. Me and Robert just came from it."

Lorna's eyes were open in the black room.

"It was me and Robert, in my car, that caused the crash two months ago, that Ford's wife died in eh?"

"Don't talk shite Jimmy."

Jimmy sniffed. Then he laughed in the darkness.

"Aye well," he said, "if you really don't want to know."

"You're saying you caused the crash?"

"Aye."

"How?"

"We were coming round a blind corner, nose to nose with a lorry."

"A lorry driver died there too," said Lorna.

"Aye. But that was a heart attack," said Jimmy. "Can't blame me for that."

Lorna felt like something had twisted in her chest. There was an excitement too though, like being privy to the solution of a great mystery.

"You killed that man's wife then," she said.

"No. It was an accident."

"But you caused it."

"The trouble is," said Jimmy, "this man, Ford, he saw our heads like, for a second. I could pass him on the street one day. I think he'd remember me."

"Why were you in his garden?"

She felt Jimmy's shoulders shrug against the mattress. He didn't answer.

"You're just winding me up, Jimmy. You weren't in anybody's fucking garden. Except maybe your mum's, or Robert's mum's."

"I know he remembers me," said Jimmy, "because if I was him I'd remember me. No way am I spending years in a cell, living around a bunch of mangy cunts, no way. No for an accident on a road."

"Just shut up Jimmy. I'm no listening. I've had enough of you doing this, stuffing my head full of shite when I'm trying to get to sleep. You wouldn't think it was funny if you had to work the next day."

Lorna turned over onto her stomach, raised the pillow, laid her cheek on it.

"Just shut up and go to sleep," she said.

Jimmy frowned in the darkness. He felt very alone. Where was the relief in confession when one was not believed? It was supposed to be good for the soul, but then people didn't believe you. What good was that? Still, it was interesting that it went that way. Perhaps it showed the flimsy nature of the evidence against Robert and himself. That was Jimmy's last thought. One moment he was staring into the darkness, the next he was asleep.

Chapter Fifteen

Detective Sergeant McPherson was sitting at his narrow corner desk, looking out a dirty window. He smelt Liz's perfume before he heard her shoes on the carpet. She placed a styrofoam cup full of coffee on his desk.

"From the machine?" he said.

"Don't be so bloody choosy. The kettle's broken."

"What? The new one? Another one?"

"Aye."

"What the hell are they doing to the kettles?"

Liz shrugged.

"Have you written up the rest of the Ford file yet?" she asked.

McPherson shook his head.

"Come on, Bill, we need to sign off on it. There's that hit and run yesterday morning."

"I thought McGregor had that."

"No. He was just doing a prelim. It's ours. McGregor's off on holiday tomorrow. Canary Islands. Some new girlfriend he got off the internet."

"You make it sound like he bought her."

Liz raised her eyebrows, pouted her lips.

"You never ever know," she said.

McPherson grinned.

The Survival of Thomas Ford

"Aye," he said, "alright. But it's the thing about the red car and the bird-faced guy, and the square-jawed guy. Ford painted a pretty vivid picture there."

"Uniform's been on the lookout for a couple like that, seen nothing."

McPherson looked over his shoulder to make sure no-one was near.

"You don't trust plod to fucking find folk, Liz. That's our job."

She laughed. Then she stopped laughing and sniffed.

"No, come on, Bill. The Inspector's made it clear. We've been on the Ford case long enough."

McPherson started tapping his desk with a pen. He tapped faster and harder, staring out the window. Liz shook her head, got up, walked away and left him to it. Out the window, McPherson could see the dual carriageway in the distance. What you'd need to do, he thought, was dedicate a car to just sitting at the roadside, looking out for a bird-faced guy. But there were too many forms to fill in now. Not enough time for anything. McPherson grabbed the Ford file, tugged it closer, read off the phone number, dialled.

"Hello, it's DS McPherson here. That's you isn't it, Mr Gillan? Alan?"

"Aye. Hello Mr McPherson."

"I'm just calling as a matter of courtesy, Alan. I'm sorry not to have anything new. We've had men on the lookout for the driver and passenger of the red car which I told you your son-in-law described…"

"Aye, well, Mr McPherson, we were actually round at Thomas' house, Thomas and Lea's house, last night."

"Oh yes, Alan? Well, that's good then, that you've all talked at last."

"Aye. There's no sign of the lads in that red car then, though, Mr McPherson?"

"No Alan. Not yet anyway. Sorry not to have anything solid to tell you, as I said."

"Aye."

There was a silence.

"Mr McPherson, do you believe like, yourself, that there was a red car there, with lads in it, like Thomas said?"

"Well Alan, I can only make note of what I'm told, and then pursue lines of enquiry."

"Aye."

McPherson felt a sudden wave of desolation, depression, come through the phone to him, from Alan. McPherson gritted his teeth and sniffed.

"Oh Alan, sorry, I have to go just now, something's come up here. But I'll be in touch again soon. Goodbye Alan."

"Aye, 'bye Mr McPherson."

McPherson started tapping his pen again. It was important to keep a distance. Otherwise you could burn out. You had to watch it, all the time. He stared at the Ford folder, then used his pen to flick the cover up hard so that the file closed with a slap.

Chapter Sixteen

Thomas woke up on the bedroom floor. He had dreamed that a great hawk was flying low over the city, shitting on everything, knocking people over with its great, sharp clawed feet. It was very hard to think of a reason to move, so he lay there for a long time. The sun shifted position in the sky as he lay still, feeling the carpet against his heels.

Eventually, he felt thirsty, so he walked down the stairs to the kitchen. He walked around the broken glass on the floor, took another pint glass from the cupboard, filled it with water. He turned to face the garden, saw Lea's little rockery. There they were in the morning light, the colours, brown stones, mauves, pinks, orange stones, grey bricklike slabs.

Thomas unlocked the big, sliding patio doors and lugged a wooden chair out with him into the garden. He sat by the rocks, sometimes staring at them, sometimes letting his neck swing far back until his closed eyelids faced the sky. It was going to be a good day, weather-wise. It occurred to Thomas that he could try to work. He hadn't been in the little studio in the loft since returning from the hospital. He had no ideas though, nothing to begin on, his mind was empty. Maybe he should do some push-ups, or yoga, but he couldn't be bothered. It was as though some thick, scaled toad was sitting just beneath his breast-bone, blocking all life.

Thomas picked up the chair and was halfway down the garden when he saw the footsteps on the grass, two sets it looked like, big feet, coming round the corner of the house and leading up to the patio doors. Some of the boot marks were left on mud, beside the grass, from yesterday's rain. Some of the marks were on the stone flagging of the patio, boldly embossed there, in dried dirt.

The mud had only been there from yesterday evening onwards. Who could have come round here like that, since then? Had they come when Alan and Jean were here? Or when he was asleep upstairs? The first thought that came into Thomas' head was that cops had been here, while he was in the living room talking to Alan and Jean. Cops out here, with Alan and Jean's knowledge, listening to the living room conversation, trying to get Thomas on tape maybe, or witnessed, as he said something new, some confession about the crash. It was possible. But then Thomas remembered Jean's eyes at the front door, as she left. Her eyes had not contained any such deceit.

Kids then, round the back, playing. Kids had big feet these days. Or burglars, burglars who knew about the empty house and had come to see. Well, burglars would have gone through those patio doors like butter.

Then the image came to Thomas' mind, the bird-faced driver and the square-jawed passenger. Thomas tried to reason himself out of it, but he saw them clearly, walking round the corner of the house, hovering out here in the garden, staring in at him.

Thomas walked into the house, sat down and picked up the phone. Then he put it down. He didn't know the police number. He would have to ask the operator. She would give him some stupid new directory enquiries number. Then

The Survival of Thomas Ford

eventually McPherson would be on the phone. Thomas tried to phrase it right, in his mind, what he would say to McPherson.

McPherson! It's me, Ford. I think they were here in my garden. The driver with the bird-face and the other one. There's footprints in the garden. I don't know why I'm thinking it could have been them. It's just a funny feeling I got when I saw the boot marks out there just now.

No. There was no way to phrase it that wouldn't sound mad.

Thomas sat back in the lonely brown chair and stared at the empty sofa. Footprints in the garden, that was all. The rest was only in the imagination.

Chapter Seventeen

Lorna woke up to the view of Jimmy's high, profiled hawk-nose. His eyes were closed and she sensed that he was truly asleep, not just feigning it to trick her. She had gone to sleep sure that Jimmy was winding her up with all the talk about causing the Ford crash. Now she woke up believing him. As though sleep had re-ordered her cells and neurones mysteriously, prepared her for this new, dark knowledge. She didn't want to know anything about it. She closed her eyes again to see if that would stop her knowing. Sleep had forced her to understand that this wasn't some new craziness come out of nowhere. She had remembered the odd questions Jimmy had asked about Thomas Ford. Even when Jimmy's stomach had been hurting that day, in Starbucks, Jimmy had still been asking her about Thomas Ford. He had asked her if Thomas Ford had said anything to her at the hospital, about the crash. It had felt wrong when he asked.

Lorna turned away from Jimmy as she got out of the bed. She felt his hand on her shoulder.

"What time are you going to work?" he said.

"I have to be there at two."

"You still cleaning that theatre?"

"Aye."

"Funny how they call it a theatre eh? Like it's just a stage production, all an act, drama and that. Bangs and flashes."

The Survival of Thomas Ford

Lorna sniffed. His hand was still on her shoulder, like some fat pirate's parrot. The weight seemed to enter her shoulder bone, then travel down the arm to her wrist. She could almost make herself feel it, a pain in the wrist from the weight of Jimmy. Not the weight of Jimmy's hand, but of Jimmy himself, and what he had told her.

"Hey," he said, "you know I was just joking last night eh?"

"I know you weren't."

She didn't turn to look at him. His hand left her shoulder like the parrot was taking off now, toward the bedroom ceiling, escaping from everything. She could see its wings and red-feathered belly. She felt hot, like the beginning of a fever.

"Don't go to work today eh?" he said.

"I have to."

"Why? So a few people don't get poisoned later by some superbug? Let them get poisoned. If that poison doesn't get them they'll just get it from another poison somewhere else. The water. The air. It's idiots in charge of everything. Let them fuck it all up eh? Just lie down here with me."

And suddenly she did feel like it, just lying back again and watching the ceiling. Maybe the ceiling, or the sky, or a flock of red parrots, would roll down towards them until she and Jimmy were crushed together here in the room. Then it would all be over.

"I need the toilet," she said.

"Go on then."

Jimmy listened to the sounds of her moving through the flat. He knew it was possible that she could get dressed quickly, without him knowing. She could open the front door quietly, nothing on it squeaked. She could run out onto the streets and tell everyone that he killed Lea Ford that day. Jimmy laid back on the bed, his neck tensed. He heard the toilet flush. He heard feet pad on the carpet, then felt her body against his side. He turned to look at her eyes. Her irises were wide and round as she looked back at him, like shooting targets at some wild fairground. Jimmy brought his bird-features close to Lorna's face. He kissed her mouth. When he was inside her and moving he found his mind back at the road by the lochside in the moment before Thomas Ford swerved his Toyota into the water. As Jimmy came with Lorna, it was Lea Ford's face he saw behind closed lids. Afterwards, as he lay and held Lorna, there was a sour taste in his mouth and an annoying slick of sweat between his shoulders and the sheets. Lea Ford's face was still there. He wanted it to go now. Her eyes were locked on him.

"Why did you tell me, Jimmy?" said Lorna.

"Eh?"

"Why did you tell me?"

Her face was in his armpit. It was uncomfortable, her face there. Jimmy felt tension all through him, his nerves.

"You must trust me, Jimmy," she said.

Jimmy felt his eyes sting. A tight lightning-flash of pain flicked through the very centre of his right eye. He twitched.

"Are you OK?" she said.

"Aye."

"You're not worried about telling me are you? Now, I mean?"

Jimmy laughed. Something pulsed in his soul like a black insect waking up.

"Well," he said, "it was a pretty fucking stupid thing to do I suppose."

"You can't hold everything in, Jimmy."

"Aye, evidently eh?"

The Survival of Thomas Ford

When Jimmy left the flat an hour later, he stared long and hard at Lorna, as she lay on the bed gazing back. There was something in her eyes that Jimmy didn't like, something lazy and satisfied, the look of a lioness that had just fed.

Lorna slept for an hour, then lay awake watching the ceiling and feeling the idea's energy grow in her. She didn't know if she had the courage. Did she dare? She lay on the bed and physically trembled, vibrated, trying to truly sense whether she had the nerve to carry out the idea, live with its consequences. She was not sure.

She looked at the clock.

There would be time to go and see Robert on the way to work.

That might help her decide.

Robert's mother was at his bedroom door. She had a strange look on her face. Robert pulled the earphones out and Johnny Cash's voice became a distant, tinny screech, as though Johnny Cash was reincarnated now, back in town as some performing insect vocalist trapped in the world's ether.

"There's a lassie at the door for you, Robert."

"Who?"

"Lorna, I think she said."

"Lorna?"

"Aye."

At the foot of the stairs, Robert saw Lorna standing, waiting. She looked up at him as he walked towards her.

"Hi Robert."

She smiled.

"Hi," he said. "Eh, do you want a tea?"

They stood in the kitchen, quite close together. Robert could smell soap from her. Lorna looked toward the doorway slyly, twice, until some instinct moved Robert to say, "My mum will no hear us. She's out in the garden."

Lorna looked at him sharply, almost coldly.

"Jimmy told me what happened," she said.

Robert stared.

"Mrs Ford," said Lorna. "The crash."

Robert's heart took a leap, like it was in no way part of him suddenly, but some alien object in his chest. He swallowed.

"Jimmy was driving," he said. "I was just the passenger."

"Aye, the silent fucking passenger who's never said a word to anyone about it since."

"Have you told anyone, Lorna?"

She shook her head.

"He only told me last night," she said. "Were you two really in that man's garden?"

Robert nodded.

"We saw his back, in the kitchen of his house. He didn't see us."

"What were you doing at his house, Robert?"

Robert shrugged.

"Jimmy said we had to do something about him."

"What did you do?"

"Nothing. Jimmy said after that it was reconnaissance, like in war."

"Reconnaissance?"

"Aye."

Robert's hands were hot with fear.

"Jimmy told me not to tell my mum," said Robert. "But now he's told you."

The Survival of Thomas Ford

Lorna's eyes narrowed into a tight horizontal strip of eye, like twin cinema screens were regarding Robert now, each showing a wide, blue desert sky, or unfathomed ocean deeps. And at the centre of each eye a black circle that Robert could sense was full of contempt. He looked down.

"I should go," said Lorna. "I should be at work. I think I just wanted to see if you'd tell me Jimmy was talking shite and it's all a wind up. But I already knew it wasn't."

"You're no going to tell anybody are you?" said Robert.

Lorna sniffed and shook her head.

"It's Jimmy that seems to be doing all the telling just now, Robert. I don't know what I'm going to do."

Lorna walked slowly along the street from Robert's house. She tried to make the walk like a moving meditation, watching each shoe plop down on the next paving-stone. She crossed the bridge over the river, not sure if she would head for the bus-stop and go to work, or was she on the way to somewhere else.

Half an hour later, as though some strange warm southern wind had blown her there, Lorna found herself standing on the opposite pavement to a large ground floor office that had the sign above it:

McCallum Homes, Builders and Architectural Consultants

Lorna stood and stared. She had been there a minute, and was on the verge of letting the warm wind blow her on and away from there, when she saw through a window the thick head of white hair, the bird-like profile, of Jimmy's dad. She crossed the street and walked in to the building.

Five minutes later, she was alone in a room with Jack

John A. A. Logan

McCallum. He was staring alternately at her breasts, then her eyes. Back and forth.

"You're doing well, Lorna, to keep putting up with that wee bugger. Most young girls would have told him where to go by now."

"I had to take him up to the hospital the other day, Mr McCallum, because you'd stamped on his stomach."

"Call me Jack, Lorna. No, I didn't stamp on him. He exaggerated. But you know what he's like. He was out of control, goading my Polish employees. Without those Poles, Lorna, I'm halfway out of business. Are you still working up at the hospital then?"

"Aye."

"Well, why not have a wee think about coming to work for me here? Surely you'd rather be doing office work than that cleaning?"

"I've never worked in an office."

"Happy to give you a job here with me, Lorna. It would be my pleasure."

It was uncanny, how much he looked like Jimmy. Lorna had never been alone with Jack McCallum before. She had met him once on the street with Jimmy, and again when she'd been out to visit Jack's big house at Culloden.

"I'm no here to talk about a job, Jack. It's about Jimmy."

Jack raised white eyebrows. Lines like corrugated iron rippled across his wide forehead.

"Aye? What about him?"

"He told me about something he's done, Jack. Something terrible. Something that would mean a lot of trouble, for him, his mum, and you too, if people get to know. He told me in bed last night."

Jack started to grin.

The Survival of Thomas Ford

"What did he tell you?"

"I'm not ready yet to tell you what it is, Jack. I'm just letting you know, that's all."

"Letting me know?"

"Aye."

"Letting me know. What are you after, Lorna? Money?"

"Aye Jack, maybe. But like I say, I haven't thought it all through yet. I'm just letting you know there's this thing out there, that Jimmy's done."

Jack let the grin spread across his face.

"You're an entrepreneur then eh Lorna? Just like myself. No cleaning work or office work for you eh? That's great. You need to be careful though, Lorna, not to get out of your depth. That can be a terrible thing too."

"Aye, Jack. I know I'm going to have to be careful."

Four hours later, after deciding not to turn up late at the hospital and phoning in sick instead, Lorna stood on the doorstep of 16 Cromwell Drive. She had been home, eaten a tasteless frozen pizza, watched a repeat of the Jeremy Kyle show, then looked up Thomas Ford in the phone book.

Now she stood on the stone doorstep, staring at the frost-glass on the door. She sniffed and rapped hard on the wooden panel, four times. There was no answer. She waited, then almost walked away. Instead, she gave the door six hard raps. A silhouette of a head and shoulders appeared at the frosted glass. Thomas Ford opened the door and stood looking at Lorna. She could see he had not been out today.

Lorna smiled at him.

"Thomas?" she said. "You remember me? Lorna from the hospital."

Thomas Ford blinked.

"Lorna? Aye. Hi."

"Well, maybe it's crazy Thomas. I just had the idea, to come and see you."

Thomas Ford stood completely still for several seconds, looking at her.

"Well, come in then," he said, with a shrug.

He stepped out of the way and Lorna walked past him into the wide hallway.

"Go on through to the living room, Lorna. On the right."

Thomas walked behind her in the hall. He watched her hair move from side to side as she walked. He could smell her. Her smell filled the hall suddenly, like Lea's used to. He remembered watching Lorna like this at the hospital, his neck loose like a snared rabbit's, as she emptied bins and her starched uniform expanded to accommodate her.

In the living room she stopped and turned towards him, smiling.

"Are you sure this is Ok Thomas? It must seem mad, me turning up at your door. But I thought, well, you never know, sometimes it's nice to have company. How have you been getting on?"

Thomas pointed through the patio glass, out into the garden.

"Well, I had some uninvited company last night Lorna, only found out today. Footprints in the garden, coming right round the side of the house, through the garden, and up to those doors there."

Thomas laughed.

"So you're no the first visitor," he said.

Lorna shook her head. Her concerned eyes narrowed.

"That's terrible, Thomas. What did the police say?"

Thomas sat in the lonely brown chair. He motioned for

The Survival of Thomas Ford

Lorna to sit on the sofa. He blew out air like an animal dying.

"Police. Well, I never bothered telling them. Nothing to tell really. Just kids probably. I had enough of police questions at the hospital Lorna."

Lorna nodded sympathetically.

"Aye, Thomas, I saw them there. I felt sorry for you, the way they'd not even let you alone, even in ITU. But you seem a lot better now, Thomas."

Thomas looked at her, raising his eyebrows. It was strange to see her sitting there on the sofa, in Lea's place.

"Do I?" he said. "All I've been doing for weeks is sitting or lying around. It must be hard to notice improvement in that."

"You looked pale in hospital. Now you look like you've been outside."

"I was out in the garden, sitting for a while. Before I noticed the footprints out there."

"That's terrible. Who do you think it was? Just kids maybe eh?"

"Maybe," said Thomas. "Kids with big feet."

Lorna smiled and nodded.

"Do you want coffee or tea?" said Thomas.

"Aye, thanks, a coffee would be nice."

Thomas was standing in the kitchen, getting the spoon into the coffee jar, when the full strangeness of Lorna's presence in the house started to pick at the edge of his brain with a paranoid surge.

"You got my address in the phone book then, Lorna?" Thomas called loudly enough so she would hear in the living-room.

"Aye. I knew you were home. I saw on the news that they'd let you go home."

"Right."

"Are you sure it's not too weird Thomas? Me turning up? I could go if you fancy being alone."

Thomas took the coffee through to the living room. When he handed her the mug Lorna saw that his hand was shaking.

"I never used to be nervous, Lorna. Now I feel like I'm just one big, long nerve, waiting for the next thing to set me off."

Lorna smiled and stared up at him.

"And now I'm setting you off?" she said.

"Maybe. A bit."

He sat down again. He had made no drink for himself. He picked at the edge of the brown chair's thick arm.

"Thomas, there is actually a serious reason for me coming round here like this. I know a lot of people in the town. I suppose it's a city now, but I've lived here all my life and I still think of it as a town. Well, I know a lot of people. I hear a lot of things. And, well, I've become privy to some information very recently. Only last night in fact."

Thomas blinked and licked his lips. He felt his attention wandering. He felt strongly that the girl was leading up to something significant, but equally he felt his attention petering out, making everything in the room seem vague. He stopped picking at the material on the chair arm. He lifted his hand to his forehead.

"Lorna, sorry. The thing is, I find it hard to concentrate lately. My mind must be all over the place. Go on though. Information?"

"Aye. And as soon as I, like, got this information, I realised that it would be really valuable, not just to one party but to two parties. And you're one of those parties Thomas. I've actually just come from a meeting with the other party, where I sort of tested the ground like, but without actually

The Survival of Thomas Ford

divulging the information."

Thomas had an overwhelming desire to laugh out loud.

"Aye," he said. "Right Lorna. Information eh?"

Lorna sipped coffee. She nodded.

"Aye Thomas."

She looked around the living room.

"You know, Thomas, you have a really nice house here eh? You must have had a nice life. That wall-paper is really lovely by the way. Was it your wife that chose that?"

Thomas nodded.

"Anyway, Thomas, you have this house and, sorry Thomas, what do you do for work?"

"I'm an artist, an illustrator."

"Really? Aye well, there you go eh? And the other party who would love to have this information I'm on about, he has a nice life too eh? A nice big house too."

Thomas blinked and frowned.

"See Thomas, I'm fucked off with this cleaning job up at the hospital. I feel like I could be doing something better, you know?"

"Is it blackmail you're talking about then, Lorna?"

She raised her eyebrows. Thomas noted that her eyebrows were each a thin line, possibly only consisting of make-up.

"Blackmail? Fuck's sake Thomas, no. I'm talking about the independent brokering of information. It would only be blackmail if I was saying this to the party that gave me the important information. But I'm no saying anything to that party. No, I told you. I'm taking this important information and I'm approaching you and a third party, who I know this information would be of value to."

Thomas blinked twice.

"But what's the information, Lorna? I mean, I might be a

bit mental after the crash, but I don't understand all this."

Lorna slapped her right leg. Thomas looked at the thick thigh.

"That's why this is difficult, Thomas. I can't tell you what the information is, at least I haven't thought of the right way to tell you what it is, without actually telling you it, if you know what I mean."

Thomas smelt something in the air. It could be body odour or it could be her breath.

"Right," she said. "Sorry Thomas. I know I'm going to have to be more direct. I've never done anything like this before."

"Maybe you shouldn't be doing it now."

"Well, like I say, Thomas, I'm fed up with that cleaning job. I'm looking obviously to, eh, profit from this exchange of information."

Lorna looked around the living room again, lingering on the patio doors.

"Aye." She nodded. "Financially Thomas."

Thomas leaned back in the lonely brown chair. He closed his eyes. He heard Lorna breathe out air.

"I know the lad who was driving the car that caused your crash, Thomas. That killed your wife."

Thomas opened his eyes.

"I only found out last night Thomas, like I said. I could have kept quiet, or I could have gone to the police eh? But...I'm fucked off with my life Thomas, you see? I want something out of this eh?"

Thomas leaned forward and rested his palms on his knees. He swallowed.

"Who is he?" he said.

Lorna sneered and laughed loudly. To Thomas it felt like

someone had just run a cheese grater across his soul.

"Oh aye, Thomas. I'm just going to tell you eh? Fuck's sake."

Thomas raised his hands and used them to hold his head. Without warning, the pain shot through his chest. Thomas moaned and bent double. He let himself slide to the carpet, onto his knees.

"Thomas!"

He rolled onto his side. It was just like some lion or starved tiger, biting his heart. Lorna stood over him and watched veins rise to the surface of Thomas' neck and forehead.

"Do you need an ambulance?" she said.

But she didn't move towards the phone. She sat back down again and bit her lip. For a minute she watched Thomas writhe and sweat on the floor. Then she stood again.

"Thomas! Thomas! Do you feel any better?"

She walked towards his huddled shape. She leaned over and placed a hand on Thomas' shoulder.

"Breathe deeply Thomas."

She had heard the nurses telling people that in ITU. Sometimes it worked.

"Just keep breathing deeply. I'll get you a drink of water."

She ran into the kitchen. Her boots clopped on the kitchen floor. She found a cupboard full of glasses. She stared at all the different-sized glasses. She pulled out what looked like a half-pint glass. She ran water from the tap into it. When she got back to the living-room Thomas was lying face-down on the carpet.

"Thomas? Do you feel better? Here, drink this."

But he wouldn't raise his face from the thick carpet. Lorna waited a few seconds, then sat back on the sofa, the water in her hand. She sniffed and took a sip. Out the patio window, there was a view of a beautiful garden. Lorna had never sat in a house before, as a guest, with a garden like that. She had cleaned some nice houses, but that was different. Thomas grunted from the floor and Lorna was surprised. She had forgotten he was there, as she stared out through the glass at the pink stones arranged in a circle far down the garden. A wee brown bird was pecking at something, its thin legs planted solidly on one of the pink stones. Thomas rolled over onto his back.

"Do you want a drink of water, Thomas?"

She saw him shake his head. She raised the glass to her lips and took another sip. Sitting in this big house was like being insulated. If Thomas and his poor wife had stayed here in the house they would have been alright. It was only out there, in the world, on that road, that they had run into Jimmy. Lorna nodded to herself, feeling the rhythm ease tension from her neck. The wee brown bird was hopping along the garden now, towards the patio window. It wasn't a worm in its mouth. Lorna couldn't tell what it had there. The bird stopped just short of the window glass. It stared in at Thomas.

"Maybe you should stay in here forever, Thomas eh? It's dangerous out there. Maybe I should stay in here with you."

"I get these wild pains in my chest now, Lorna. It's like some big fucking beast has hold of my chest and is biting me there, chewing. It passes though."

"Did the doctors say you were alright, to come home like that? You've got to watch them Thomas. I see how they treat folk. They're bastards for wanting the wards cleared of folk, especially ITU. You're lucky you made it all the way home. Some old ones only make it as far as the first roundabout."

"They say it's in my head. Radthammon, the cardiologist,

The Survival of Thomas Ford

he just wants me to see a psychiatrist."

"Radthammon, he's a prick Thomas. He only cares about his fees and this new house he's getting built."

"New house?"

"Aye. Up in the hills. A beautiful view."

Lorna's mind froze for a second. She waited for Thomas to ask how she knew about the view. Jimmy had told her about the site. Then she realised it was alright, she could say it was gossip she'd heard at the hospital, or Radthammon himself boasting. Thomas lurched sideways and got up onto his knees. His face had a wounded expression, like a footballer who'd just been fouled. Lorna held out the glass of water to him. He took it and gave her a fast, hard look. Then he was clambering back up into the brown chair. He flopped back there and sipped the water.

"Do you want me to get you an ambulance Thomas? I would have done, but I wanted to give you the chance like, to right yourself. I know you won't be wanting to end up back there if you can help it."

"I'm alright. It's maybe all in my head like they say."

"Anyone would be driven mental by what's happened to you, Thomas. I'm no saying you are mental like. But no-one would blame you."

She watched him sip the water.

"What do you illustrate?" she asked.

"I've done all sorts. Children's books, graphic novels."

"Aye?"

Jimmy loved graphic novels and had tried to show her some. Maybe Mr Ford had done some of the drawings that Jimmy stared at.

"I liked drawing in school," she said. "Art."

"My wife, Lea, liked sculpture and carving more. What's

his name Lorna?"

She grinned.

"I went somewhere else today Thomas, like I said, before I came here. I went to the lad's father. He has a business in the city. So I let him know something was up, without giving away too much. I think what you'd say is, I'm open to bids now for the information. From his dad to keep me quiet. From you to tell. See?"

Lorna shrugged. She looked out the window again at the bird. It was staring back in at her, like it could read her thoughts.

"You must think I'm a right bastard, Thomas. But I just need to make the most of the opportunity."

"Bids," said Thomas. "Did the boy's father make a bid then?"

"I didn't tell him hardly anything, Thomas. He probably got left thinking I was mental. I just told him there was something he would want to know. That's all."

Thomas finished the water in a gulp.

"I could tell the police what you're up to," he said.

"I know," she said wistfully, staring at the bird's eyes through the glass.

Thomas shook his head and looked down.

"What kind of bid?" he said.

She blinked. She gnawed at her lower lip. Then she said, "I'd take this house. Or if you let me move in and maybe marry me later. Well, you'd definitely have to marry me, or pass the house to me legally otherwise. The boy's dad's rich as fuck you see. He can bid that high and higher, without noticing. But I don't like the dad, or even the boy much. I like you, Thomas. We could do business that way. Then you wouldn't have to be alone here eh? You could keep drawing,

The Survival of Thomas Ford

and I'd just stay in and sit here and look out at the garden and the birds."

Chapter Eighteen

Robert recognised the four hard raps at the front door. His mum was out. The usual dread at hearing Jimmy there was absent. Robert almost charged forwards, grabbed the handle, muscled the big door wide open.

"Robert," said Jimmy.

He paused and stared for a moment at Robert's narrowed eyes.

"Robert, eh, I've done something a bit mental, man."

But Robert had grabbed Jimmy's jacket lapels. He was pulling Jimmy into the house. Jimmy's shoulder scraped along the edge of a brass mirror in the hallway, nearly knocking it off the wall.

"Lorna was round here!" shouted Robert. "You've told her you bastard! She knows about me! You told me not to tell my mum and now you've fucking told her!"

Jimmy was too shocked to fight back. His first response was a deep laugh, but it never reached his mouth because Robert punched it. Jimmy's head jerked back and bounced off the wall. The hallway had gone almost completely black. Jimmy raised a hand, then felt his knees wobble.

The thumping sounds woke Jimmy up. He felt so thirsty. He started to open his eyes but a shooting pain went through his whole head. He swallowed and took several breaths, then

The Survival of Thomas Ford

made an effort to raise his head. He didn't try to open his eyes this time. He got himself up onto an elbow, then the eyes seemed to pop open quite happily. Robert was four feet away, sitting on the stairs. He was punching regularly at the stair he was sitting on. He was looking down.

"No need to go fucking mental, Robert. We've got to stay focused eh?"

The equilibrium in Jimmy's head vanished again. The elbow slid away and Jimmy hit his head on the carpeted floor. It hurt, even though the carpet felt soft and thick.

"You didn't see Lorna," said Robert. "She was round here, going on about it. I'm no going to jail for you, Jimmy. I couldn't cope."

Jimmy raised himself up again.

"Aye. I know," he said. "I know. But you think I'm going to jail for this eh? No."

"Why'd you fucking tell her then?" Robert screamed.

Jimmy looked at Robert's tear-stained face.

"I don't know man," he said. "I was in bed with her."

"So what?"

"I must have gone soft like."

"Soft?"

"Aye. After shagging and that."

Robert's eyes seemed very wide open.

"Robert, you better calm down man, eh? I hope your mum's no here."

Robert's head shook.

"Well, that's one good thing then. Come on, give me a pull into the kitchen and put some coffee down me before she gets back eh?"

Robert shook his head again. He got up off the stairs and walked toward Jimmy. Jimmy flinched momentarily as

Robert's boots got level with his face. Robert leaned over and took hold of Jimmy's elbow, helping him up.

"You hit me quite hard there, Robert."

"Sorry."

"No, no, it's good to know you've got that in you. If we have to go after Ford and that."

"What's the point? Lorna knows now."

"She won't tell anyone."

"You didn't see her," said Robert. "She looked like she could tell someone, Jimmy."

"She knows I'd fucking kill her if she told anyone."

Jack McCallum was sitting in his office. He tapped the side of his forehead regularly with the gold pen. He'd had to take several calls since the girl's visit. Now he was trying to replay in his mind exactly what she had said to him. How had she worded it? Something terrible that Jimmy had done. Something that would mean a lot of trouble. Trust Jimmy to be screwing a blackmailer and not even have the sense to keep his mouth shut about whatever this was. There was something wrong with the boy right enough. The girl was attractive though, nice thick thighs. Jack imagined having them wrapped round him, here in the office, on some quiet afternoon. Maybe after the blackmail he could still employ her. Mind you, if she had something that was really worth paying for, it could all get expensive. Not too expensive though surely, a girl like that, she'd be happy to get crumbs maybe. Jack stopped tapping his head. He remembered that hungry look in Lorna's eyes.

He picked up the phone.

"Cathy, is Jimmy there?"

"No Jack. Is everything alright?"

"Aye, of course. Do you know where he is?"

The Survival of Thomas Ford

"He said he was going round to Robert's house."

"Right. See you later love."

"Jack…"

Jack started to put the phone down, then lifted it again.

"Cathy? What's that Robert's address?"

"I'm not sure Jack."

"Look Cathy, you'll still have it somewhere from when you sent the Christmas cards out. Find it and call me back."

Robert was dropping three sugar cubes into Jimmy's coffee. Jimmy was sitting at the kitchen table. He kept blinking. It was like the centre of himself had been displaced.

"That's some punch you've got eh Robert? Didn't know you had it in you."

Robert handed Jimmy the mug. Jimmy's hand was shaking.

"I'll put it on the table just now," said Robert. "Look, Jimmy, what if Lorna's at the cops right now, grassing?"

Jimmy frowned.

"Why would she do that? I admit it was mental, telling her, but she wouldn't have a reason to go to the cops."

"She told me she didn't know what she was going to do."

"That's just talk," said Jimmy. "Everyone talks shite most of the time, Robert. Otherwise they'd have fuck all to say."

Jimmy raised the mug but his hand was still shaking. The coffee splashed on the table.

"You've done some job on me here, Robert. Now, if you're really worried about Lorna you should just get hold of her and do the same eh?"

"How?"

"I thought you didn't want her talking. Slam her in the head, Robert, and she won't be talking or grassing on anyone."

"She's your girlfriend."

"Up to a point," said Jimmy.

He managed to bring the mug to his lips. His jaw hurt when he opened it.

"I didn't think she was a grass," said Jimmy. "It changes my feelings."

"We don't know she grassed yet."

"She came here and grassed to you."

"That wasn't pure grassing. She knew I already knew. We don't know she's done any real grassing yet."

"If she has, she's dead."

"If she has, it'll be too late, Jimmy."

"You mean we should kill her before she can grass?"

Robert looked down. He saw that one of his boots was unlaced. He stooped over to tie it. He had the first lace in a circle like a rabbit snare when Jimmy's boot came up between Robert's legs and connected hard with his balls. Robert exhaled with a moan and sank to the floor.

"Not so hard now eh cunt?" said Jimmy.

He drew his boot back and kicked in deftly against Robert's rib-cage. A sad little sigh of air got expelled from Robert's mouth. Jimmy kicked again, trying to find the same spot, but this time there was no exhalation. Robert must be empty now. Four hard raps came at the front door and Jimmy's boot froze in the middle of a kick to the head.

"Who's that?" said Jimmy. "Eh cunt, who will that be?"

Robert made no answer. Jimmy stamped on his leg.

"*Cunt!*"

Jimmy sat back down in the kitchen chair. He felt dizzy. The door was knocked at again, down at the other end of the hall. Jimmy leaned back in his chair, stared down the hall. The silhouetted head at the frosted glass seemed familiar somehow.

The Survival of Thomas Ford

Jack McCallum gave another series of ratatats on the door. He waited a few seconds then walked around the side of the house. There was a little grey gate leading to the garden. Jack flipped the catch and looked at the neat hedges. He closed the gate quietly behind him and made his way along the pebble-dashed wall to the kitchen window. He hated pebble-dashing. No McCallum Home would ever have pebble-dashing. It scraped the edge of his hand as he poked his face against the kitchen window. He saw the back of his son's head. The boy was sitting in a chair, leaning back dangerously. Jack saw something move on the floor, a dog maybe. He walked along to the back door and turned the handle. The door opened and he shoved it in. He entered the kitchen with a loud sniff. Jimmy turned a set of shocked eyes his way. It wasn't a dog on the floor. It was a lad. It looked like Robert Ferguson.

Jack shook his head.

"See, Jimmy, you can't get along with anybody eh? Doesn't matter if it's at my building site or in this poor boy's house. You just bring a squirt of trouble wherever you go. Have you hurt this lad? Has he hurt you lad?"

"What the fuck are you doing here?" said Jimmy.

"Have I no a right to come and see my own boy, check what he's been up to? It looks like you need checking on, Jimmy. Anyway, that lassie Lorna was round at my office today. She says she knows something about you, Jimmy. She says you've got yourself mixed up in something serious."

"Lorna?"

"So I thought I'd come and see you and let you tell me what she's on about, ok lad? No in front of Robert of course. Sorry to come in like this, Robert, but you know how it is. Families and that. Hope you feel better, son."

Jack grabbed the collar of Jimmy's leather jacket. He twisted and pulled. Jimmy felt the dizziness intensify as Jack pulled him out of the chair, then out of the kitchen. Jack let the side of Jimmy's face scrape along the pebble-dashed wall, then he battered Jimmy's head against the grey garden gate. He pulled Jimmy's head back then rammed it against the gate again. The second time the flip-catch split from the wood and the gate opened. Jack pulled his son through the gate and along the side of the house, through the front garden and onto the pavement.

Jack kept Jimmy bent over, his face not far from the concrete. He searched in his pocket for the keys to the Subaru. An old man with a stick was walking past slowly. The man turned red, wet eyes on Jimmy, then on Jack. Jack stared back hard. The old man shook his head and walked on.

Chapter Nineteen

Jack and Jimmy McCallum were sitting in the Subaru, at the edge of the high woods overlooking the city.

"Is that not a wonderful view, boy?" said Jack. "That's development see? Twenty years ago that town was a piss-pot. In twenty years time who knows what it could be? Would you not like to be part of that, Jimmy? Building up the place?"

Jack turned to look at his son. Shreds of bloody skin were peeled back here and there from Jimmy's cheek where the pebble-dashing had got him. Jimmy didn't look back at his father. Jack sniffed.

"You were so clever at school eh? That's what I don't understand, Jimmy. Your mother was just too soft with you. She indulged you. There's a price to pay for things like that and now we're all paying it."

"What price?"

"I don't know, Jimmy. But maybe that wee lassie of yours knows."

Jimmy felt like he was sinking.

"How do you mean?"

"I don't know. She wouldn't tell me any details. Eh?"

Jimmy swallowed.

"*Eh?*" shouted Jack.

He slapped Jimmy's cheek. He held up his hand to slap him again. Jimmy cringed. Shreds from his bloody cheek had come off onto Jack's hand and were glistening in the sunlight like grated rubies.

"I should pound your face in, Jimmy. I've never really done that. Maybe it would get through to you. Nothing else did. But this is business, boy. You're my son. What do you think I'm working for, my old age? I'll probably just fall over on a site one morning and that'll be it. It's all going to be yours boy. But it'll be a man I leave it too, not a boy. This lassie Lorna comes to me and says, *I know something terrible that Jimmy's done, Mr McCallum.* I'd offered her a job before she even says that Jimmy. But no, she wants to go into business for *herself* eh, mangy little Council house cunt. And she wants the McCallums to front up cash for her first deal."

"Cash?" said Jimmy.

Jack shook his head.

"She wants paying son. Paying for not grassing about whatever it is you've done. I wouldn't mind paying. But the paying never ends you see boy?"

Jack slapped his palm down on top of Jimmy's head in an almost loving gesture. Jimmy's black parrot plumage of hair was ruined.

"Why do you no comb your hair forward Jimmy like normal people?"

Jack sighed.

"She said she was going to grass?" said Jimmy.

Jack sat back in his seat and focused on the view.

"That's what she meant," he said. "She wants to be an entrepreneur. Can't blame her. Who doesn't nowadays? So anyway, son, tell me what it is you've done."

Jack looked at Jimmy's sly eyes.

"No boy," he said quietly, "don't make up something that you've done. Tell me what it really is she's got on us."

The Survival of Thomas Ford

Jimmy tried to make a face that would look like he was racking his brain, trying to imagine what it could be.

"Right, out of the car."

Jimmy didn't move.

"Out Jimmy."

Jimmy opened his door and pushed it. The late afternoon air had a wonderfully clean smell. A warm breeze filled the Subaru. Jimmy stepped out of the vehicle. He was standing on brown earth. He heard his father opening the driver's door, then he saw his father's white-haired head rise as he stood. His father started to walk round the front of the Subaru.

"Look dad, I don't know what the fuck she must have been on about. She's mental. I think she should maybe see a psychiatrist eh?"

Jack shook his head.

"You're a stupid wee bastard, Jimmy. I've put up with you and I've tried with you."

"Come on dad, you were saying eh, that all your work's for me eh? What's the point of always clubbing fuck out of me all the time eh? It doesn't make sense man."

"You'll no cooperate Jimmy. You never would. I give you the opportunity like, drive you up to a nice place, ask you nicely, and you tell me shite."

"I'm no telling you shite!"

Jimmy opened his eyes and the sea was below him like he was falling from a plane. He was terrified. There were grey whales in the sea, hundreds, families of them. He felt sick. No, that was the sky up there, not the sea. He was here on the ground, looking up at the sky. That's what was happening. The grey whales were just clouds. There was pain and then disbelief. Jimmy realised he had been knocked out for the second time that day. Outrage filled his cells as he closed his eyes again.

He felt Jack's shoe jab his shoulder.

"Come on, son, stay awake. This is all for your own good. You don't need that wee lassie running around knowing stuff about you, any more than I do. You've got to grow up, Jimmy. Tell me what she knows and then I'll know how to take care of her, see?"

Jimmy opened his eyes again. He saw his father's upside-down face high over him like God. He got up and leaned on his left elbow. There was grass there, shifting in the wind, and a dandelion just by his elbow, quivering on its stalk.

Jimmy looked at the dandelion for a long time. Then he said, "We were just out for a drive by the loch. That's all it was. But I overtook this lorry, just before a bend. And a car came round the corner. Do you remember in the papers, that crash, out by the loch, that woman who died? That's all it was though, we were just out for a drive."

Jimmy shook his head. The dandelion seemed to vibrate now in the sunlight.

"That's all it was," said Jimmy again. "Honest to God, dad. I know the woman died. Aye, I know. But it was all just an accident."

Chapter Twenty

Robert Ferguson was still lying on the kitchen floor. His balls throbbed and sent regular electric pulses up his abdomen to his brain. The nausea was a bloated sea that he kept sinking down into, then rebounding upwards from. He hadn't vomited. He didn't know that he still couldn't move until he heard his mother's key in the front door. Then he tried to move and the electric pulses became galvanic surges that threatened to make his head detonate in a rupturing blasted charge that would leave him vegetabilised there on the laminate flooring. He drew in a thin breath as though through a miserly straw, then blew out the air loudly. He heard his mother enter the hall and the rustle of plastic bags. She walked into the kitchen and past him. He heard her put bags on top of the work surface. She turned to open the fridge door, then she saw him.

"Robert! Robert!"

"It's alright. I fell."

His voice was a wet gurgle.

"I'll get an ambulance love!"

He felt her hand on his neck.

"No! I'm alright. Just let me alone a minute."

"Robert!"

"Let me alone!" he screamed.

He heard her feet leave the kitchen and go into the hall. He heard her pick up the phone. He dragged himself into a foetal position. It felt like one of his balls was connected to his abdomen with a piece of string and that if he straightened himself the string would pull the ball up into his belly. But he got to his knees and crawled until he could see her at the phone.

"Put the fucking phone down! I'm alright I said!"

He saw her blink. Then she put the phone down. She stood looking at him for a few seconds.

"I fell," he said. "I just knocked something. My balls. On the chair. But I'm feeling better. I don't want an ambulance, I just want to rest."

"Alright love. Lie down there. I'll get you a pillow."

He lay on his back and looked at the ceiling. Jimmy's dad had said that Lorna had gone to him and said she knew something about Jimmy. That was it all over then. He could try killing himself maybe, overdose his medication. Or go on the internet, find something more sure to do the job. If he just hadn't been in the car with Jimmy. Once he'd gotten in the car, it was all written in stone somewhere what would happen. There was no free will after that, only fate. Robert didn't feel strong enough to live with the consequences of falling foul of fate. He already wasn't strong enough just to live normally, day by day, not without the medication to keep him calm and steady. None of it seemed fair. The only way out would have been to have gone straight to the police about Jimmy, the day after the accident. Robert frowned. But he could still grass now. Yes, grass now. It sounded like Lorna had only half-grassed to Jimmy's dad, told him only half of the truth or even less. Jimmy's dad obviously hadn't known any details.

The Survival of Thomas Ford

Robert closed his eyes and saw the car coming round the corner and the two heads above the bonnet. He focused on the female head in his memory. It was the female head, the dead one, that mattered. Robert might owe a huge debt to the man, Thomas Ford, but the major debt was obviously to the woman. His presence, his silence, his complicity. But it had been an accident, part of his brain started to say…

No, the silence had not been an accident. Robert had felt the evil dust in the silence. He had stayed longer and longer in the shower each morning, to try to shift that unshiftable sensation of the evil dust on his skin. But the dust was beneath the skin, somewhere deep.

No, luck was not with them. The universe hadn't done one of its errors of omission, not over this debt. Robert could hear the gears and chambers of the universe's engine, rolling terribly towards him out of the future.

"Mum! Mum!"

He heard her feet running on the hall carpet.

"What?"

She was breathless.

"There's something I want to tell you about," he said.

Chapter Twenty-one

Lorna was sitting in Thomas Ford's garden. Her ankle was near the first of the large pink rocks. Sunlight reflected off the rock, making the edge of her ankle seem to glow pink. The high fence and hedges gave total privacy. Lorna couldn't remember the last time she was outdoors and felt that total privacy. She started to worry and try to think back. Maybe she had never felt it before. In the countryside, yes. But not here in the city. This garden in the city was like a machine for escaping the city.

She looked back toward the house. She could see Thomas Ford sitting on the sofa in the living room with a frozen, stunned expression showing at the side of his face and in the angle of his head. She looked up at the roof, the bedroom dormer windows. She would like to go up there soon, but for now it was pleasant here in the garden.

The only thing spoiling the view was the two sets of muddy footprints trailing round the side of the house and up to the patio doors. She stared and tried to tell Robert's prints from Jimmy's. Robert must have the bigger feet. She wondered for a second if that meant he would have the bigger cock. That little bird was still bouncing and hopping around the garden. Maybe it lived here then. Maybe Thomas or Mrs Ford had been feeding it. Lorna looked around the garden, hoping to see a bird-table to complete the idyll but there was

The Survival of Thomas Ford

none. Still, maybe they used to throw it scraps and now Thomas is home and he has forgotten to start feeding it again.

The bird bent over and jabbed mercilessly at a worm.

Thomas sensed the bird's jerky movement with the edge of his left eye. He wasn't consciously aware that it was a bird out in the garden that had moved. His brain might have taken it to be Lorna out there making some predatory passes at the air. What the girl was trying to do here was beyond belief, but there was something refreshing about it. After all the indirect suspicion Thomas had felt for weeks, from doctors, nurses, police, Lea's parents, news announcers, journalists, here was someone being straight with him, in her own way. That's not to say Thomas felt comfortable having her out there in his garden like this.

Thomas blinked. He was afraid too, he realised. Afraid to know the identity of the driver of that red car. What would he have to do once he knew the man's name? Now that the mystery could be solved, Thomas felt nostalgia already for the days of ignorance. But the girl could be lying. She might know nothing.

Thomas got up and walked through the patio doorway, out into the garden. He passed Lorna and went up to the edge of the high, brown fence. He stood and looked over it, at the clouds, keeping his back to her.

"How do I know you're not just making all this up?" he said.

"I'm not."

"How do I know?"

"Do you remember the driver's face?"

"Aye."

"Well, you'll recognise him then, won't you, if I lead you to him?"

"I don't know if I want to see him again."

"That's fine too, Thomas. Just let me know and I'll go to the driver's father and he'll pay me to keep quiet anyway. See, I can't lose Thomas, that's why I came here."

"Maybe I do want to see him," said Thomas.

"Then you see him, after you pay me."

Thomas looked down and laughed.

"I'm no joking Thomas. If you want to know who he is you have to pay me."

Thomas turned to look at her. Her brown hair was being blown against her shoulders, bouncing in a light wind that found its way round the edge of the house.

"Anyway, there's more to this than you're realising Thomas. I didn't want to say but, those footprints outside your window there, that wasn't kids or burglars. That was the driver and the passenger, they came round here to scope you out last night man. They might have even come to do more than that, but they bottled it I think, shat themselves and backed off."

"Now you're just making it up," said Thomas.

"Am I? I'd no be so fucking sure if I was you. Twenty minutes after he was in your garden that driver was in my bed, Thomas, telling me about the day of the accident and how he'd just come from your house."

Thomas stared at her eyes. Perfect little green circles with clear white borders. There was a cant of realism in the eyes. He felt himself believing her.

"So it's no just a question of do you want to find this lad Thomas, this lad is on the hunt for you."

"Why?"

"Why! Because you're the only living witness to him causing death by dangerous driving eh? And don't forget the passenger. He's a quiet lad, but, to be honest, I don't think he's all that stable a character either. Both those boys are waking up sweating Thomas, thinking you'll identify them. They shited last night and left you alone but that doesn't mean it would always go that way."

Thomas remembered getting up from the kitchen floor last night. There had been a moment when he had sensed that someone was behind him, in the garden. Then the footprints today. Kids or burglars hadn't quite made sense. This crazy story was making pieces fit together.

"Aye, you're starting to take me seriously now eh, Thomas? That's OK. I'll even throw in the passenger's name free, once you've paid for the driver."

"Pay you how?"

"You know how. A house. A home. One or the other or both. I told you."

"You're not getting my house Lorna."

Thomas laughed.

"It's either that or you move me into your life," she said.

Thomas shook his head.

"These boys could be back here tonight, Thomas, and just stick you in the back of a van and drive you off into the hills and no-one would ever even find the body. They're at snapping point now I think."

"Maybe I'm at snapping point."

"Aye, maybe, but the difference is they know what direction to snap in. You don't yet. I could be in a manky hospital operating theatre this afternoon, Thomas, wiping detergent over surfaces. Not to save people from getting infected, no, just to keep some manager's arse safe until the next inspection. After the inspection, they'll just let the dirt come back. Everyone's like that, Thomas. You keep things clean only as much as you can afford. Only enough to stay safe."

"And you think I'd be safer with you here then?"

She looked over at the hopping bird.

"You're safer already Thomas. Now that you know about the danger. Thanks to me. Do you ever feed that bird, Thomas?"

Thomas looked round at the bird.

"No. Lea used to sometimes."

"We should put out some nuts or fruit for it, Thomas."

"There's nothing in the house."

"Well, let's go to that Tesco's at the bottom of the road then. We need some food in. So does that bird, if it's used to being fed here."

Thomas shrugged. In a way he would have liked to be alone. In another way, this was better.

Chapter Twenty-two

Jack McCallum was sitting in the driver's seat of the Subaru. He tapped the steering wheel with a finger. He had read about the Ford crash in the newspapers of course. Something about it had never quite added up. Now Jack had found out that the anomaly in the equation was his own boy. Yes, it would be enough to bring everything down. It was worse than anything he'd been imagining since the girl came to his office. First Jimmy would go down, then Cathy would follow. In the centrifugal fallout from that, Jack wasn't naïve enough to think he could survive himself. And if he went down, McCallum Homes and the future went down too.

Jack couldn't let that happen. If that happened then men like Lanski would fill the gap, evolve from foremen into entrepreneurs like the fulfilment of some terrible Darwinian prophecy.

Just like this girl, Lorna, was trying to achieve the evolutionary leap from cleaner to entrepreneur, in one afternoon. Jack couldn't allow it. He had worked too hard and long.

"So you thought the only way out was to kill this man, Thomas Ford, eh Jimmy?" Jack said loudly.

His voice carried over the grass and earth, going into Jimmy's ear. Jimmy was still leaning on an elbow, staring dully at his father in the car.

"Come here!" growled Jack.

Jimmy took a deep breath, levered himself up from the ground in stages. He limped over towards the Subaru. He tripped on a hard root, embedded among the dandelions. When he reached the vehicle he leaned his face, his cheek, on the metal roof.

Jack turned and looked up at Jimmy's armpit.

"You still think that's what it'll take to make us safe, Jimmy? Killing the man?"

"I don't know dad. It's all fucked."

Jack shook his head. He grinned.

"No, boy, it's no all fucked yet. No yet. But safety's harder to buy than you think, boy. Oh aye. I've had the same problem on the sites for years. You've got to balance safety with expediency, profit. And you've got to take risks sometimes, for the sake of the future. The girl will have to go too, Jimmy. You can see that eh?"

Jimmy sniffed.

"Eh?" said Jack again.

Jimmy nodded, without taking his cheek off the roof metal.

"And that lad, Robert, him too," said Jack. "He's weak, Jimmy."

Jimmy closed his eyes and saw a broad, narrow black slit.

"He might have told his mum," said Jimmy.

"Aye?" said Jack. "Her as well then."

Jack held the Subaru steering wheel in his hand. He looked out the windscreen, at the beautiful view, and imagined himself driving round a corner like Thomas Ford had done, to be suddenly faced with Jimmy's head above a red car bonnet. It stuck in Jack's brain for a moment like an indigestible plant; the idea of his son's head being the last

The Survival of Thomas Ford

thing some poor woman saw. Jack had been at Jimmy's birth, against his better judgement, some whim of Cathy's. He had seen Jimmy's head coming out into the world, already covered in a little carpet of vertically spiked black hair. Now he was talking to his son about murdering people. Where did the time go? Jack hadn't murdered anyone for years. He'd thought that was all behind him.

"Is there anyone else, Jimmy?"

"No."

"You didn't tell your mother did you, Jimmy?"

Jimmy took his cheek off the Subaru roof. He looked down at the edge of his father's right eye.

"Of course not," he said.

"Good," said Jack. "Good. Well, it's just a matter of deciding who to start with then, isn't it?"

Chapter Twenty-three

Robert was still lying on the kitchen floor. One of his balls was still sending out regular pulses of complaint. His mother was hunched forward in her chair, frowning at the laminate floor.

"See mum? I need to go to the police, tell them everything, before Lorna does."

"You can't risk going to the police, Robert. You'd never survive even a week in jail."

"But if I tell them everything, make a deal, I wouldn't go to prison over it."

His mother was shaking her head.

"I don't think that girl intends going to the police, Robert, or she'd have just done it. She wouldn't have gone round to Jack McCallum if she meant to go to the police. Oh, she'll threaten to go, aye. But only until she gets Jack to pay up. She came here before she went to Jack. That was her checking the story, wasn't it? Do you think she'd have done that, Robert, if she ever intended going to the police herself? No."

"Do you think?"

"It's the safest bet for us, Robert. You going anywhere near the police could be the one thing that gets you in trouble now."

She shook her head.

The Survival of Thomas Ford

"Why did you have to keep hanging around with that boy? I told you what he's like."

"I know. But I thought we were friends."

"A friend wouldn't leave you in all this trouble, Robert. Or lying on my kitchen floor like that. And his dad coming in here too. I could never stand Jack McCallum, Robert. None of the folk in our class at school could stand him. He was always fighting or bumming off about what a big man he was. Even when he was fucking eight years old."

Robert felt frightened, hearing his mum swear. His mum never swore.

"And anyway, Robert, who's to say you were in that car at all? Where's the evidence? Jimmy's word? Thomas Ford seeing you for a second? Hearsay from some blackmailing hospital cleaner? No, you just keep your mouth shut about it, Robert. And never admit a thing, not to anyone, never again."

Robert's mum stood up. She sniffed.

"I've got to get this kitchen cleaned up, Robert. Are you going to stay there on the floor, or do you want to try crawling through to the living room? The Rockford Files is on ITV3. You like James Garner. Go on. I'll bring you in a herbal tea. You've got to try to calm down, Robert, or you'll just make yourself ill over all this and then it won't matter if you're in prison or where you are."

Robert twisted to the side and found that he could lie comfortably on his belly. He tried to get to his knees but that invisible string from his ball to his stomach drew too tight and he couldn't stand up. He got back down on the floor again. His mum was right. It was easier to crawl on his belly to the living room.

Mrs Ferguson stood alone in the kitchen and watched her son crawl along the carpet until he turned left and started to disappear into the living room. She kept staring at her son until, finally, his heels vanished from the hall. Then she stared at the place where the last heel had been until she heard the television being switched on. She walked across the narrow kitchen and stood at the sink, staring out into the garden. Jack McCallum. His stupid taunts and bullying had spoiled half of her childhood. She hadn't been the only one, oh no. And if she had been a boy, well, she had seen the kind of treatment Jack McCallum could dish out at school to the boys he didn't like.

Then one day Robert had started hanging around with Jack McCallum's son. Jack and Cathy's son. Marie had been in school with Cathy too. Cathy had always been a nice, quiet girl. No-one had understood what she saw in Jack McCallum. But then Jack's little housing empire had started to flourish on the high hills around the town. A lot of girls must have thought twice then, about saying no to Jack back at school. Marie had never regretted saying no, though. Even if it had led to years of abuse from him and his little gang.

Marie bent over and started emptying a bag of shopping. The image of Robert in Court or in a prison visiting room flashed across her eyes for a second and she felt dizzy. If only Robert's father was still here. George could have put a stop to Robert's association with Jimmy and none of this would be happening now. But George was dead and gone, his body never recovered, somewhere at the bottom of the North Sea after a helicopter crash that wiped out a full crew of oil workers on their way out to a fortnight shift on the rig.

It made no sense to Marie.

Men like Robert's dad dying so young, while a man like Jack McCallum grew fat on housing profits. Jack had grown so rich so fast there had even been a TV documentary about

The Survival of Thomas Ford

him a few years earlier. Jimmy had been young then but Marie still remembered him on the TV as a wee lad following his dad around the building sites.

It had been funny, seeing Jack and Jimmy together, like different sized clones almost, even then, except Jack's hair already white.

Now nothing about the McCallums was funny any more, or could ever be again. Marie grabbed the fennel out of the plastic bag and stuffed it roughly against the back of the fridge shelf.

Chapter Twenty-four

Lorna put her fork through a halved tomato and looked across the table at Thomas Ford.

"I'm no used to this, Thomas. Sitting at a table and that, to eat like."

Thomas raised eyebrows.

"No?"

"I always eat in front the TV. Habit eh? Shovel it in and stare at some story."

"We could take it through to the living room if you want."

"No." Lorna shook her head. She took a sip from her glass. "No," she said. "I don't mean I don't like it."

She smiled at him. It seemed to Thomas her eyes bulbed out and there was a strain in her as she looked back at him. Maybe she was finding it harder than she thought, carrying out her crazy plan. Thomas preferred to illustrate characters like that, the ones who had big ideas but not enough nerve to sustain the necessary action. He would draw them with that same strain in their eyes.

"My wife and I had problems here, Lorna. It wasn't a fairy tale marriage by any means. Especially not the last eighteen months. But I did love her."

Lorna nodded. She looked down at the dark-wooded table top.

The Survival of Thomas Ford

"You don't have to tell me anything, though, Thomas. It's not my business."

"She was very ambitious, Lorna. Nothing satisfied her for long. I suppose I got frustrated at that sometimes. Well, I know I did. I wished she could just relax and enjoy what we had here. Tension crept in and just wore us out I suppose. But I think we were on the mend and we could have worked it all out. If the accident hadn't happened."

"Life's always like that though, do you not think?" said Lorna. "Always throwing something at you. I was headed for going to college or maybe even university, then my mum died when I was fifteen. I wasn't right in the head for years after."

"Was your dad not there for you?"

Lorna shook her head as she chewed on a slice of cucumber. "No. He was never there for us. I never even met him, except as a baby but I can't remember that. Anyway, I've no idea where he is now. He could be dead. He was an alcoholic. My mum wasn't like that though. She took good care of me. But she had cancer. At first she never even told me that's what it was. She was always just tired. I knew something was wrong. She only lived two months after she told me what it was."

Thomas nodded.

"Is your mum and dad alive, Thomas?"

He shook his head.

"No. When I married Lea, it was a bit like her mum and dad, Alan and Jean, became mine too for a while. But that was the honeymoon period. Alan soon started seeing my faults and letting Lea know."

Thomas waited for Lorna to ask him what his faults had been. She just looked at him so he said, "My mum was good to me too, and my dad. My dad was a train driver. My mum stayed at home."

"You don't have any brothers and sisters?"

"No. Have you?"

"Nah. It was just me and mum. Now it's just me."

"You must have a boyfriend."

He saw her blush and he grinned.

"So how would that work, Lorna? You wanting to stay here with me and your boyfriend too?"

Lorna felt confusion. It was the first time she didn't know what to say next. She looked down at her plate. She blinked, then looked back up, directly at Thomas.

"It's him," she said.

Thomas frowned and leaned back in his chair.

"The driver?" he said.

Lorna nodded. Her cheeks were still blazing with hot blood. Her eyes seemed hot too now, like an animal just snared, or just escaping a snare.

"I fucking hate him, Thomas. I didn't really know, not until today, how much I hate him. He can be a laugh, and it's not like he's ever really done anything terrible to me, but…there's some part of me that, like, he makes my skin crawl, part of me. Part of me likes him, fancies him, but there's always something fucked up about it. I feel like I might not ever get rid of him unless I really properly get rid of him. Like, he needs flushed down a toilet or something. That's how I feel."

Thomas knew suddenly that something inside himself was getting tugged towards her. It was a tide within him, a wave starting up and moving inevitably in her direction. He knew she must be seeing it in his eyes. She didn't look away. He reached his hand across the table and put it over her hand

The Survival of Thomas Ford

which was by her plate. His mouth was open and he could hear his own loud breathing in the quiet room. Her cheeks were still bright red. Her hand was hot against his palm. She turned her hand over so her palm met his palm.

"I don't really think there are accidents," said Thomas. "I hated it at the hospital, every time they said 'the accident'. Lea used to believe everything is just accidents, coincidence. But I don't see it like that."

"What do you see?"

"There's patterns to things. Like, here you are and I'm glad you're here just now. And you know who he is. You know who made Lea go into the water. And you want rid of him. I want rid of him too. I see him in dreams. Him and his mate beside him. Above the red bonnet. I hate him a lot more than you ever will. The police and the hospital and Lea's parents, they think killing's an accident, or else they think it was my fault and I'm lying about the red car. And your boyfriend thinks killing's a game or a sport maybe."

"I don't really know what he thinks," she said. "Not really."

Thomas laughed.

"I'm not really sure I ever knew what Lea was really thinking."

Lorna sniffed.

"No, it's no like that. Your wife at least wasn't mental, Thomas. Jimmy..."

Lorna shut her mouth. She swallowed. Her cheeks blazed.

"You better go and put your face in cold water, Lorna. Jimmy eh? I wonder how hard it would be for me to find him now. Still too hard maybe. But I don't know. I know where you work, easy to find out where you live. I could ask your neighbours about Jimmy."

Lorna shook her head.

"My neighbours know nothing about me."

Thomas shrugged and smiled.

"It doesn't matter anyway, Lorna. You can stay here if you want to. I don't mind the idea at all. Lea's parents might find it very strange, and the police when they find out, but I like the idea. I'll need a lot more than his first name. If I'm going to fix this little bastard properly I'm going to need to know everything about him that you know. So tell me."

"No, I says before, you'd have to get a document drawn up legally, entitling me to this house, or you'd have to marry me. I wasn't joking."

"Neither am I joking, Lorna. Tell me about him. Then you can stay."

Lorna frowned and sat back heavily in her chair. She grinned suddenly.

"You've got nothing, Thomas. A first name. It's nothing. I can still go to his dad and he'll give me a house just to shut me up."

"His dad has a spare house?"

"He has money."

Thomas felt a sharp stabbing sensation in his chest. He nearly panicked, expecting the pain to return fully the next second. He breathed in deeply. Then out slowly. Lorna watched him.

"Are you alright?"

Thomas nodded.

"Aye. But we've got to stop arguing about all this."

"Thomas, if you can't cope with arguing, you're no going to be able to cope with handling him, are you? I said he was mental, but I didn't say he wasn't hard."

"Hard?"

The Survival of Thomas Ford

Lorna nodded. It was the one quality in Jimmy that couldn't be denied, an elemental toughness. There was a solid core at the centre of all his bullshit. That was the trouble with him. That was why you had to watch what you did to him.

"His dad's hard too," she said. "See Thomas? You're up against so much here and you don't even know it. Jimmy wants rid of you in case you can ever identify him. But if Jimmy's dad finds out then you've got even more to worry about. His dad would never let this, or anything, fuck up their lives. Your only chance, and my chance, is to fuck up their lives first. Really."

Thomas looked at the green eyes. Saucer circles of honest intent drilling back at him over the table. Yes, he'd like to draw her. It was almost worth all the trouble and agony, what had already been and what was still to come probably, just to have these moments sitting with her. He had realised her quality at the hospital, watching her as she moved among the forest of metal beds, emptying bins, picking up used Lucozade bottles. For a brief moment he compared her to Lea. The thought shocked him, something sacrilegious in it.

"Fuck up their lives first," said Thomas. "I like that. Except it was him that fucked up my life first, and Lea's."

"Aye, well you don't know him like I know him Thomas. He can do a lot more if he gets the chance. This time last night they were standing out there in the garden Thomas, looking in the fucking window at you eh?"

Thomas turned his head toward the patio windows and looked out onto the shadowed garden. The bird was still there, hopping around. It seemed wrong to Thomas, the bird being there so late.

Chapter Twenty-five

Jack McCallum turned the ignition key back and the Subaru engine died out.

They were parked on the opposite side of the road from Thomas Ford's house, but much further down than Jimmy and Robert had been the night before.

"We can't see anything from here dad eh?"

"We can see enough."

They had just spent two hours parked outside Lorna's flat, waiting for her to come home. Every few minutes Jack had sent Jimmy into her building to rap on her door in case she was in and asleep or just not answering. Then, on the way to Thomas Ford's house, Jack had taken a detour to pass Robert Ferguson's house and Jimmy had clearly seen Robert and his mum sitting in their living room, ghostly shadows from Coronation Street flickering across their white visages.

Jack had grunted and said coldly, "They'll keep."

Now Jimmy was staring at the pavement outside 16 Cromwell Drive. A woman passed suddenly with a dog and Jimmy recognised the dog from the night before. Jimmy was cursing his weakness now. Something about being in Thomas Ford's garden had broken him, seeing the man there in the kitchen. He still hadn't recovered. The fall-out from that had been landing on him ever since. That was why he had told Lorna everything.

The Survival of Thomas Ford

It had only taken 24 hours for it all to come apart and now here he was stuck in the Subaru with his father. The worst thing about Jack McCallum tonight was the cold calm that had entered him. Jimmy had grown used to verbal abuse and beatings. But this calm iced demeanour was difficult to get used to.

Jack sniffed. Then he said, "We only need to be close enough to see if someone comes or someone goes. And without us getting seen. You got too close last night. You don't ever get that close, Jimmy, not unless you know exactly what you're going to do. You had it all arse backwards. But maybe it's for the best."

Jack tapped the steering wheel rhythmically with his forefinger. He looked up and down the long, broad road of Victorian and Georgian properties. This was the cream of the city's real estate. Jack himself owned three of the larger properties on this road, under a company set up using the alias, Graham Farnham. As Graham Farnham, Jack was a respected shadow or sleeping partner in a good percentage of the city's business, and all without any conflict of interest charges ever arising. Often Graham Farnham's company would acquire land one week that Jack McCallum started building on the next. These Poles who came and went, even the clever ones like Jack's foreman, Lanski, they didn't have a clue what they were getting involved with in this city. Same went for men like Radthammon or even that other doctor, Nissen. Jack regarded them as only half-men, a form of transient adolescent flashing across the landscape. They wouldn't last. Only men like him lasted and made a mark on their time and place. Now the boy had done something stupid and threatened the edifice somewhat. But he would learn.

That was a father's responsibility after all; to show by example, not just talk.

"What's the fucking point of sitting here eh?" said Jimmy. "It's Lorna that's the real danger just now, worse danger than Ford eh?"

"Aye? Is that right? How do you know that? Fucking assumptions. How do you know that lassie isn't sitting in that man's house right now, telling him everything?"

Jimmy looked stunned.

"Why would she do that?"

"She came to me eh? What's to stop her going to him? She's trying to come up in the world, boy. You should take a leaf out her book eh? She's discovered the joy of being an entrepreneur. I almost envy the lassie. There's no buzz like it. She has to go back and forth from me to Ford, until she gets the offer she wants, see?"

"What if she's already seen him then, and got the offer she wants?"

"No, boy, it doesn't work that fast. She'd come back to me again, before she made the decision. She'd need to give us a chance to outbid Ford. That's business, son. That's what I've been trying to teach you."

Jimmy sniffed. Just then, Thomas Ford and Lorna appeared together on the pavement outside 16 Cromwell Drive. Jimmy blinked and stared at them. He was trying to make himself believe he was really seeing them, that they weren't his imagination playing a trick. Thomas Ford and Lorna turned their heads and seemed to look directly at the Subaru.

"Dad! Fuck's sake. It's them together. Fuck's sake. Are they seeing us?"

"No if you stay still. We're just shapes behind the tint from where they are."

"What if they come down this way?"

The Survival of Thomas Ford

"Then they'll see us."

Jack bit his lip and raised his eyebrows. He tapped the steering wheel twice. Thomas Ford and Lorna started walking along Cromwell Drive, away from the Subaru.

"He's holding her hand!" Jimmy shouted. "How the fuck's this going on? No, this is no right. Eh?"

"Shut up, boy. I'm trying to think."

"That's them off to the police," said Jimmy. "The station's up that way."

"Aye, five miles up that way."

"We've got to see where they're going! Fuck's sake!"

"No. What else is up that way?"

"The off-license. The park."

"Maybe just out for a walk," said Jack.

"Out for a fucking walk! She doesnae even know that cunt!"

"She knows him now, boy. She's holding his hand. No, we sit here and wait on them. They'll be back."

There was a warm tingling in Thomas Ford's fingers as he walked along beside Lorna. It felt like he'd been transported somehow, into a new place. The last few weeks seemed to be washed away from him, a layer of old skin dropping off. It amazed him how his steps were synchronised already with her steps. Lea had always done that thing of walking a half-step in front, no matter how fast or slow they would walk together. Lorna didn't do that and Thomas felt guilty for noticing the difference and liking it.

"This whole area is so peaceful, Thomas. Is it always like this?"

"Aye. Nothing much ever happens round here."

"Look at these beautiful old trees."

"Aye, there's character in them isn't there? I draw them sometimes. You could imagine them coming to life and walking off."

Lorna laughed.

"That one looks angry," she said.

"Aye, but not that one."

"No, not that one. That one's nice."

"You've never been in this park before?"

She shook her head and kept her eyes on the tree.

"I think it's the city's best park," he said. "Even when I lived on the other side of town I would come here to go for walks."

"Is it safe at night?"

He shrugged and laughed.

"Safe as anything else."

"That's not saying much, Thomas."

"No. I suppose not."

"I do feel safe with you, though," she said. "I haven't really felt safe for ages."

"Why?"

"Him. Being with him. Around him. He's not safe. I don't think he's right in the head."

"Maybe I'm not right in the head either."

"Aye, but if you're not right in the head, Thomas, it's because of him."

Thomas sniffed and looked up at the dark sky.

"He's not here, Lorna. Forget about him for just now."

"I bet you can't really forget about him."

"Just now I could. Walking here just now, with you, it's the first time in weeks I could forget about him."

"Aye?"

"Aye."

The Survival of Thomas Ford

He felt her hand squeeze his palm.

"I'll shut up about him then," she said.

But Thomas Ford was lying. In his brain the indelible image of the erect black hairstyle, black eyes, birdlike nose, still loomed. Framed by the blue sky above and the red bonnet below, Jimmy's head, incandescent, searing, a grotesque human torch illuminating Thomas Ford's ravaged mind.

"What are you thinking about?" said Lorna.

"I don't know. This has been a strange day. For you just as much as for me."

Lorna nodded. Her eyes were on the path at her feet, the angled toes of her boots.

"All the days have been strange though," said Thomas, "since I woke up after the crash."

"You were asleep six weeks weren't you? I remember when they brought you in. Then I was cleaning round your bed for weeks and weeks."

"Aye, six weeks," said Thomas.

"I watched you sleeping sometimes. Some of them aren't nice to watch sleeping. But you looked like you were enjoying the sleep."

Thomas laughed.

"Aye?"

"Oh aye. The nurses said that too. That you looked happy asleep there."

"I don't remember anything from it. Not even any dreams."

"I'd like to go to sleep for six weeks, Thomas. Sometimes I think I'd just like to go to sleep forever. Do you ever feel like that?"

"No. Six weeks was long enough."

John A. A. Logan

At the edge of the park, where Cromwell Drive met Fortsmith Road, Jack McCallum and Jimmy stood like newly-exorcised and roaming ghosts, staring in through the metal railings at the distant walking silhouettes of Thomas Ford and Lorna.

"This is fucking unbelievable," said Jimmy.

"Shut up," said Jack.

Jack was trying to run through the permutations in his mind, the series of moves Lorna must have made today to have ended up here, walking in the park with Thomas Ford. But it didn't make sense. Jack couldn't make it add up, no matter which way he spun the dice.

"Something's fucked up here right enough boy," said Jack. "This is what you get when amateurs step into the playing field. Unpredictable odds. Give me a hardened professional to deal with every time, son. They might beat you, aye, but at least it will make sense afterwards when you're licking your wounds back at the ranch eh?"

"What are we going to fucking do?" Jimmy almost squealed.

"You find your balls for a start eh son? Come on, get a grip. It's no even the end of round one yet."

Jimmy stared longingly at Lorna's shape in the park. He had never wanted her like he did now, not even when she wore the boots and went on top. The pain of seeing her with Ford was starting to turn him on, bizarrely, against his will.

"I loved her," said Jimmy. "I really loved her. I didn't realise until now."

Jack looked at his boy with disgust.

"Don't talk shite, Jimmy."

Jack sniffed and shook his head. He looked away from the couple in the park. He gazed down Cromwell Drive. It

The Survival of Thomas Ford

seemed very quiet. No people. No traffic. Not even a stray cat. Jack tried to remember if that was normal for this street.

"Was it this quiet here last night?"

"How do you mean?" said Jimmy.

"The street boy! Last night. Was it this quiet?"

Jimmy looked at his dad, then back down Cromwell Drive.

"I cannae mind. Aye, I think so. Just a woman walking a dog was all."

"No son, this doesn't feel right. This could be a set-up. The cops could be watching us right now. I think it's a trap boy! That's why they're in there. She's grassed."

Jimmy stared at his father. He saw fear in his father's eyes.

"You're just shiting it!" said Jimmy. "Cops wouldn't be here for us. They'd be straight round the house, no here!"

"I don't know, boy."

Jimmy watched his father's neck crane like a terrified, hunted beast.

"I don't know, Jimmy. It doesn't feel right boy. Let's back off the now. I need time to think."

Jimmy shook his head. This was as useless as the visit to the garden the night before. Where was all his father's big talk now?

"We haven't got time to think any more," said Jimmy. "There she is in there with him now eh? What are we going to do?"

"I didn't plan for this," Jack hissed. "She's moving too fast. Doesn't smell right."

Jimmy stared at Jack, focusing hard on the fear in his father's eyes. From a branch in a tree high above their heads, a lonely bird screeched aggressively into the night. Jimmy looked away from his father and up into the branches.

"Did you hear that?" said Lorna.

"What?" said Thomas Ford.

"That bird. It sounded angry."

"You seem to have a thing about birds."

"I like them. Aye. Tomorrow I want to get some bread for yours in the garden. Is that OK?"

"None of my business," said Thomas.

"Oh, you want it hopping round your garden all day starving do you?"

"I never notice it."

"That's not very charitable, Thomas. You've got to try to take care of wee things."

Lorna turned towards the tree she had heard the bird call from. For a moment, she thought she saw shadows there, like people standing near the tree, outside the park, on the pavement. But then the shadows were gone.

"That's strange," she said. "I thought I saw something."

"What?"

"Nothing. Just a shadow."

Thomas looked over in the direction she was indicating.

"Tell you the truth, Lorna. I'm starting to worry about this Jimmy. I sort of forgot it for the last hour. But what if they come back to the house tonight? What if they're there now?"

"He wouldn't be there with the lad from last night, Thomas. I saw him today. He didn't look like he wanted any part in it any more."

Jack and Jimmy had edged themselves round the railings a few feet, to shelter behind the tree with the screeching bird.

"They didn't see us," said Jack. "If they did, they'll just think it's people passing."

The Survival of Thomas Ford

"We've got to get them before they go to the police," said Jimmy.

"They might already have been."

"Phone mum. If the police haven't been to the house, then no-one's grassed yet."

Jack felt the slick of sweat above his eyebrows. He hadn't thought of the phone. Jimmy heard Jack's horny fingernails clumsy against the keyboard.

"Cathy!" hissed Jack quietly. "Cathy, hi. Everything alright at the house?"

Jimmy heard his father do a false laugh into the phone.

"No, no, no reason for asking. No visitors today then? No calls? Quiet day then eh. That's good. I'll be home soon love. Jimmy's with me too. We'll be back soon. No. No. OK. Bye love."

"See?" said Jimmy. "This is the chance."

"OK boy."

Jack reached in his pocket for the Subaru keys.

"Aye, Jimmy. You're probably right. Run back down, get the car, bring it up and park beside the gates there."

Jimmy squeezed the keyring.

"What are you going to do?" he said.

"Just get the car. Run boy!"

Jimmy's feet slapped the pavement on the way back down Cromwell Drive. It felt like battery acid in his veins, or the wrong oil, not blood. This was all happening too slowly. It wasn't like the day of the crash when everything happened in a sudden blitzkrieg of action. Jimmy ran past Thomas Ford's driveway. He kept running. He ran past the Subaru. He didn't even look at it there, parked on the opposite side of the road. He kept on going. He ran faster. He passed the woman with that strange, old dog on a chained lead. The dog's eyes glared with manic danger at Jimmy under the orange lamplights. It was only properly a nightmare for Jimmy, now that his father was involved. The two separate worlds had collided. The dinosaur in Jimmy was faced with its final nemesis comet moment.

Anything could happen now.

Chapter Twenty-six

Robert's eyelids were drooping heavily in front of the TV screen's mesmeric flicker. His mum watched him as she knitted on the big leather chair that her husband had loved. The chair was split in so many places now, but Marie would not give it up.

If the chair went, everything could go.

"You should be off to bed, Robert," Marie whispered when she saw her boy's head nod on its thick neck.

"I want to see this programme."

"You've slept through half of it."

Robert sniffed. He raised his torso up higher on the sofa back. Jimmy McCallum's face appeared suddenly at the living room window, like someone had just thrown his wet head there from the street and it had stuck to the outer glass. Marie Ferguson screamed and Robert stared. Jimmy's mouth was working like a ventriloquist's dummy's wooden, churning lips. Through the double-glazing nothing could be heard. Robert stood up and his balls throbbed in complaint.

"No, Robert! Just stay where you are!" said Marie.

Robert shook his head and walked into the hall. He was careful how he moved on the way to the front door, trying to keep his thighs off his balls. He opened the door and Jimmy seemed to collapse into his arms like a relieved damsel in a fairy tale, except Jimmy was lathed in sweat. Robert held him up and got him into the house. He closed the front door with a bang, surprising the old grey cat that sat on their driveway wall every evening.

It was like a fever. Jimmy didn't remember sleeping, but now he was waking up in Marie Ferguson's bedroom. He recognised the smell, the wallpaper, the furniture, that mirror with the Elizabethan influence. Often Jimmy had masturbated with his head full of Marie Ferguson and this room.

But it wasn't Marie standing over the bed. It was Robert.

"Robert man!" Jimmy whispered.

Robert watched Jimmy's eyes make a long, slow roll of the room before focusing on himself.

"I'm sorry I did your nuts like that man! I'm sorry. It was fucking stupid. Forgive me man eh?"

Robert tried to imagine what could have happened to Jimmy tonight to leave him talking like this. It was like seeing a stranger there, lying on his mother's bed.

Now Jimmy was reaching out towards Robert with a pawing hand.

Robert stepped back.

"No, Robert man, no, I mean it. I'm sorry. You're the only friend I've got man eh?"

Jimmy's eyes came into clear focus. Robert believed it.

"Friend?" Marie Ferguson shouted from the doorway. "Friends don't get people into the kind of trouble you've got my son into, Jimmy!"

Jimmy looked at her and Robert expected an outburst.

But Jimmy only said, "I know, Mrs Ferguson, I know. I'm sorry. Look, I'll do whatever you want. I'll go to the police and tell them Robert had nothing to do with it. I mean, I'll say I was alone in the car. They'll not care about a passenger."

The Survival of Thomas Ford

"That girl knows Robert was there," said Marie.

Jimmy nodded.

"Aye. She's with Thomas Ford right now. In a park. My dad's there too. He's gone properly mental now, I think. I didn't know what he was going to do. I ran off."

Jimmy looked from Robert to Marie.

"I was frightened," said Jimmy. "I've always been frightened of my dad."

"What did you think he was going to do?" said Marie.

Jimmy shook his head and looked at the thick carpet.

"What's Lorna doing with Thomas Ford? Has she grassed?" said Robert.

Jimmy stared. His eyes were desperate black pools as Robert looked into them.

"She was holding his hand," said Jimmy.

Chapter Twenty-seven

Jack McCallum had been waiting, hunched down just inside the park gates, for a long time now. He kept looking down Cromwell Drive for the Subaru. There was no traffic. The air was still. Jack knew he hadn't even heard the engine start and he was sure he could have heard it from here.

The boy just couldn't be relied on. It was a terrible fact. His own boy.

Nevertheless, the insane optimist in Jack, the part of him that had sanctioned several McCallum Homes building projects on steep south-facing hills with poor drainage, that part of him kept looking down Cromwell Drive, expectant still of spying the Subaru's metallic nose.

"Cunt!" said Jack under his breath. "Little cunt."

He couldn't even take comfort in alleging the boy was not his own. Cathy was boringly faithful, like a Labrador, and anyway the boy looked like a younger version of himself. No, the problem was located in the boy's brain, some kind of cross-wiring, or incompatible programming. The boy had the hardware, but the drivers needed upgrading, something like that, something impossible to fix with a human head to date. All that talk about solving this problem with murders. It should be the boy getting murdered. Jack opened his mouth in a sudden snarl. Orange lamplight glittered on his crowned incisors.

The Survival of Thomas Ford

Jack took a deep breath and let it out.

The boy wasn't coming.

Jack stood up straight. He wasn't sure whether to walk out of the park and down Cromwell Drive, or go further into the park. He couldn't see Thomas Ford or Lorna. If he stayed off the path, in the trees, he ought to be able to find them, maybe even get close enough to listen to them. Yes, that wouldn't be a waste of time. Far from it.

Thomas Ford and Lorna were passing over the short stone bridge.

"Are you sure we're safe in here, Thomas?"

"I've been walking here for years at all hours."

"Aye, but the city's changed man. There's piles of folk here now."

"But you're saying we're not safe at the house either," said Thomas. "Where would you feel safe tonight? Your place?"

"Uh uh. Jimmy's probably there now, battering at the door."

"So we're not safe anywhere now, except if we go to the police."

"Do you want to?" said Lorna.

"It would stop them thinking I'm crazy. It's been bad, everything just being my word."

"Now there's my word too," she said.

"Will you come to the police then?"

"No Thomas. You wouldn't have to pay me anything once I'd told the police. If you go to them I'll deny anything. I'll say you're mental, that you've had a fixation on me ever since you watched my arse in the hospital when I was emptying your bin."

"I didn't watch your arse."

"Aye you did. Two nurses told me."

Thomas felt himself blush.

"You can stay with me," he said. "I want you to."

"Aye, but I need something in writing. Something formal."

"That would take time. I'm not sure how to even go about that. It probably wouldn't be legally binding."

"You'll have to find something that would be legally binding. That's what lawyers do isn't it Thomas? They find ways to sort out things how you want them to be."

Thomas shook his head.

"You're living in a fantasy world," he said.

"Maybe," she said calmly, "but you want to know what I know, one way or another. You need to know."

"You're not safe either. Not until you tell either me or the police."

"For me it's a calculated risk."

There was a sudden rustling sound in the bushes nearby. Thomas and Lorna stopped walking.

"What was that?" said Lorna.

"Who's there?" called Thomas.

They stared at the trees and bushes for moments. The noise didn't come again.

"Probably a cat," said Thomas.

"Let's go back to the house."

Thomas nodded.

From deep in the bushes, Jack McCallum stared out at the couple. He saw them turn back and head for the stone bridge again. He hadn't been able to hear what they were talking about. Trying to hear, he had come too close. But they looked awful cosy together. This afternoon, at the office, had

The Survival of Thomas Ford

she already been to see Ford by then? They looked like they'd known each other for years. What was going on here? Now they were headed right back to the park gates. What if they run into Jimmy there, just arrived with the Subaru? Or maybe the car hadn't started and Jimmy was trying to get it going down by the house. They'd hear the engine coughing and spluttering all the way down Cromwell Drive, then they'd see him surely.

There were too many variables and Jack sensed the softness in his head. His head was soft where it used to be a machine, because Jack had passed the real thinking on to men like his foreman, Lanski. Jack clenched his fist and realised this was the first time in months that he had to face reality without Lanski to bail him out of a problem.

It was frightening how quickly you lost your strength when you stopped using it.

Then when you needed it again it was gone.

There hadn't really been a plan. Jack had no idea what he would have done next if Jimmy had shown up at the park gates with the Subaru. There would have been momentum at least. Now there was no momentum. Jack could hardly even bring himself to stand up behind the bush and follow Ford and Lorna back to the bridge.

Chapter Twenty-eight

"He's really gone mad though," said Jimmy to Marie and Robert Ferguson. "I've never seen him this bad."

"He's always been like that, Jimmy," said Marie. "He was like that in school, primary school I mean. He would always take things too far. Bullying people, getting ideas into his head."

Jimmy nodded.

"He's battered me all my life," said Jimmy. "My mum couldn't stop him. No-one could stop him."

"Cathy shouldn't have let him away with that," said Marie.

"No-one can stop him," said Jimmy. "No-one on the sites could ever stand up to him. Even folk buying houses are frightened of him. They take houses off-plan but then he tells them what they're going to have in the houses, they get no choice. If people go to lawyers he frightens the lawyers. If people get the police nothing happens. All the high-up police know my dad eh?"

Marie nodded. It was true. Two of them had been in their primary school class and had joined in when Jack shoved her. They were even worse bastards than Jack. There was always the chance that now the town had supposedly grown into a "city", there might be some top cop there who had their mind on their job, not their next Free Mason meeting, but Marie doubted it.

The Survival of Thomas Ford

"Maybe we should still go to the police though," said Marie.

"You said no police, mum."

"Aye, Robert, but now Jack's involved."

"We were in the park watching them," said Jimmy. "The park at the top of Thomas Ford's road. We could see Lorna and Thomas Ford, in the park. We couldn't hear what they were saying. But they were holding hands. I don't know what's going on. Neither did my dad. Up to then I thought he had a plan. But when we watched them in the park together I could tell he was going more and more mental. He told me to go and get the car and bring it to the park gates. I don't know what he was going to do with it. I ran here instead."

"I'll call the police," said Marie.

But she didn't move. Jimmy and Robert were silent, waiting for her to move.

"They're all his mates, Mrs Ferguson. Honest to God," said Jimmy.

She looked at him. He said, "It's no that I'm worried about getting in trouble any more. But they're round at our house all the time like, cops, they drink whiskey with him for hours. They all live in his houses."

"I thought all that had changed," said Marie.

Jimmy shook his head.

"No, Mrs Ferguson. I think it's worse now than ever. There's folk up from London and that, high up guys, worse than the ones before. There's so much money around now eh? That's what's really changed."

"What's he going to do then," said Robert, "to Thomas Ford and Lorna?"

Jimmy shook his head. The high plumage of his black parrot hairstyle shook beneath the energy saving bulb attached to Mrs Ferguson's living-room ceiling.

"It's no just Thomas Ford and Lorna he's after now," said Jimmy. "It's all of us."

Chapter Twenty-nine

"Lanski," Jack McCallum said into the mobile. "Lanski. Wake up! It's McCallum."

"Mr McCallum?"

"Do you know where Cromwell Drive is, Lanski?"

"What, Mr McCallum?"

Jack heard a woman say something in Polish in the background.

"Get out of bed, Lanski. I've got a job for you. Meet me right now, outside 16 Cromwell Drive, you understand? Don't drive all the way here. Park on Booth Road, then walk round the corner past the park gates, and down to Cromwell Drive, outside number 16. Walk quiet, Lanski. Don't make a sound when you get here. I'm in the Subaru on the other side of the road from 16 Cromwell Drive and about 20 yards downhill. You'll see me. Now move it, Lanski."

Jack terminated the call. He sat far down in the driver seat of the Subaru. His eyes on the windows and door of 16 Cromwell Drive were the eyes of a cat near feeding time. Jack had been a long time between meals. He suddenly realised he was getting into this. He felt five years younger. Then he frowned. Maybe not. Maybe he only felt relief now that Lanski, his best man, was getting on-board.

Fifteen minutes later, Jack saw his lanky Polish foreman coming down Cromwell Drive. Lanski had on a blue thermal jacket, a wool hat, and his work boots. He saw Jack in the Subaru, just a forehead and a strip of white hair above the steering wheel. Lanski half-smiled inside. This was like smuggling meets back in Warsaw. He counted the house numbers as he walked down the street. When he knew he was passing number sixteen he took care not to look over at that house.

Nearing the Subaru, Lanski saw McCallum's hand unlocking the passenger door and silently shoving it open. Lanski caught the handle in long fingers and with a tug and a swerve of his hips he was in the passenger seat, hunched down low like his boss.

Except this wasn't his boss. Lanski sensed the difference immediately. It was like a smell in the car. Lanski knew that this was his boss' shadow. The Wolf within McCallum had risen to the surface now and taken over. The flesh at Lanski's neck crawled. The last thing Elena had shouted as he left the flat was to be careful. Yes, he was going to have to be very careful. Lanski looked at McCallum's face beneath the orange streetlight nearby. Only the lower half of the nose and mouth were visible. The rest was in shadow, or had become shadow itself. Lanski's grandmother had told him stories about the men who had holes inside themselves and how the hole could grow larger and larger until the man himself became nothing but a hole. Lanski's mother had hated her own mother filling her boy's head with those old-country stories which all seemed to be about the fatality of life, the uselessness of struggling against it.

Lanski's mother had taught him, no, struggle. Never stop struggling, that is what she had taught Zbigniew Lanski who looked so much like his own father now.

"Mr McCallum?"

The Survival of Thomas Ford

"They're in there, Lanski. That house. Number 16. A man and woman who can bring everything down, Lanski. What I've worked for, and what you've worked for too. You don't want that to happen do you, Lanski? No, of course not."

Lanski swallowed and stared over at the unlit house.

"A business problem?" said Lanski.

"Aye. And worse. Much worse. Family trouble, Lanski. Enough trouble brewing in that house tonight to bring my whole family to the ground I think. And if that happens I go down with it. And if I go down with it you go down with it. So it's family trouble for both of us."

Lanski frowned.

"But what can anyone do to hurt you, Mr McCallum? You are a secure man."

"I thought so too until today, Lanski. But we both know there's always been a potential danger in my life eh?"

Lanski blinked. The boy. McCallum meant his boy, Jimmy. The boy has done something. A light came on suddenly in the living room of number 16. Lanski saw a man's silhouette pass behind thin drawn blinds. A woman's shape followed.

"What is it you want of me, Mr McCallum?"

"You're an ambitious man, Lanski. If you help me tonight I'll take care of you and your family, your whole family, aunts, uncles, nephews, illegitimate bastards, your old widowed mother, your wives and girlfriends, whatever you've got, I'll take care of it all for the rest of your lives, Lanski. If you help me here tonight our families will be bound together, Lanski. Everything you've been working for and would take you thirty years, I'll give you it for one good night's work."

And then Lanski knew beyond doubt that the Wolf at his side had killing in his heart. Lanski licked his lips. There was really nothing to consider. Somehow just by getting in the car he was already too far in to turn back now. Lanski swallowed loudly.

"We have to get them out of that house tonight, Lanski. I have a place no-one knows about. We get them there. It shouldn't be too hard. Then the problem will have gone away. That's all we need."

"It is only a man and a woman there?" said Lanski.

"Aye. Both young enough. But the man's been in hospital after a car accident, he's weak. Big though. It's the bitch I'd expect the worst trouble from."

Lanski heard McCallum laugh. After the laugh there was a long silence.

"Are you ready?" said Jack.

Lanski didn't answer. He opened the passenger door and levered his weight smoothly out onto the pavement. The light was still on behind that blind in 16. Lanski heard Jack's driver door opening. He looked across the Subaru roof at his employer's white hair, tinged with the orange from the streetlight. Jack nodded at Lanski and they both walked up Cromwell Drive.

In the living room of number 16, Thomas Ford was kissing Lorna's neck as he stood behind her. It was as though there were some juice beneath the skin that he felt he could extract with his lips. Time in the living room seemed to have slowed. Lorna had her hands at Thomas' hips, feeling behind herself. She twisted her neck until he kissed her mouth.

She didn't taste like Lea, of course. Still, there was a shock, as though Thomas had expected her to taste like Lea. This taste was less rich, more sweet. Lea had been, in many ways, a savoury dish. Lorna, so far, seemed more to do with

The Survival of Thomas Ford

the fruit family. Her two breasts truly like warm melons in Thomas' palms. Her earlobe plump and firm-fleshed now between Thomas' teeth. There was a quick insane desire to bite the earlobe and make it pop and split and burst and bleed forth, to taste her juice perhaps.

But still, there it was in Thomas' mind, the black-haired driver with his bird nose and fathomless eyes. That head, floating through Thomas Ford's brain like some guillotined aristocrat.

"Do you want to go upstairs?" said Thomas.

"No, here. Here."

Jack McCallum and Zbigniew Lanski were silent as they travelled the length of the side wall to Thomas Ford's house. Their shoulders grazed the wall like floundering organic spirit levels trying to find some flat, final mathematical truth before the day ended. Jack eyed the pebble dashed wall with distaste. A house in a good area like this should never be allowed to go pebble-dashed, even at the side elevation. He made a mental note to get on to Lizzie at the Planning Office about it. Then Jack saw that Lanski was leaving the wall's corner and entering the garden. Jack sprinted forward and slapped his palm onto the Pole's shoulder.

Lanski spun round. Jack raised a hand, patted the air, telling Lanski, wait, in that unspoken language they had evolved through countless building projects.

Jack put his head round the corner. The garden was bathed in light from the house. Something moved in the garden just as Jack started to look for the living room window. Jack stared at the grass and saw a thin bird hopping around. The bird was glaring at Jack and Lanski.

"Look," said Lorna. "No, stop. Look."

"What?" Thomas said breathlessly.

She was indicating out the window, at the garden.

"The poor wee darling," she said. "Come on, Thomas, we've got to put out something for it to eat ok?"

Thomas saw the small bird bouncing and stamping around in the light from the living room.

"What, now?" he said.

"We've got to, Thomas. I can't just watch it out there, starving. I thought it could wait but that's it desperate now. Just let me get some bread."

Thomas had to raise himself off her as she started to get up from the floor. Her thick thigh almost struck his face but he saw it coming and dodged just in time. Thomas let his weight bring him onto his back. He watched the ceiling. He spread his arms wide and turned the palms of his hands down to rest on the carpet.

"Don't give it everything," said Thomas. "Remember to keep some for us."

"Do you think it will be happy with bread on its own? Will it need water?" she called from the kitchen.

Thomas sniffed.

"Give it water in a bowl," he said.

"Poor wee thing."

Thomas could hear her moving around in the kitchen. He looked over as she walked back in. She was naked, her long hair flowing. Her breasts and thighs were huge, luscious. Nothing like Lea's petite control. This new woman was an entirely different continent from Lea. As she walked her left breast nudged at the edge of the stack of sliced bread on the plate.

Thomas laughed.

"You're going out into the garden like that?" he said.

The Survival of Thomas Ford

"Just long enough to feed it. How? Can neighbours see in here?"

Her face looked apprehensive suddenly.

Thomas shook his head.

"No," he said. "But I know a few who would want to."

She grinned. As she reached a hand out towards the patio door she tossed her head and the strands of thick hair rippled and flew. Thomas rolled onto his belly, raised his face, and watched her.

"Careful he doesn't rape you," said Thomas.

There was a sweeping lined curve where her hip met her back. Thomas would draw it later, from memory. It would be good too, if she would pose for him. Lea had never liked posing, or even being drawn on the move.

Jack and Lanski were well round the corner and several feet along the back wall of the house when they heard the patio doors opening. Jack didn't know it but his boots were positioned in the mudded prints left the night before by his son. Lorna walked out onto the patio paving. She looked down and was careful to keep her bare feet away from the mud left by Jimmy and Robert. The bird saw her and didn't hesitate. It reached her in three long hops.

Lorna set the plate down and removed the little bowl of water she had been balancing at the plate's edge.

"There you go," she whispered.

This bird was absolutely fearless, totally accustomed to being fed by somebody around here.

Jack and Lanski watched the naked woman's squatting form. Her buttocks looked inhuman somehow, there framed against the garden and shadowed by the light from the house. Jack and Lanski were too far along the back wall to retreat now, or to move in any direction. They stood frozen against the pebble-dashing, limbs at awkward quivering angles, afraid even to breathe or move their eyes off the woman and the bird.

The bird jabbed savagely at the bread, tearing off far more than it could hope to chew. Its beak gaped.

"Thomas!" called Lorna.

She laughed.

"Thomas, you've got to see this."

Jack and Lanski heard a man's voice from inside the house say, "No. I'm alright here."

"Aww, little love," said Lorna.

Jack saw her reach out towards the bird's thin breast with a curled index finger. The bird hopped back, letting a large crumb fall to the grass. Lorna withdrew her finger and the bird advanced back to the bread. Jack saw the girl's buttocks swell as she flexed. Lanski saw the young woman stand up. It seemed she stood very slowly. Her hair covered all of her back as she stood straight.

The light from the living room made shadows dance around the crack of her arse, as Thomas gazed out at her. She was worthy of a proper painting, a portrait in oils like the old masters. She turned now and Thomas' senses were filled with the impact and grandeur of her heavy breasts, the mound of V in hairs below. Her hips and thighs were a wide, replete symphony of shapes, a Pythagorean glory of natural geometry, God speaking in whispers through the flesh rather than in bellows of stone Cathedral.

As she turned, her thick hair flew up and around her face, hiding the shapes of Jack and Lanski against the wall. She raised her hand to fling the hair away, but as she did she turned to look back over her left shoulder at the feeding bird.

"Night love," she said.

The Survival of Thomas Ford

Lanski watched to see if Jack, who was closest to her, would stop her. But Jack only watched her body move past him, take three steps, and enter the living room again. The patio doors closed with a quiet thud.

Jack breathed out. Lanski breathed out. The bird was tearing a piece of bread to fine shreds, confident now that no-one would take the prize away. Jack moved back along the wall until he was next to Lanski.

"Couldn't take the bitch outside," he whispered against Lanski's long hair. "One scream and the cops would be out."

Lanski nodded.

In the living room, Lorna was sitting astride Thomas Ford. He sighed out air. Even through the condom he could feel her heat. It had made Thomas wonder, the condoms she had in her bag. Specially for him, or always there for opportunity that might arise?

It was as though Thomas was being washed inside as she moved up and down above him. He placed his palms on her thighs.

Lorna was enjoying the change from Jimmy. No requests to wear boots. No bird-like face below her. No black eyes simmering with unknown meanings. This man inside her was a professional, middle class, with a nice home of his own. A beautiful garden with its own little bird. It was all like a dream really. Only this morning Lorna had been on her way to another day at the hospital. Then something inside her had made her go to Jack McCallum instead, and that had led to this. Lorna gasped out air as she felt the first wave of excitement. Thomas gripped the flesh of her thighs. She could feel his fingernails bite into her skin. She liked it.

In the garden, Jack and Lanski and the overfed bird stood watching the girl's rhythmic motions. The bird continued to chew. Its beak clicked lightly. Lanski heard his employer's breathing noticeably accelerate. Lorna's face, viewed through the clean glass of the patio doors, was in profile. Her eyes were closed and her top teeth nibbled down on her bottom lip in a charming overbite expression. She tilted her nose up and her neck back as she bore down again on Thomas Ford, filling herself. Jack heard Lanski swallow. The girl's thighs were so thick. Jack had never seen anything like them. They should almost make her appear grotesque, but they didn't, not at all.

As Lorna came, a shuddering passed through her shoulders. Lanski saw her breasts jiggle. She hung her head forward and her hair fell across Thomas Ford's face, which was already angled away from the patio doors. To Jack and Lanski it seemed now that the woman was consuming Thomas Ford, draining the force from him, filling herself with his life. From the edge of his eye, Lanski saw Jack lick his lips like the wolf he was.

The girl was off Ford in one movement, lying in his arms at his side now. It was only luck that she hadn't seen the two men standing outside the windows. Jack and Lanski stayed where they were. They saw the girl's hands remove the used condom from Ford, tie a knot in it, and throw it on the carpet.

It only seemed a matter of moments before the man and woman on the floor of the living room of 16 Cromwell Drive were asleep. Somehow, Lanski and McCallum knew, beyond doubt, that the couple slept now.

Lanski saw McCallum's hand raise then and move toward the handle of the patio doors.

Chapter Thirty

Detective Sergeant McPherson woke from a violent dream to the sound of his wife snoring beside him. He heard his own rapid breathing. The sweat was a lake on his back, the organic cotton sheet saturated.

Bill McPherson didn't approve of the organic sheets. He thought his wife, Sarah, had gone too far with that.

The dream though. The dream had been that woman, Lea Ford, her skeleton shimmering in the sunlit current of a shallow river. It had been as though Bill stared down at her remains, from high above the water.

Strange. She had died in deep, black waters. Her body had been recovered the same day, many weeks ago.

Bill thought it must be guilt, from closing the case before the right time.

But that was how everything was now, you had to keep moving forward, like a shark, headed for the next thing, the next target.

It wasn't about doing the job right any more.

Bill closed his eyes as Sarah exhaled a rasping, long breath. That fucking noise. He could understand murder, sleeping beside Sarah and the snoring. Bill let his mind turn to Detective Constable Liz Davies. Her blonde hair instead of Sarah's black. Her smell. Her petite elbows. Oh, if he only could. But Liz had knocked him back too many times for it to be just playing hard to get.

Lea Ford's face drifted into Bill's mind. Then a black-haired bird-boy driving a red car. If Bill had his way, they'd have found that wee bastard. Unless Ford was only making up the boy in the car. Bill knew that Thomas Ford's father-in-law suspected that, but Bill could never tell whether there was a real basis for it, or was it just the man not liking his daughter's choice.

Sarah's parents had lamented long and hard over her choice after all.

Alan and Jean Gillan were lying awake in the night too.

"Can't you sleep?" said Jean. "I wonder how Thomas is doing, Alan?"

Alan blinked in the darkness. He didn't care about Thomas Ford. If it were not for Thomas Ford, their daughter would still be alive.

"He'll be alright," said Alan.

"You think so? Maybe I should give him a phone tomorrow, invite him for tea."

Alan sniffed.

"Do you believe him then?" said Alan.

"About what?"

"All that about a boy in a red car looking like a bird."

"Of course," said Jean.

She couldn't see her husband's twisted sneering snarl in the darkness. Alan often assumed extreme facial expressions lying in the dark like that. It allowed him to release something that might otherwise build up to an explosion. But what if an explosion was what was needed? Something was certainly needed.

The Survival of Thomas Ford

"You can't keep blaming him, Alan. It'll eat you up inside. You'll end up just old and bitter. It was an accident."

He heard her swallow in the darkness. He lifted his arm like a wing and she shuffled down in the bed until she rested on him. He put his other arm round her as her body began to heave, swelling and emptying again, with sore tears.

"Sssssh darling. Ssssh."

He kissed the hair at the side of her head.

At the corner of Church Street, in the city's centre, dozens of varied objects and crafted figures sat silently behind glass shop windows and the sign that read:

WORLD NATIVE ARTS
Proprietor Lea Ford

In the orange glow from streetlights outside, a carved wooden head from New Guinea stared solemnly. A hollow, twisted horn from Sierra Leone lay casually abandoned on an oak table-top nearby.

Like themselves, their owner, buyer, and would-be seller, the late Mrs Lea Ford, was now without life. The array of old objects she had chosen with loving care and discretion had been orphaned in the same way by generations of possessors already though, so there was no shock for them. Only a continuing river of existence, neither hot nor cold, wet nor dry, an unerring, unbelievable, endless median.

A Hell in a way, unless you could weather it, and the gathered artefacts of all the world's corners in Lea Ford's Gallery had proven they could weather it.

Wood, and bone, and stone, inert and unchanging.

Chapter Thirty-one

Lanski was driving.

Thomas Ford's body was lying across the broad back seat of the Subaru, enveloped in a two-man tent that Jack McCallum had found at the back of the utility room in 16 Cromwell Drive. Some areas of blood had already succeeded in seeping through the synthetic material.

On the floor of the Subaru, resting against the plush velvet carpet, Lorna's body lay in an attitude of mild genuflection, like an advertisement page for a Swiss Army knife. She too was hidden, by swathes of blanket and duvet cover.

The hardest thing had been carrying the bodies from the house to the vehicle, but the street had been silent, empty, unmoved.

"Left," said Lanski's boss now, and Lanski flicked up the indicator. The orange light on the dashboard flashed, the electronic clicking filled Lanski's ears.

Lanski steered the Subaru through the roundabout. The city was still, peaceful, asleep. The few cars they did pass seemed unreal to Lanski, as though these were only the shadows or ghosts of cars, not solid. Lanski knew there was a good chance the Ford man was dead already, or dying now on the rear seat. McCallum had hit him very hard. But the girl was only unconscious. This made Lanski nervous. He kept expecting to hear sound from the blankets, or movement, but she was still.

The Survival of Thomas Ford

Jack McCallum stared directly ahead.

"Follow the road. Over the bridge and straight on past the golf course," he said.

Lanski was glad he didn't know where they were going. It was better like this. He could pretend for long moments that nothing was wrong, they were only on the way to some late emergency job, subsidence at a new build or leaking gas.

The Subaru passed over the canal bridge. The golf course was a black shape, an expanse of dense shadow, bordered by old oaks.

"Left," said McCallum.

Lanski raised his right wrist and the vehicle abandoned the boundaries of the growing city, its headlit nose pressing eagerly against the skirts of the night.

In Marie Ferguson's living room, tears glistened on Jimmy McCallum's leathery young cheeks.

"He says to me he's going to kill all of yous," said Jimmy. "Aye, Thomas Ford, Lorna, you Mrs Ferguson, and Robert too. He even asked me if I'd told my mum about any of it eh? He's gone off his fucking head. Nothing's gonnae stop him now eh?"

Jimmy sniffed and observed the fear in the eyes of Robert and Marie Ferguson. He choked back tears and shook his head.

"No," he said, "this has all gone far enough eh?"

Convulsively, Jimmy stretched an arm out to the phone on the table by the settee.

"I'll phone the police, Mrs Ferguson. It's my dad. I'll tell them what's really going on."

Marie watched Jimmy take a deep breath, then he looked back at her.

"I'll dial the local cops, Mrs Ferguson. They're just up the road. My dad says it's faster than 999 eh?"

Marie watched Jimmy's fingers tap out figures on the handset of her phone.

Jimmy blinked. The living room was so still and silent now that Marie and Robert could hear the phone's ring-tone over the beating of their respective hearts.

In the Subaru, Jack McCallum's mobile rang out violently. Jack flinched and fumbled for it in his pocket. Lanski's mouth had fallen involuntarily open. The blackness of the huge, monstrous loch flashed by steadily to their left. The road ahead was a dark beast's belly. The Subaru seemed to move forward against the beast's throat through a narrow tunnel of light. Lanski had the impression that the night was swallowing them all and there would never be another day.

Jack pressed the button on the phone.

"Hello," he heard Jimmy say. "I'm calling from 72 Broomfield Road. I need to report a crime that may or may not have happened yet. A murder...murders."

In the living room of Broomfield Road, Marie bit her lip. Robert felt odd in his stomach, his medication rendered temporarily impotent by events.

In the Subaru passenger seat, Jack McCallum frowned heavily. Lanski whipped his head to the left for a moment, to watch his boss' expression.

"Please send officers here right away," Jack heard his son say. "72 Broomfield Road, Marie and Robert Ferguson's home. And to 16 Cromwell Drive. It's Jack McCallum, the builder, he's gone mental. Thank you. Bye."

Jimmy put the phone down.

The Survival of Thomas Ford

"They're on the way," he said to Marie and Robert. "Two minutes, they said."

Jack flipped his mobile closed. As though in reaction, Lorna's body twitched and shuffled at the back of the Subaru. Jack tapped the phone twice against his chin. He needed a shave. He hated letting all the white hair grow in there on his jaw, like Santa Claus.

"There might be hope for that boy yet, Lanski," said Jack. "He seems to have started Phase Two of this operation under his own initiative."

Jack nodded his head. Aye, hope for the boy yet. Jack's eye drifted to the Subaru's speedometer.

"Easy, Lanski. Stay under fifty. We're no exactly set up for a stop by the cops eh?"

Lanski blinked and eased his foot a degree upward. The Subaru was coming up to the corner where Lea and Thomas Ford's car had left the road, taking part of the roadside's low stone wall with it. In the headlights, Jack saw the joins in the stone where the Council had repaired it. A sneer crossed Jack's face. Fucking amateurs. If Jack or Lanski had repaired that wall the mend would be invisible.

"Watch this blind corner, Lanski. It's a dangerous one. There was an accident here not long ago. A woman was killed."

In the living-room of 72 Broomfield Road, Marie Ferguson was experiencing an odd, nervous nausea in her stomach. Something was wrong. Something more than the obvious. It was the way Jimmy had spoken to the police, something in his tone.

Marie looked over at Robert. Robert was staring at Jimmy, as though waiting for an instruction. Marie looked at

Jimmy. The boy's black eyes glared back at her. Jimmy blinked and it was as though some hostile spark slipped out for a moment, from behind the mask of expression.

Then Jimmy grinned like a shark in the sea.

"What was my dad like in school, Mrs Ferguson? Can I call you Marie? I've always thought you were very attractive, Marie, for your age."

"Come on, Jimmy," said Robert. "Cut that out eh? The police will be here in a minute."

Jimmy nodded.

"I bet my dad was a bastard in school," he said. "He must have always been a bastard."

Marie breathed in slowly. Outside the living-room window, the cat gave out a long, low moan.

The Subaru was entering the village.

"Right after the bank," said Jack McCallum. "Then right again."

Lanski indicated. There was another brisk shuffle from behind them. Jack turned and stretched to reach the blanketed form on the rear floor. He pounded his fist into one end of it and hit the girl's foot. A cry came from the other end of the blanket roll. Jack punched that end and the girl went quiet.

Jack turned to face the road again.

"Here!" he shouted. "Here! I told you, right again!"

Lanski jammed the brakes on hard. He gave an anxious look, belatedly, into the rear-view. It was alright. No-one behind. Lanski brought the vehicle around and started along a narrow tarmac road. Within a minute, the headlight tunnel was penetrating the purest darkness Lanski had seen since his grandmother's village as a boy.

The Survival of Thomas Ford

"Stop," said McCallum. "I'm driving now. Go round."

Lanski opened the driver's door and walked around the front of the Subaru. From the corner of his eye he saw his boss shuffling across from the passenger seat to the driver seat. For a second, Lanski was caught in the headlights, blinded. It occurred to him that McCallum could run him over and leave him on this road in the blackness. Then Lanski was getting into the passenger seat. As he pulled the door shut, Jack revved the engine. The Subaru screamed, then lurched forward, its rear wheels stirring up gravel and mud.

Jack brought the car around a left turn.

In the headlights, Lanski saw a sign:

CHALET RECEPTION

McCallum pulled the Subaru's nose into a passing place opposite the sign. He did a three-point turn until they faced the sign and a one-storey building. Jack drove hard at the building and Lanski thought for a moment his boss intended to ram the structure, but at the last second Jack twisted the Subaru's nose to the right. Lanski felt the suspension grind against rough track. The gradient was sudden and steep, reminding Lanski again of the hill path to his grandmother's village, her wooden house.

It seemed to Lanski he was slipping back in time as the Subaru churned the earth and its well-studded tyres bore them all up into utter blackness, except for the shuddering headlight beam.

Lanski looked to the right and saw Jack McCallum's head grinning. The Subaru ripped its way up the steep hill and, beyond Jack's head, Lanski saw abandoned vehicles pass the driver's side window. There was a tractor, illumined by the kiss of the headlight's edge. It was an old tractor, fifty years old, just like the richest man in Lanski's grandmother's village had owned.

Lanski looked forward again.

Jack looked at him and laughed.

"Ah!" Jack shouted. "And you thought you'd come to fucking civilisation eh, coming over here? No, Lanski. This is what's under the surface man. It's the same fucking everywhere."

Jack ground his teeth and absorbed a jump from the Subaru as it bounced over a knotted tree-trunk. It seemed to Lanski they were climbing an impossible gradient now, the chassis and themselves at a forty-five degree angle to the proper earth.

"I was going to build a house up here, Lanski. I lived here with my family, when I was your age, for two years. Aye, I was just like you, Lanski. We had fuck all. Just a caravan on this hill and a dream. But I'll tell you, the boy was fine then. Jimmy. He was no problem at all when we lived up here. It was when we got the money, Lanski, that's when it all went to fuck. You remember that, Lanski."

Jack pulled the Subaru around a left turn and Lanski thought for a moment his boss had oversteered and they would roll the vehicle now, all the way back to the bottom of the hill behind.

Then they were ploughing upward again, straight, at an even more unlikely tilt.

Jack had had no four-by-four to attack this hill with twenty years ago. No, back then it was a third-hand Triumph that Jack, Cathy and Jimmy had arrived with. And here it was, the Triumph, coming up in the headlight beam, rusted and dead. Jack laughed loudly and took his right hand off the steering wheel to point out the wreck to Lanski as they

The Survival of Thomas Ford

passed it. But Jack didn't explain anything to Lanski, just let him stare out the window.

"In the end, Lanski, I had to borrow, no, hire, the bastard charged me twenty quid to rent his tractor for the day, that was how I got the caravan up."

The Subaru's engine was struggling against the gradient, moaning and roaring in turns.

"Fuck," said Jack. "I think we might do it."

But exactly then the rear wheels lost purchase on the rooted track. For a few seconds the front axle ground down and took the slack, but it wasn't enough. Jack felt the vehicle's nose slip and slide off to the right. He fought back and got the steering wheel twisted left again, but the momentum was gone. Jack depressed the brake pedal, pulled up hard on the handbrake.

"Fucking good try though," said Jack. "Closest I ever saw anything get except that tractor. We're close enough."

Jack opened the driver's door, stepped out onto the track. The Subaru's headlight shone a white tunnel up the track at an odd angle, as though Jack had been looking for some animal in the trees. Lanski heard the rear door opening.

"Come on!" said Jack.

Lanski got out of the Subaru. He stood straight for a moment, looking up the hill against the blackness that enveloped the headlight's narrow slice of brilliance. There was a cool wind flicking gently against Lanski's cheeks. He could smell the birch trees and hear their rustle. It was just like home. This Scottish hill was more like the country home of his childhood than any Polish town or city had ever been. Lanski felt the energy come up from the soil, through his boots. He looked back at Jack but Jack was only a shadow on the other side of the Subaru. Then the shadow shifted, lurched, walked uphill several paces. The shadow had a hunched back for a second, like a creature in a folk-tale, then Lanski saw that McCallum was carrying the girl, still wrapped tight in her blankets. Lanski watched this strange man-girl beast walk directly into the headlight beam. Nothing seemed real about it for a long moment and Lanski clenched his fist until his fingernails broke the skin of his palm.

"Lanski!" shouted McCallum. "Get Ford! Hurry up!"

Lanski swallowed. He walked around the back of the vehicle. The rear door was still open, swinging in the light wind. The Ford man was only a shadow on the back seat. Some sense of horror in Lanski made him hesitate. He didn't want to touch Ford. He didn't know which end was Ford's head and which his feet. He couldn't remember which end had bled through the tent material. He didn't know if Ford was alive or dead.

"Lanski!" came Jack's hissed shout through the black air.

Lanski looked uphill. McCallum was gone. There was no sign of him. He had walked beyond the headlit zone.

Lanski snarled and reached far into the back of the Subaru to get his arm underneath Ford's body.

The man was heavy and awkward. Lanski had to bend his legs deeply, lean hard against the side of the Subaru. He jerked at Thomas Ford's dead weight. It was difficult to even shift the body on the seat, let alone lift it.

Lanski straightened up. There was no other way. He grabbed the near end of Thomas Ford's tent covering with both hands and pulled abruptly. He gave a second jerk and Thomas Ford fell heavily from the rear seat of the Subaru to the vehicle's floor. The thud terrified Lanski and rocked the vehicle. Lanski stood still in the darkness and listened to the squeaking of the suspension.

The Survival of Thomas Ford

He pulled again, a long, driving tug, and Thomas Ford left the Subaru. He landed on the rooted earth and knotted grass like a huge, newly-landed fish. Lanski could only just see the elongated shape on the ground, in the furthest reach of the headlight's grace.

Lanski shook his head. He felt dizzy. A wave of weakness washed through him. He should have been able to lift Ford and carry him, but Lanski felt certain he couldn't manage it. His hands and thighs shook as he stared down. He grabbed one end of the long shape, planted his feet firmly, and started to pull Thomas Ford slowly up the hill, dragging the load painstakingly and reluctantly as though some force from the forest might rescue him, all of them, at any time, so long as there was this reluctance to do the job.

Far up the hillside, Jack McCallum was carrying the girl easily. There was no light to see by, but Jack was sure he could remember every step of the way to the old blue and white aluminium caravan. There had been something healthy about this place, living here, planning to build here. This was the only build Jack had ever planned for love, rather than money, but he had never completed it. The site had been abandoned when the first big money offer came along. Jack could feel the girl's arse-cheek under his palm as he climbed the hillside blindly. Certainly a healthy girl. Jimmy had good taste in that at least. She should have taken the offer of the job at the office in town. Jack could even have set her up in a flat near the job, visited her there. He had that going with a couple of the other lassies from the office.

But this girl Jack was carrying now had thought she was too good for that. Not too good for wiping up piss and blood at the hospital, but too good for Jack McCallum eh?

Jack adjusted her weight violently on his shoulder.

He heard a dry crack and wondered if it was one of her ribs. Women had one rib more than men, didn't they? So she could live without it.

Jack stopped walking. He stood still and listened to the wind.

"Lanski!" called Jack.

Far behind, dragging Thomas Ford's inert weight, Lanski froze in dread at hearing the wind whisper his name. His heart felt like a shard of ice had pierced it.

"Lanski!" came the wind again and Lanski breathed as he recognised McCallum's animalistic tone.

"What?" called Lanski in a repressed shout.

Lanski was too terrified to call out properly. It was his grandmother, all those stories she had filled his head with. All the stories were still in there, reviving now, like decayed skeletons rising from the tombed cells of Lanski's brain. His mother had been right. The old grandmother should never have been allowed to put all that folklore of werewolf and ghost and vampire into a boy's skull. The grandmother had never been bothered by any teacher, had never needed to read or write. She had little curiosity for the modern world's developments. The developments had never reached her village to affect or help her anyway. But the grandmother could milk any beast, knew which herbs would heal and which would kill, and she knew the old stories as well as the old ways.

"Get up here, Lanski!" the wind screamed as Lanski stared ahead, unseeing.

Lanski bent over and got a grip of Thomas Ford's tent shroud again.

He pulled, his back aching now already, still not knowing which end of Ford he had hold of. He couldn't see Ford except as a shadow by starlight, unless the shadow was something he

The Survival of Thomas Ford

only imagined out of the need to see something there. How long ago had it been since Lanski was lying safe in his bed with Elena in his arms? An hour? Two hours? Ford's body wasn't shifting. Lanski dug his right heel into an impression in the earth by a tree-root. There was a moment of shocking strain, then Lanski had the big body moving again, up the hill, away from the already distant Subaru headlights.

Jack McCallum stood alone in the darkness waiting. Although the girl was heavy, Jack was hardly conscious of the weight being a burden. She seemed to fit there snugly enough, on his shoulder, like a pirate's parrot, sleeping, its head hood-covered. There was a lot of potential action in the weight of her long, drooped body and Jack felt an exhilaration suddenly. He could hear rustling in the trees. That had always been there at night. Jack had always put it down to the gang of cats that lived beneath the family caravan, the rustles in the night, out in the trees. Surely, the cats couldn't still be up here living could they? Great descendants, feral, insane, alone in the silver birches. Then the memory came blazing and alive before Jack's eyes. The first day he had known something was wrong with Jimmy. He had found the boy, hardly past the toddler stage, standing alone by a tree, his little brown-sandaled foot pressing down on the skull of one of the kittens. Jack could see its grey fur. Poppy. Christ, its name had been Poppy, Cathy had named it, that was it. The whole thing had made no sense. Poppy was Jimmy's favourite kitten too. Jack had walked away, hadn't let the boy know he'd been seen. The wee thing was better off dead by then anyway.

Later, when Cathy had spent days in the trees, looking for the kitten, Jack had said nothing. He had only looked at his son's tiny face, trying to read it.

Cathy never found the kitten and Jack had gone back to the place but there was no sign except a little patch of different shaded earth and then Jack knew the boy had buried it.

That had been the beginning of everything turning bad, it seemed now to Jack.

Within a year of it, Jack had had to take care of his first piece of really filthy business in the town. Some Irish bastard builder had tried to muscle him out of a job and Jack had snapped. It had been a meeting on a hill about a planning application problem, nothing should have gone wrong, then the Irishman had started swearing and Jack had killed him in a moment that seemed now the fastest moment of all his life.

For an hour, Jack had stood over the Irishman, crying, shaking.

Only when he had remembered Poppy's little grave by the trees on the hill, did Jack stop shaking. It had been his own boy that gave him the idea.

Tears sting Jack's cheeks in the darkness. He can hear Lanski coming now and he knows by the sound that Lanski is dragging Ford up here, not carrying him.

"Come on, Lanski," Jack whispers into the wind. "Come on, man, and I'll show you where the bodies are buried. You don't know a place or a business until you know that."

Chapter Thirty-two

Jimmy was sitting on Marie Ferguson's couch, his shoulders hunched forward.

"I'll make us all some tea eh?" he said.

He looked up as he spoke, straight into Robert's eyes.

Robert felt a searing twist in his testicles, then it was gone.

It seemed to Marie that time had compressed in the living room. The room also seemed to have shrunk. She blinked to see if the sensation would go away, but it remained. Now Jimmy turned his grin on her.

"Cup of tea, Mrs Ferguson?"

She swallowed, as though she wasn't sure her mouth would work if she tried to speak. She nodded.

Jimmy nodded back and stood up slowly from the couch. It was like the unfolding of an animal. No, a snake, if a snake could just suddenly choose to grow feet and stand. Marie could imagine his secret scales as she sat watching him.

Jimmy walked out of the living room without looking back. He turned right in the hallway. Soon Marie and Robert could hear the slamming of drawers, the clanging together of spoons and cups. Marie and Robert sat silently, occasionally looking at each other. The kettle could be heard now, building up through its powerful crescendo.

"It's alright mum," said Robert. "The police will be here in a minute."

"They should have been here by now, Robert."

Marie's eyes were restless, vibrant. Robert nodded.

From the kitchen, the sound of loud whistling overwhelmed the kettle. Jimmy was doing a little dance on the laminate flooring. He had his arms raised in the air, one higher than the other, as though he waltzed some invisible partner around the small floor area. In Jimmy's right hand, a thin spoon. Clenched between his teeth were three teabags. Jimmy was whistling through the perforations in the bags, enjoying the acoustic challenge. The kettle finished boiling with a final violent bubble, then a pop. Jimmy spat the teabags out onto the work surface.

"Do you want sugar?" he bellowed toward the kitchen door. "For the shock and that?"

In the living room Marie shook her head. She stood up.

"This isn't right," she said.

Robert watched her walk out into the hall. He was ashamed at the fear in his knees that stopped him following.

"Mum," he whispered, but she was already gone.

Jimmy saw her coming in to the kitchen and raised his eyebrows.

"Aye, Mrs Ferguson, I'll need a hand right enough. Can't find the sugar lumps and I'll need a tray to carry it through."

"That wasn't the police you phoned, was it Jimmy?"

"How do you mean, Mrs Ferguson?"

"Who did you phone, Jimmy?"

Marie Ferguson's blood had started to feel odd. She believed she knew who Jimmy had phoned.

"Mrs Ferguson, Marie, you're getting too stressed out about all this."

Jimmy saw Robert come out of the living room, over Mrs Ferguson's right shoulder.

The Survival of Thomas Ford

"Robert, man, tell your mum everything's going to be alright now eh?"

Jimmy grinned and looked directly into Marie Ferguson's eyes. Windows to the soul, but Jimmy's were frosted. He had bathroom glazing over both pupils. The black circles round the pupils only emphasised it. You couldn't trust eyes like that even if it was only your dog that had them.

"It all just is what it is, eh Marie?" said Jimmy. "Just let it be, Mrs Ferguson, eh? Like The Beatles and that. Times of trouble. Bridge over water and that."

Jimmy blinked. He saw Robert frown.

"Don't take it all to heart, Bobby, for God's sake. We're all just whizzing round and round on a big moving ball called a planet eh? It's a set-up designed so some folk are bound to fall off and get hurt eh? There's merry-go-rounds designed with more safety in mind. Naw, we're here for the ride boy. The buzz. You bet on it. Maybe next life will be the one with the slippers and armchairs."

Jimmy reached his hand out slowly towards the kettle full of boiling water. Robert watched Jimmy's hand travel. It seemed to take hours to move through the air. When Jimmy's fist clenched to grip the handle, Marie Ferguson noticed the perfectly groomed fingernails. There was so much time to move away or move towards Jimmy but the molecules in the air around Jimmy seemed to have densened, making travel anywhere in the room hard suddenly. It seemed to Marie also that the air had grown thinner, her head felt light, and wasn't the kitchen darker now? Had she blinked or did the energy-saving bulb in the long lampshade at the centre of the kitchen ceiling flicker on and off for an instant?

Jimmy raised the kettle and poured water into a mug over a teabag. Marie breathed out stale air. *It could have been my face. He could have thrown the kettle of boiling water in my face. He was ready to do it. It was going to be my face but he changed his mind.*

Robert stared. He felt as though he had missed something happening in the room.

"There you go, Mrs Ferguson. You don't take sugar, do you?"

Marie reached her hand towards the mug and was surprised to see it steady, not shaking.

"Thanks Jimmy," she said.

Jimmy didn't look at her. He looked down into Robert's mug. But a wide grin spread across Jimmy's cheeks, compressing them and stretching them simultaneously, like some paradoxical shift in weather on a satellite photograph taken from space.

Chapter Thirty-three

Jack McCallum was trying to get the generator working. There were some kinds of job you couldn't manage in the dark. You had to see what you were doing if you needed to be sure you wouldn't leave any traces.

Jimmy hadn't known about that when he was wee, not leaving any traces. He'd left Poppy's grave obvious where the replaced earth stood out in a patch. No, you had to blend the earth, you had to blend everything.

Jack was trying to remember the last time he was out here. He sniffed at the fuel cap. Summers ago, it must have been. All the petrol was evaporated now then.

Jack blinked into the total darkness. He had sent Lanski back to the Subaru for the spare petrol can. Jack had laid the girl out at the bottom of the caravan, by the hole where the cats used to crawl under for shelter. Jack had felt the old hole with the edge of a rough hand. He wasn't sure what Lanski had done with Ford before he went back to the car. Jack was half-sure that Ford was already dead anyway.

A rustling sound came from the trees.

"Lanski?"

Jack sniffed.

"Lanski!"

No answer came. Jack tried to feel around the floor of the shed by the old generator engine. There should be something here, even just a spanner. Wind tore abruptly through the leaves above Jack's head, but he knew that sound.

"Lanski!"

The Pole could have run out on him. If his own boy could do it, then the Pole could too. Jack felt an enormous loneliness that shocked him. Tears pricked his eyes. He wanted to phone Cathy, or even the boy, but he stopped himself reaching for the phone in his pocket.

Jack clenched his fist. It was the place. It had too many ghosts now. That lawyer, Shandlin, he had screamed out here, like an animal, Jack knew the village down below the hill must have wondered that night what it was up here. But even then, no-one had come. People don't come to find out about sounds like that.

Another sound, not the rustling, not the wind. This time Jack was sure, he recognised Lanski's tread, even here.

"Lanski!"

Lanski heard the fear in McCallum's voice.

"Reach the can out to me, Lanski! Pass it to me! Say something man!"

"It's alright. It's me."

"Where's Ford? Find him. Is he where you left him?"

Lanski walked another step toward McCallum's voice. Another. Another. Then he felt McCallum's hand knock against the can.

"There," said Lanski.

"Got it. Find Ford."

"You heard him move?" said Lanski.

"No. But find both of them, make sure. Until I get this done."

Lanski turned his back on McCallum's voice. He managed two steps towards where the caravan was, or where he hoped

The Survival of Thomas Ford

it was, then he walked into a group of thin, long, sharp branches. Lanski screamed. He believed it was the girl, free, raking his face with her fingernails. Jack was feeling for the fuel hole in the generator lid when Lanski's scream nearly made him drop the can.

"Get a fucking grip on yourself!" Jack hissed furiously into the darkness.

Lanski stopped flailing at the branches. He stood still. He raised a hand steadily until he could feel the wood and his own blood there from his scratched face.

"I walked into a tree," said Lanski.

"Find Ford where you left him. I put the girl by the caravan, near the hole in the bricks. Just check them until I get this going."

Lanski glared around himself. He thought he saw some huge shadow in the darkness. It was hardly his eyes seeing it, he didn't know what he was seeing it with. But he felt it must be the caravan so he headed that way, more careful now.

Jack had the petrol can tilted, almost ready to commit to where he felt the generator tank opening had to be. There was always the risk, if you tried this in the dark, of mistaking some other bump in the generator housing for the fuel hole and pouring all the petrol away against the outer surface. Jack had done that before, once, and always remembered to bring a torch since then, until this night. Jack started to pour. It sounded alright, like the liquid was falling through some space before the gurgling sounds. He tried to estimate half the can. He would keep the other half back, in case he was pouring the first half in the wrong place.

At the caravan, Lanski had found the girl. He had his hand on the outer layer of blanket covering her. He knew she was alive, without knowing how he knew or what part of her body he was feeling her life come through the blanket from. He pulled his hand away. He raised his weight and leaned against the caravan. It rocked noisily for a second. Lanski drew back. Keeping his hands light now against the aluminium wall he felt his way along towards where he thought the tree was where he had left Ford lying across a thick root. Lanski's hands left the caravan, felt empty air, then his boot knocked against something. Lanski bent. No, not Ford, some rotted tree trunk.

Jack pulled violently at the generator cord. It snapped in his hand. Lanski heard McCallum swear.

"Rotted through," Jack whispered to himself. "Like everything fucking else."

Jack felt around on the generator roof until he found the snapped cord. He started to curl and twist it against the broken-off end he still had hold of. Jack tried to take his time with the knot, then he tugged tight.

He was almost sure the cord would just snap on the next go too, but it didn't. Jack's arm whipped all the way back and the generator spluttered reluctantly. The cord ran back into its housing. Jack pulled again. Another dry hack from the machine's guts. On the third pull the generator exploded into clanging life. Light flooded Jack's taut face, the caravan, and the girl's prone blanket-covered form. Lanski's broad back was highlighted against a silver birch's gnarled roots where he had been searching for Thomas Ford's tent-covered body.

As Jack turned and Lanski stared around himself from tree to tree, both men realised that Thomas Ford was gone.

Chapter Thirty-four

Thomas Ford had not come to anything so lofty and evolved as true consciousness while he lay by the silver birch near the caravan, swathed in the materials of his own tent. It had been more the passing from one level of dream to another.

Swimming gestures of his arms and legs as he lay on the dead leaves had released him halfway from the tent. Jack, over at the generator, had accepted the sounds as just another ghost on the hillside, or the wind. Maybe even the soured spirit of Poppy the kitten, returned for justice.

But it had been Thomas Ford, crawling along the forest floor, through the darkness. That is, partly Thomas Ford, and partly the reawakened animus within Thomas Ford, the same raw and primitive slice of Ford's brain that had left Lea to die alone in the car in the loch that day.

And Thomas Ford remembered it now, the moment of decision as he left his wife, abandoned the idea of saving her, and turned instead to the business of living. He did not know that he was crawling along a forest floor. He was passing through the glassless windscreen again, kicking, grasping at black water, pulling. His body replicated those swimming movements among the dead leaves and Thomas Ford travelled smoothly past tree trunks, magically missing them with his already half-shattered head. Instinct turned his torso to face upwards and Thomas Ford climbed the hillside as though the trees were the ripples in the body of the loch, the reflexes of its peristaltic belly.

Now the forest vomited Thomas Ford's body upwards, just as the water had once done.

Then he stopped crawling and became still on the forest floor.

What was he doing, leaving Lea behind like this? He did not want it.

His remaining healthy eye blinked. He could feel the binding tent material tight against his hips and stomach. He rolled and kicked, trying to free himself, not understanding what was on him. He took the tent to be soaking wet, heavy clothes, full of the loch's water, or drenched in Lea's blood.

Ford turned full circle on the leaves.

Lea. Something was wrong.

They had been in the house, not in the car. Lea had been making love to him, like before, before she hated him.

Lea, but this Lea in his mind's eye was big, heavy, different. Thomas bent his neck and pressed his face against the vegetation. The smell of the leaves choked him.

A roar filled the air, as though some beast, the loch's monster, or that great black bird from Thomas' earlier dream, had arrived to tear the world apart between its taloned feet. Thomas raised his face and light flooded his good eye, blinding it.

He blinked and a little howl came up from his throat.

He heard men's voices on the wind, it sounded like church singing somehow for a moment, until one voice separated itself out into a barking, commanding roughness. Thomas held his breath at the rage in that voice.

He didn't know where he was or why but he knew now he wasn't in the water and this was not the day of the crash.

The Survival of Thomas Ford

He remembered the hospital suddenly but this was no hospital despite that white, glaring light.

The thing to do was get out of that light. Thomas crawled and changed the angle of his shoulders. He could hear boots now, crushing the leaves, grinding them against the earth.

Lanski and McCallum found the discarded tent. It lay on the leaves like the slewn-off skin of some great serpent that had passed. McCallum looked at the tent and shook his head.

"Lanski, I'm going back to the girl before she fucks off too. Find him Lanski. Find him fast. If he reaches the village down below, or one of the chalets up above, we're finished."

Lanski stepped over the tent and walked without hesitation up the hillside, not sure what he would do when he reached the natural border of the generator's light.

Above all of them, invisibly, the clouds were shifting like thoughts in a disturbed soul. The wind shoved and tugged mercilessly at their vapours and gasses. High in the firmament stars blazed while a full moon reflected effortlessly the hidden sun's power. Like the theatre lights of drama or medicine they waited expectantly for the curtain below to raise.

Thomas Ford was crawling downhill now. He did not know he had already passed the caravan and Lorna's blanket-covered body. He only wanted to escape the perimeter of the roaring, monstrous generator bulbs.

Soon his bare feet and wriggling toes left that light's caressing edge.

Ford was confused again, not sure whether he moved through air or water, not sure if this was the day of the crash.

Then his head bumped hard against the Subaru's front right tyre. It was a puzzle to him. Something in his head, at the top of it, seemed to have exploded. The shock travelled down Thomas Ford's skull and entered the vertebrae of his neck. With that sudden compression of nerve and bone, a red light erupted deep within Thomas Ford's eyeballs. He groped upwards with his right hand and grabbed the Subaru's headlamp. It filled his palm like one of Lea's breasts. The headlamp still shone bright and was hot as fevered flesh. For some time Thomas Ford had been free of the generator's perimeter of light. He had entered the Subaru's headlights without knowing the transition.

Ford raised his head and the Subaru's light glared him down into snow-blind submission. He crawled to the left instinctively. Grabbing handfuls of earth and leaves he bypassed the huge vehicle.

Lanski had gone as far uphill as he dared in the darkness. It was pointless anyway. Nothing could be found in a place like this, not without luck, and there was no luck in this situation for Lanski. His grandmother would have told him the spirits of Fortune were against him tonight. But he did not need her here to tell him that. There was a sound in the air now, new, running water. Some stream or even river that had been hidden away among these trees. Lanski started to head for the sound. Ford might have headed for it. It was not that Lanski really wanted to find Ford, but he was accustomed to obeying McCallum. The habit ran deeper than Lanski had understood.

Jack McCallum stood over the girl's still, blanket-covered form. The light from the generator bulbs made the caravan and the covered girl look very unreal. At least the girl was still here. Jack sniffed and raised his face to the sky. For a moment he thought he felt the beginning of raindrops. It was only the wind. Some stars were breaking through the clouds above. The

The Survival of Thomas Ford

generator's light masked them but Jack could pick out some familiar patterns of pinpoint white dots above him, like holes in a black fabric. Holes in everything, thought Jack. Holes in me. Holes in my marriage. Holes in my boy's head. Holes in plans. Holes in the ground on this hillside to bury my mistakes in. Jack bared his teeth and turned his back on the caravan and the girl. He headed for the generator housing, to look for the long shovel he had left there last time.

Thomas Ford was crawling downhill in the darkness. It was like sinking down in the loch's water, or falling from the talons of the great bird through the sky in the nightmare. He had left the light from the generator, and the light from the Subaru, far behind now. He had not looked up for some time when, again, his head crashed hard against an obstruction. Ford whimpered and pushed his face deep down against the rotted leaves. He let out a howl of frustration, not caring who might hear. He was near the edge of himself now. He thrashed again on the earth, then lifted his head viciously, expecting to see nothing. But the starlight and moonlight had broken through the carpet of clouds above. In silver light, Thomas Ford clearly saw that his head had bumped into a huge metal object. He tilted his face, presenting his good eye to the object, letting the silver light bathe the eye.

Ford looked behind himself suddenly, up the track, which was visible now in the moonlight and oddly familiar. He tried to stand and managed to bring himself onto his knees. Nausea swept through him and he swayed there for a moment. Then it seemed his whole being steadied and solidified as he stared at the old, abandoned tractor in the moonlight. His breathing stopped. His bad eye tried to open but it couldn't. McCallum had hit it much too hard for it to ever work again. Out of the eye he had left, Ford gazed at the tractor in front of him. Its rust was a crisp, ragged coating that glinted in the silver light.

Ford turned his neck and a shooting pain jolted him so that he rocked back on his heels. But he kept the good eye open and, just behind the tractor, impossibly, he saw the other vehicles, abandoned, like animal skeletons picked clean of once-plump flesh. There was the van, like an old Post Office van but its markings rotted off. And beside it, flat and embedded in the rotted compost of leaf and tree, the metal wheel rim Thomas Ford had last seen that day while Lea had stood a little way down this hillside track, waiting for him, that day when there was no way she could know she was waiting to be taken to her death.

As though of its own will, Thomas Ford's eye lingered on the area of silver space just beside the broken and twisted, earthbound wheel rim.

Like bubbles burped up from the earth's belly into the silver air, Thomas saw the gas emission that had puzzled him and absorbed him that day weeks, or months, or lifetimes ago, when he had made Lea wait as he stood over it and stared down. That day the earth had been brown, not silver, and he had seen what seemed like gas coming up. It had shimmered in the cold sunlight. There had been no smell.

Now the air seemed clear again and Thomas swayed forward. His head hung low, almost all the way to the leaves. This was Ardlarich then, the hillside. This was real. He remembered the hospital, Finlay had driven him home, no, he had not made it home the first time, he had thought he had seen the bird-faced driver on the pavement. He had tried to chase him.

Thomas Ford whined and a sudden clump of vomit burst from his lips, skidding down the front of his bare chest. He

The Survival of Thomas Ford

looked down at himself. He was covered in filth, except for a tangle of artificial tough fabric swathed around his waist and hips and thighs. That fabric seemed familiar too. Ardlarich. The hospital. Lorna, the cleaner. Lorna. It was like electricity in Ford's spine. He remembered Lorna coming to his house, talking to him about money, information, the bird-faced boy. The house. Lorna had been at the house with him, they had been together in the living room. Someone must have come there, done this, taken him here and Lorna here. That was what she had warned about. She had been saying it, that the bird-faced boy and the passenger had already been to the house, planning something like this.

Ford opened his eye. The gas bubbled up from the earth again and Ford told himself it was not real. He told himself it could not be gas or it would have a smell. What if it was a sign? What if it had been a sign that day, causing him to make Lea wait? If it had been some warning from God or the Universe, slowing him down, he should have paid more heed to it. If he had stayed to understand the sign then Lea would still be alive.

But equally, if the strange gas had never been in the air here, to distract and delay him, they would have driven away earlier and passed that deadly corner safe, too soon for the bird-faced boy to do them harm. Thomas Ford laughed in the moonlight, air whistling between his remaining teeth. At that second, something light as air kissed his cheek. He froze, believing it was Lea's ghost here with him on the hill, here to help him. Then he blinked his good eye as a second kiss came. Something tiny and fast made the air flicker in front of Thomas Ford's face. The butterfly danced back and gave the half-broken man room to see it. Its wings were silver now, not white, and yet somehow the clean whiteness could still be sensed. Ford's body gave up beads of precious moisture it could ill-afford now, there was a wet sensation in his chest, then the good eye filled with water until tears rolled down his filthy cheek. It felt like he was being washed inside, some lump passing that had been there since waking at the hospital. Even while the throbbing pain in his head and eye and mouth intensified, that other pain deep within him was relieved and released.

As the butterfly flew higher and higher above Thomas' head, he looked up after it, raising one shaky leg which took his weight, and then the other, until he stood.

He blinked his eye as the butterfly seemed to disappear among the clouds overhead. He raised his palm and rubbed the salt tears into his cheek like an anointment. He turned his head to look back up the hillside. At a distance, the Subaru headlit zone represented one area and further up the hillside the perimeter of the generator's light arc could clearly be seen.

Thomas Ford twisted his neck and clenched his fist. He started to walk back up the hill towards the lights. He had already left one woman behind to die. He could not do it again.

Chapter Thirty-five

In the living room of 72 Broomfield Road the telephone rang out suddenly and violently. It seemed so loud to Marie Ferguson. She could not believe that its ring was always that loud, that insistent.

Marie and Robert had been sitting, pretending to drink tea.

It was Jimmy's hand that reached out and lifted the phone. "Hello?" he said.

At first, all Jimmy could hear in response was the dull roaring of some great insect or engine.

"Have you got everything under control there, boy? You better have. Look, I was going to send Lanski there, but now Ford's gone missing here, see? So you'll have to deal with the woman and the lad yourself, alright boy? Can you manage it?"

Jimmy lowered the phone and placed his palm over the mouthpiece in a gesture of great politeness. Marie Ferguson watched Jimmy's eyebrows raise almost all the way to his vertical black hair.

"There's been a terrible road accident," said Jimmy. "Out by the hospital. All the officers from this side of the river have been sent out to it. They think it'll be half an hour before they can send anyone here."

Jimmy shook his head and shrugged. Robert frowned. Jimmy lifted the phone to his ear again.

"Are you there, Jimmy!" he heard his father shout into the phone.

Marie and Robert heard the shout too. They also heard the strange buzz of the generator on the hill.

"Yes, Sergeant."

"Well, boy, can you handle things there?"

"No, Sergeant. We really need an officer here right away. It's urgent."

"Look, boy, do you know where I am? I'm on the hill. Ardlarich. The hill, boy. The caravan. Remember?"

"Yes, Sergeant."

"Ford's fucked off, Lanski's chasing him, and I've got a shovel and I'm standing here and I'm about to put your wee lassie in a hole in the ground here on this hill. Do you understand, boy? In a hole on the hill. You know all about that, don't you boy?"

Marie Ferguson watched Jimmy blink four times as though he was suddenly paralysed except at the eyelids.

"I can't come to help you, Jimmy. Lanski can't come to help you. You're on your own."

"No Sergeant, we really need an officer here right away now."

"You stupid little…"

"Thank you, Sergeant," said Jimmy.

Like a skull, Marie saw Jimmy grin widely and replace the phone in its cradle.

"They won't be long now," said Jimmy.

He lifted his mug of cold tea to his lips.

"Who was that on the phone, Jimmy?" said Robert.

"It was the police, Robert. I told you."

Jimmy shook his head.

"Robert," said Marie. "Go and make some more tea. Mine is cold. Jimmy's must be too."

The Survival of Thomas Ford

Robert looked over at her. She looked back at him with clear, bright eyes. She nodded.

"Go on, Robert."

She held out her mug to him.

"Get some biscuits too, Robert."

Robert took her mug. Jimmy held his mug out to be taken. Robert stared at Jimmy for a second, then took the mug. He walked out of the living room.

Jimmy smiled at Marie Ferguson.

"Aye," he said. "They won't be long now."

Marie smiled back and nodded at Jimmy.

"How's your mum these days, Jimmy?"

"My mum? Aye, she's alright, Mrs Ferguson. She's fine."

"I should keep in touch with her, Jimmy. We were good friends when we were young, your mum and me. Before she started going with your dad we'd be up town every weekend, your mum and the rest of us."

Jimmy grinned.

"That right?" he said.

"Oh aye. Your mum was happy when she was a girl, Jimmy. We all were really. Everything was a laugh then. It's when you get older that it all changes."

"Aye, I know what you mean."

"No, Jimmy. You've no idea what I mean yet."

"My dad battering me and that, Mrs Ferguson. I know what you mean well enough."

"Ok, Jimmy. Maybe. But should that not mean you need to get right out from under your dad now? While there's still time. Before it's too late."

"Is that no what I'm doing now, Mrs Ferguson?"

"I don't really know, Jimmy. I'm not really sure what it is you're doing."

Jimmy sighed out air.

"Aye well," he said.

Marie licked her upper lip.

"We'd help you, Jimmy. Me and Robert. We'd not turn our backs on you."

Marie watched the boy's eyes change. It was as though some great and intense heat from deep within the boy had suddenly erupted into the black eyes. In that moment half the hope in Marie's heart seeped away, like a liquid that had spilled out of the soles of her feet and down into the thick carpet.

In the kitchen, Robert was opening the knife drawer. He took the wooden handle in his palm and pulled out the long, curved, serrated knife that his mother used to cut turnips and pineapples. The knife shook in Robert's hand. He was due for his next injection. His eyes swivelled to the left slowly, then they scanned to the right as though Robert was reading some invisible document suspended before him in the kitchen's air.

Chapter Thirty-six

The full moon hung over the hill at Ardlarich like a wounded, sightless eye.

Jack McCallum stood in the light from the generator bulbs, alone apart from the blanket-covered girl on the leaves at his feet.

He tapped his phone thoughtfully against the edge of his jaw. Then he shook his head and clenched his fist.

"The boy's no good," he whispered to himself.

Jack let himself sink down until he crouched over the girl's body.

"The boy's no good. The boy's no good."

Jack punched the middle area of the blanketed girl.

"Did you know that, lassie? Your lad's no good. He's weak. A weakling. A wee shitey weakling."

Jack heard leaves crackle behind him. He turned and sprang to standing, facing the direction of the sound. The sound came again, but seemed to change position.

"Who's there?" Jack growled.

A tall, pale figure began to materialise at the border of the generator's light. Then the figure faded away again, back among the tree shadows.

"Who the fuck is it? Is that you, Lanski?"

Jack licked his lips and stared at the place where the figure had been. Or had he imagined it? He tried to be sure but it was impossible to be sure, not without lying to yourself. He looked quickly at the girl's blankets. She hadn't moved. Jack sniffed. The wolf within him bristled tightly from its tail to its long snout. A grin spread across his face, much like his son's grin. But the next moment it vanished. Jack had trained it not to appear. Cathy's husband couldn't grin like that. Neither could the owner/director of McCallum Homes, or any of the business aliases Jack went under in the city. Only here, on the hill, could Jack McCallum reveal his true nature, yet even here he masked it.

Again a ghostly figure seemed to take shape, but this time ten feet to the left of where the first one had tried to come through. Jack took three steps on the dead leaves. His ankles were trembling.

"Lanski!" Jack hissed.

Lanski's long, lean form emerged from the forest.

"I couldn't find him," the Polish-accented voice declared. "I followed all the way to that stream that comes down the hill. I looked all along it and zig-zagged back and around but the man is not here."

Jack frowned. He turned his torso to face the hill above.

"He must have gone up there or…"

Jack reversed himself, his feet still planted in the leaves, his ankles still secretly vibrating.

"…or he's down there, maybe at the road or the village already…run down, Lanski. He could have passed out, before the Subaru, or just after it. You'll see him…"

Jack tilted his body back far now, presented his breast and neck and face to the moon above which was only a dim impression because of the glare from the generator bulbs.

"That moon there will be showing it all up, Lanski. Once you're past the Subaru you'll find him, if he's gone downhill. Go!"

The Survival of Thomas Ford

Lanski stared for a second, then turned. He had walked all the way to the generator's light perimeter when he stopped and looked back.

McCallum sensed the movement and twisted his face.

"What?" he said.

Lanski only stood silently.

"What?" said McCallum again.

"The girl. What will you do?"

McCallum spat on the leaves.

"Find him, Lanski. Find him or it's finished for all of us."

Lanski turned and walked out of the light. He tread slowly and carefully down the steep track, stumbling sometimes, nearly falling once, until his eyes got used to the moonlight.

Then he heard a roaring shout from behind. It was McCallum.

"Lanski!" screamed McCallum's voice.

Lanski turned and ran back uphill. He ran into the arc of the generator bulbs again, sure he would find Ford standing over McCallum, revenging himself. Lanski did not know what he would do if that was what had happened. But McCallum was only standing quietly where Lanski had seen him last. His face seemed different though, even in the harsh light here that held no subtlety or nuance.

"It's just, the boy, Lanski, Jimmy, my boy. Take the Subaru and go to 72 Broomfield Road, in the city. If you see Ford take him back here first. But if you don't find Ford go to 72 Broomfield Road. Jimmy's there with a woman, Marie, a right bitch. And her son, he's a weakling, like my boy, but he's big too. You'll need to help Jimmy sort out that house, Lanski. Then get back here fast, bring the boy, bring Jimmy, bring him back up here, alright Lanski?"

Jack turned, inclined his body uphill again.

"I think Ford's up there, Lanski. There's something in a dying animal, wanting to hide, I think it would take him up there, above us. What do you think? You were brought up in a forest weren't you? Your grandmother's village."

Lanski could not remember telling McCallum ever about his grandmother or her village.

"That was why I looked along the water," said Lanski. "The dying will sometimes seek out the water. I don't know if they will seek height."

Lanski shook his head.

"72 Broomfield Road," said McCallum.

Lanski nodded.

"See my boy's alright, Lanski. Then bring him back to me. I'll be finished with this by then."

McCallum jerked his neck in the direction of the girl under the pile of blankets on the ground by the caravan.

Lanski let his eyes look directly at McCallum's eyes for a long moment. Lanski turned again and walked steadily downhill. He couldn't remember telling McCallum anything about his home or childhood. He had told other Polish men on the site these things. One of them must have told McCallum. Lanski said the address, 72 Broomfield Road, out loud to himself twice, to prove to himself that he remembered it. He tried not to think about what was happening to the girl by the caravan. She was not his business. He was not his sister's keeper. Lanski walked down the silver-lit area of track between the generator lights and the beginning of the Subaru's headlight area which was still in the distance as though some giant had abandoned their torch here on the hill. Lanski's eyes were just becoming used to the silver light from the moon and stars above when he nearly walked headlong into Thomas Ford who was coming up the

The Survival of Thomas Ford

hill. Lanski and Ford both stopped walking at the same time and stood looking at each other. Lanski could see that one of Ford's eyes was ruined, but the other eye shone back moonlight at the Polish foreman. Lanski parted his lips and nearly swallowed, but the swallow didn't come. He waited for fear, or anything, to start in himself, or for Ford to move, but Ford was absolutely still. Lanski could see that Ford was naked and barefoot, apart from the shredded remainder of tent material around his waist and upper thighs. He could see this without ever taking his own eyes off Ford's one wide glittering eye.

"Where is she?" said Ford.

Lanski waited long seconds before answering.

"She's up there at the caravan. He's going to kill her."

Ford's single eye blinked. He nodded, but not as though the nod was about the girl at all. He seemed to be thinking of something else. Ford's head dropped and his whole body shuddered. Ford exhaled a long breath that was audible above the wind that still whistled there on the steep slope. Lanski watched as Ford raised his head again and that single eye focused on Lanski's eyes.

"And you?" said Ford. "Which one are you? Are you the passenger?"

"I'm going to the car behind you. I'm going to the city."

Ford's eye seemed to swell as Lanski stared at it. Lanski felt smaller and smaller as the eye regarded him. It seemed to Lanski that this was hardly a man at all. He was unsure. Was this even Ford? Then Lanski swallowed and his heart shrunk in his chest.

"I'm going to the city," said Lanski again.

Ford's eye shone with silver light. Lanski looked down. Suddenly Ford shifted all his weight to one side. He moved out of the way on the track, with an enormous and slow courtesy, making a space for Lanski to pass.

Lanski's eyes and chest felt wet for a moment. He took two steps down the steep hillside but stopped as Thomas Ford spoke again, so quietly that Lanski only just heard the words over the wind, "Don't come back."

Lanski couldn't move for the next few seconds. When he could move he took more steps down the hill. He kept walking on the silver leaves until his boots turned white from the Subaru's headlights.

Lanski got in the driver's side of the Subaru and found the keys in the ignition. His hands were shaking too much to turn the key. He sat there for a minute, then looked out and up the hillside for the first time, to see if Ford was there. Ford was gone.

Lanski shook his hands. He clapped them together. He blinked and said his grandmother's name out loud. Then he had the Subaru started and began reversing down the hillside.

Chapter Thirty-seven

Alan Gillan was still lying awake, thinking of his poor, lost daughter.

How could this be reality? There was nothing real about this. If it wasn't for Jean, Alan knew he would be considering suicide seriously by now. If only to be reunited with Lea, or have the possibility.

The moonlight was coming in Alan's window very strongly. He could see his wife's hair on the pillow beside him. It looked like the silver tail of a merry-go-round horse. Lea had loved the merry-go-round when she was a wee girl. Alan and Jean hadn't been able to get her off it at the end of days on the beach. It was like she wanted to ride off somewhere far away on the wooden horse that took her in circles.

And now she was gone, so far away that Alan couldn't imagine it.

Cathy McCallum was lying awake too, half in anger at her husband and half in fear over her son. Jack must be with one of his little office whores now. He would make up some story about Lanski and him being needed at some late-night gas-leak on one of the many sites he always had on the go, so many sites that Cathy had long since stopped listening or understanding when Jack talked about the business.

In the early years she knew she had been a help to him, he couldn't have got it all done back then, not without her. But something had changed, after they had left the caravan on the hill and Jack had started making what he called "real money".

Cathy had thought she'd known what that meant, she had enjoyed the new life too. But ten houses had become a hundred, then hundreds, and something called MCCALLUM HOMES started being talked about in the town, because it was only a town then, she had seen signs outside houses saying MCCALLUM HOMES in loud, shouting type. She had seen adverts in the newspapers, on television.

Jack had forgotten then, to take care of Jimmy. He had thought of it as Cathy's responsibility. Well, if it was her responsibility alone, then Cathy supposed she had messed it up, because even she knew that something wasn't right in her son.

He had been so happy in the caravan though, as a tiny boy, on the hillside, out at Ardlarich. It hadn't been easy for Cathy, taking a wee boy up that steep hill track to get home every day, passing all those abandoned tractors and vans. But it had all just seemed natural then, normal, and the walks kept you fit.

Cathy frowned and bit her lip. She thought of Jack, in some bed right now, some flat or hotel room, a girl young enough to be his daughter would have her legs wrapped round him. Cathy laughed and shook her head. It wasn't even that she really cared, not now. But it still hurt her pride.

The silver light came in the bedroom window and Cathy's eyes sparkled in it like strange organic jewels.

The wind picked up across the city and, outside 72 Broomfield Road, the old grey cat that chose to spend its

The Survival of Thomas Ford

nights reclining on the low, stone wall bordering Marie and Robert Ferguson's front garden stretched its forepaws out ahead of itself as tightly as it could at its age.

The wind didn't really bother the grey cat. Its aged owner rarely bothered to groom the beast any more. Its fur was a thick, matted pad of insulation, proof against rain and wind on most nights. The cat shifted its neck to look out of its large, round head at the living room window of 72 Broomfield Road.

Something there caught the cat's attention. Its claws, all except the right forepaw's claws which no longer came out, twitched and expanded and met the night air. A little cry came from the mouth of the grey cat as it looked at the glass of the living room window of 72 Broomfield Road. The woman in there sometimes came out with bowls of warm milk or sweet treats which hurt the cat's bad fangs. Hesitantly, the cat positioned itself to jump down from the low wall. This took a lot of careful preparation. When it felt all its joints were optimally aligned to cope with the shock, the grey cat allowed its considerable weight to leave the wall. It landed on the short grass with a thump. It trotted along the garden and looked up at the window sill. It wasn't sure it could manage any more but with a remarkable spring from its hindquarters the cat found itself standing solidly on the stone outer sill of the living room window.

It looked in. Its grey-green elliptical irises reflected back the light from the living-room. For a long time the cat watched, transfixed. It forgot its age and where it was. Sometimes its neck twitched violently from side to side as it reacted to the events in the living-room. The cat made no sound.

On the road along the loch-side, from the hill back to the city, Lanski drove the Subaru at a consciously steady, sane, regular pace. It was very important, he felt, to keep the outward appearance of control. Let the insides do what they liked, it was Lanski's duty, at the moment, to maintain some control of the externals.

It seemed he had only blinked an eye though, barely a moment had passed, and already the Subaru was passing the golf course and going through the roundabout.

Lanski was back in the city. Houses shot by on left and right. The occasional MCCALLUM HOMES sign loomed.

How easy it had been then, in the end, to just walk away from the dream. The dream of one day being a rich man like McCallum. It had passed and fallen from Lanski's hands as lightly as a leaf. He would go back to the flat, give Elena some of his money. She would cry, perhaps worse. But by tomorrow, Lanski knew he would be back in Warsaw, with his wife and children again. It was the right thing. There was no doubt in Lanski. He could hear the warm voice of his grandmother, deep in his soul, already welcoming him home to the land where she was buried.

But still, Lanski found himself indicating left at the sign for Broomfield Road. His heart started to speed up as he drove steadily along the old avenue of oak trees. He counted off the even numbers until, just around the corner, he saw a large 72, metal letters stuck above a solid door with frosted glass panels. With the eye McCallum had trained his foreman to have, Lanski noticed the pebble-dashing along the side of the house. There was also something odd on the living-room window-sill, some large, oval, grey object, perhaps a stone or ornament.

Lanski parked the Subaru and turned off the ignition. He sat very still and made no move to open the car door. The

The Survival of Thomas Ford

grey object on the window-sill of the living-room of 72 Broomfield Road moved suddenly and Lanski blinked. It was a cat. Lanski thought it was shifting position on the window-sill, getting ready to spring down. But now he saw from the way it moved its hips and back that it was an old cat. It wasn't preparing to jump. In fact, Lanski wondered from the painstaking movements the cat made now whether it had ever managed to jump up there on its own. Perhaps some children had left it there as a cruel trick. The children in this country could be like that. The cat moved again, almost in a flinching, cowering way. As though something it saw through that living-room window was affecting it.

Lanski placed his hand on the handle of the Subaru's driver's door. But he didn't open the door. He just left his hand there. He could stay in the vehicle. He could drive away. What business was it of his any more? McCallum had sent him to this house to help Jimmy deal somehow with some woman and another boy, but Lanski knew he had no intention of helping the McCallums now. So why had he come here then? He was being a fool. It wasn't necessary for him to be here. He should leave the city right now. It wouldn't even be necessary for him to stop by at the flat and see Elena. Lanski's debit card and passport were never kept at the flat. All the Polish workers from the site stored their valuables at Zebitov's house. Zebitov's house was safe. No-one messed around with Zebitov, not even the native Scottish in the city.

But Lanski felt his hand depressing the button on the door. He wasn't doing it. The hand seemed to be doing it by itself, with a will so mysterious and deep that Lanski dared not interfere. He pushed the door open. He stepped out onto the empty road. He kept his eye on the cat and closed the door gently. The door did not fully close. The cat did not react. Lanski stepped onto the pavement and walked along it in the direction of 72 Broomfield Road, the garden, the gate, the window and the cat.

He kept his eyes on the cat and the closer Lanski came to the cat the more familiar the animal seemed. Lanski felt a tingling sensation in his cheeks and neck. Somewhere in his head, at the top of his skull, something seemed to warm, then tighten, then burst and flush away. An emptiness followed that sensation as Lanski stared at the cat's grey fur. Its round head. No, this was too strange now. Lanski nearly turned back and returned to the Subaru, to his passport, to his debit card, to his family. But he scratched his thumb against his index finger and walked a few more steps towards the cat on the windowsill.

Lanski was at the gate to the front garden of 72 Broomfield Road. The cat made no sign of knowing he was coming towards it. Lanski recognised the cat and his lips were suddenly dry. The cat was Ixor. Ixor, the cat Lanski's grandmother had had in the village of Lanski's childhood. Lanski, who had been little Zbigniew then, little Zbiggy they had called him, he had always been frightened of Ixor, the big, old, heavy cat that sat on his grandmother's lap through the afternoon and on her doorstep through the evening. Lanski told himself to stop being stupid, this was another cat, it only looked like Ixor.

But then the cat turned its round head towards Lanski. Its eyes were orange in the streetlight glow. Its eyes locked onto Lanski's eyes perfectly. There was no difference. These were Ixor's eyes reflecting the orange lamplight. Lanski was six years old again, pee on his thigh from a dribble he had just taken against the old elm tree by his grandmother's porch.

The Survival of Thomas Ford

The cat's eyes bored into Lanski. Why had his grandmother loved that horrible, evil cat so dearly? The stench of ancient, corrupting knowledge had seemed to come off Ixor like steam under the sunlight that shone down on the forests of Lanski's childhood. And here was Ixor back again, perhaps only for a moment, looking through this other British cat's eyes at Lanski the foreman. Ixor the unkillable. Ixor, the potent terror of Lanski's infant nightmares.

Lanski stood still at the gate of 72 Broomfield Road. He knew his hands were shaking. He started to remember why he was here. The cat swivelled its huge head and looked away from Lanski. It was staring back in through the living room window of the house. Lanski felt the impulse again, like a surge of electricity, to turn back to the Subaru and escape.

Instead, he walked into the garden. He expected the cat to jump down or react and at least turn its head toward him again. But the cat was still as Lanski stepped on the paved path and walked up it until he was at the front door. Lanski looked through the frosted glass. The hall light was on. The number, 72, stood out boldly in black figures. Lanski walked along the front wall of the house, listening. He had almost reached the windowsill and the huge, old cat, when instinct told him again to go back. His feet stopped walking. Lanski stared at the cat's grey rump. He should go back to the front door of the house, try the handle. He had not thought of it when he looked through the door's glass. Neither had he thought of knocking, or ringing. No, Lanski realised, the idea must have been there, blocking him from doing those other things, the idea of seeing first, whatever it was the cat was staring in the window at.

That was it. That was the thread keeping Lanski from turning away now. He wanted to know. Perhaps that was why Granny had loved Ixor, her cat, for the knowledge in Ixor's vast eyes. The knowledge must have passed, some of it, from Ixor to herself.

Lanski walked towards the windowsill and the old, grey cat. He wanted the cat to respond normally now, at last, jump down, run or stagger away into the night. But the cat stuck there as though superglued to the stone sill. The cat seemed so heavily embedded there on that window ledge, Lanski imagined its paws sunk into the stone by now, like wet concrete. He saw how dirty and matted its thick fur was. He saw its heavy, distended belly. Again, he wondered how it could ever have jumped up to the window-sill. Lanski pretended to himself that it was the cat he was curious to see up close, all the while he was edging along the front wall of 72 Broomfield Road to get level with the window.

Lanski was close enough now, to have reached out and touched the cat, though he had no desire to do it. Still the cat made no movement. It did not turn to watch him. Lanski could see the inner panel of the double-glazed living-room window. It seemed to have an odd tint, like rose-glass, or the high cathedral windows in Warsaw. Lanski couldn't see into the living-room from where he stood. The angle was still wrong. Just another step, maybe two, and he would be able to see in. Lanski did not take the next step though. He wasn't past it yet, the point of no return. He could still go back to the Subaru and drive away without ever looking through this window. The options danced at the front of Lanski's brain like teasing nymphettes whirling in a private ballet of the soul. Lanski watched the edge of the cat's left eyeball. That old eye was still looking in the window. Lanski tried to see some reflection in the eye but that was impossible. He took three quick steps, pivoted on his toes, and stood right outside

The Survival of Thomas Ford

the living-room window, directly behind the cat's broad hips and long, thick tail which hung over the window-sill like a grey gallows rope.

The cat did not react to Lanski's arrival at its back.

There was no tint in the glass. It was only blood. Lanski looked at the glass, and through the glass. There was nothing different here. This was only the same as McCallum's hill. McCallum's hill, and now this house, it was all the same. One was a hill and one was a house but Lanski knew what they were and that they were both the same. They were both the Valley of the Shadow of Death that Lanski's old grandmother had talked about often.

Lanski and the cat remained quiet and looked into the Valley as the full moon swelled far above them.

Chapter Thirty-eight

Jack McCallum had found the old shovel at last. It had fallen right down the back of the generator's side panelling. For a while, Jack had thought he might not be able to reach far enough down to get hold of it, but he had persisted.

Jack inspected the shovel's flat blade in the generator light. He couldn't be sure if it was rust or blood embedded in the metal. He decided it must be a bit of both. Shandlin had bled a lot. Screamed a lot and bled a lot. That little bitch from Greenock who wouldn't keep her mouth shut, she had bled a lot too. What colour had her hair been? Blonde, Jack remembered, with a touch of a Farrah flick though she probably hadn't modelled her hair on Farrah's, no, this had been a nineties girl. What a mouth on her though, and the stupid little bitch thinking Jack was the sort of man who could be blackmailed. Well, she had learned. And now here was this new one, Lorna, she was about to learn.

Jack looked away from the shovel blade and over at the girl's long shape by the caravan base. Normally, he would take her out of the blankets first, try to have some fun, but with Ford out here somewhere, loose, this wasn't the normal situation.

Jack knew suddenly that he shouldn't have sent Lanski off like that, to help the boy. Lanski should have been kept here, on the hill, until Ford was found. The girl and Jimmy could

The Survival of Thomas Ford

have waited. Ford was the priority. So why had Jack sent Lanski away? Fear and confusion had set in. Jack tried to get his mind straight. Should he dig the hole for the girl now, or should he leave the girl here and go looking for Ford?

If Ford finds people, help, then Jack knows he will hear them coming up the hill. There will be warning. Jack knows he can disappear into the forest if they come. The Subaru is gone now, Jack had heard Lanski go with it, so they can't find it if they come. Did the girl tell Ford who Jimmy is, or who Jack himself is? That is the only important thing. Even that, though, might only be hearsay. Except that Jack owns the land here, and if they start digging it up...

It might all be over already then.

On the other hand, the girl was a certainty. She knew everything. Jack squeezed the shovel's wooden handle. He walked into the trees, ignoring the girl. He let his belly lead him through the shadows and birches until he found a spot that seemed fresh, unused. He jammed the shovel's blade against the rough earth and put his weight down hard.

Only twenty feet away, the family of feral cats froze in rapt attention, still, tense as metal cable, listening to the shovel break the forest earth. Such a huge intrusion into the night's peace here was a rare thing. Most of the creatures listening, with their short, wild lives, had never heard such a thing. Only some of the older, more crazed-looking cats, felt dim memory stir, from earlier burials. It had been a comfort for Jack, Cathy and Jimmy, twenty years earlier, having the family of cats sleeping and purring in the gap below their caravan. The animals had provided an insulation, not so much from the cold, but from the loneliness of the forest and the hill. Even before Jack McCallum's madness had filled the earth here with the bodies of his enemies, there had been ancient ghosts to contend with for anyone who tried to live on the dark hillside. It was an old place. Something in it had attracted many people over the centuries, and they had tried to live here, but no-one had stuck.

Only the cats had stuck for so many generations, taking possession of the land and the trees for these twenty years.

Now they tolerated the intrusion of Jack's shovel chopping at the earth.

Jack was finding a rhythm in the work. Thoughts of Jimmy started to race through Jack's mind, Jimmy at that house with the woman and that boy, Robert. Of course Lanski had to be sent there. What would have been the point of finding Ford here, only to have something happen to the boy in the city tonight? Cathy would never forgive it. Jack's unspoken contract with his wife was that, no matter what else, the boy had to be kept safe. If anything happened to Jimmy all bets were off. And anyway, for Jack himself, even with Jimmy's shortcomings, it was true when Jack told the boy that all the work had no meaning unless it could be passed along to Jimmy. Jack's hands paused. He stopped digging and the shovel hovered in the darkness. It was as though reality suddenly penetrated Jack's mind. The odds were so heavily against him now, against McCallum Homes, against the future that Jack had planned out. On paper, it looked almost hopeless now. Too many variables to control; too many genies let out of too many bottles.

Jack snarled. Paper odds had never meant anything to him. Paper odds were for cowards, who wanted an excuse for not trying. If you were going to dare to try to shape the future you had to forget about such things. You had to try to change your mind into a machine that could create diamonds, then you had to use the diamonds as tools to cut your name, your family's name, into the glass surface that other people called the future. Then other people would read your name there.

McCallum Homes

There wasn't anything else to it, not that Jack could see.

Of course, this meant you had to have a shovel on nights like this, and arms to lift the shovel, and a mind and heart that could live with the holes on the hillside.

But had it not been his own boy who had made the first hole for that kitten?

It was destiny then. Something irresistible and mighty that could not, and should not, be denied. Jack allowed destiny to use his hands to remove the next shovelful of earth from the hillside.

Chapter Thirty-nine

Lorna awoke to terror. Her head and shoulders, half-suffocated in the swathes of thick blanket, were scratching and thumping among the tree-roots and stoned earth that Jack McCallum was dragging her across to get her to her grave. He had hold of her good foot in one hand and in the other he gripped the foot he had broken earlier that night with a punch. The broken bone in Lorna's right foot was an inexplicable white-heat, searing, but the terror eclipsed it.

Jack McCallum looked up quickly as muffled screams started from the other end of the blankets. He laughed.

"*Oh girl of the forest*," Jack began to sing in a surprisingly high, clear, ringing voice, "*why do you pine so you pine so…oh girl in the forest why not pine for me!*"

Jack blinked and stopped singing. He laughed again.

Thomas Ford stood absolutely still, a statue bathed half by the moonlight and his remainder drenched in the edge of the generator's bulb perimeter. He waited for the singing to come again, so he could judge direction by it this time and try to follow. But there was no more singing.

Ford started walking again. It didn't occur to him to be careful. He simply walked into the aura of the generator lights. Long, blinking seconds passed as he walked higher, blindly, then his eye adjusted. He saw the wrecked caravan. The generator engine roared. Ford looked all round the area

The Survival of Thomas Ford

slowly. He looked for the bird-faced driver but he was not here. He looked for the square-jawed passenger. He looked for Lea until he remembered not to look for his dead wife. He looked for Lorna, a sense of urgency returning now as his mind focused again.

Lorna.

Thomas Ford walked up to the caravan. He put his hand on the door handle and pulled. The door came away in his hand. He let go of it and let it fall to the earth. The thin door landed silently there as the generator engine screamed.

Thomas stepped up and into the caravan. It was all rotted away inside. No-one was in there. Thomas backed out of the metal shell. He walked across to the generator housing.

He stood and stared around but there were no signs on the ground, no tracks. He looked at the edges of the generator's light perimeter. He would have to go out there, into the darkness of the trees again. Somewhere in the moonlight he would find her and with her the bird-faced bastard. Thomas looked down as the pain in his head and eye threatened to win. He let it build and gnaw at him. He let it almost take away his reason. Then he firmed himself again and raised his head. He chose a direction for his feet and he walked to the edge of the unnatural, searing white light.

Chapter Forty

In the city, outside the living-room window of 72 Broomfield Road, the house that Marie Ferguson's dead husband had left her, Zbigniew Lanski and the old, decrepit, grey cat remained silent and still beneath the silver moon.

The smeared coating of blood on the living-room window made everything inside the house on the other side of the soiled glass seem a rose-hued nightmare scene, not real at all. Lanski tried to make himself understand quickly and thoroughly that it was real nonetheless, but his brain refused to clank into gear and accept this.

Only when one of the seemingly dead bodies on the thick, red living-room carpet moved in a swift, convulsive spasm did the grey cat flinch and howl lowly. The spell shattered for Lanski too and he moved quickly away from the window, jogged along the front wall of the house. The door handle turned easily and Lanski was still running when he entered the hall. It was a well-decorated passageway. Lanski noticed the ornate mirror on the wall. His own reflection there was a surreal blur as he passed. The living-room door was almost closed. Lanski shoved against it but the door wouldn't open. Something heavy was obstructing it.

Lanski pushed harder. The door moved slowly and steadily towards opening. Lanski put his shoulder to the door and followed through on the shove. The momentum brought the

The Survival of Thomas Ford

door halfway open. Lanski heard a dull thud as the body that had been blocking the door finished its roll on the carpet. Lanski got his head into the room. A woman's thick black hair made a luxurious tendrilled splash against the red carpet. Her body had been blocking the door. Her arm was at a funny angle now, as though she deliberately hid her face from view. Lanski looked at the big man sprawled across the worn-out leather chair. Too big for Jimmy. Strangely, it was Jimmy's moving form on the carpet, by the electric fire, that caught Lanski's eye last. The boy's erect hairstyle was intact, but a large knife was inserted neatly in his side. Blood flowed freely there. Lanski watched the boy's eyes. Black circles. They looked back at Lanski with a curious little fire at their centres.

"Lanski?" said McCallum's boy.

Lanski nodded. He took a high step and made his way over the woman's body. He went to the man on the leather chair first. He put his fingers to the base of the man's thick, square jaw. He kept his eyes on the man's hands. There was no pulse in the neck.

"Did I do him, Lanski?" said Jimmy. "See? See? You tell my dad eh, tell him, tell him I did the both of them eh?"

Jimmy lay his head back down on the thick carpet.

"Tell him the future's secure eh? Tell my dad, Lanski. Tell him the future's alright now."

Lanski turned his neck to watch Jimmy. A moan came out of the woman. Jimmy jerked his head in her direction.

"Finish her, Lanski! Finish her man."

Lanski raised his eyebrows. He walked over to the woman and crouched beside her. He could see her face now. Her eyes were tormented. She must know the man on the chair is dead. Lanski can see that her eyes are in hell already. Lanski sees that the eyes are the eyes of a mother. She is the right age to be the mother of the man on the chair. Lanski sees that her face is beautiful, even now. She is still moaning. Her eyes are on the dead man on the leather chair. She has not focused on Lanski at all.

"Do her, Lanski!" hissed Jimmy.

"Shut up," said Lanski.

The Pole stood abruptly and walked across the blood-stained carpet until he stood over Jimmy. Jimmy craned his neck and looked up at the man who towered over him.

"Where's my dad?"

Lanski didn't answer. He bent over and took hold of the handle of the knife in Jimmy's side. Jimmy's mouth opened and a high squeal filled the living-room. Lanski twisted the handle a little. Jimmy screamed. On the window-sill outside the living-room the old, grey cat emitted a low howl. It jumped down onto the front garden, jarring its hip-joints. It ran home. Lanski's face in the living-room was set like a block of East European granite. To Jimmy's tear-filled eyes, Lanski's head was an Easter Island statue, floating above him in the room's ether. Lanski pulled and the big knife came out with a wet sound. Lanski tossed it away. He took Jimmy's jacket in one hand and his shirt in the other. He pulled back folds of material until the wound was exposed. Lanski pressed his palm by the wound's edge and blood welled up. Jimmy screamed again and his whole body shuddered.

"You're lucky little Scottish bastard. You only cut your skin I think."

He prodded the open wound again with finger-tips.

"No organs see? Just your skin boy. Just the edges of you."

Lanski laughed.

"You some kind of fucking vampire boy eh? My grandmother would have liked you."

The Survival of Thomas Ford

Lanski stood up. He left the room, walking over the woman's moaning form. He walked along the hall and guessed at the bedroom. He opened a drawer and found a white shirt. As he walked back along the hall, he ripped the material into strips. He walked back over the woman and grabbed Jimmy's shoulders. He pulled his boss' son to a sitting position. When Jimmy understood what the Pole was doing, he raised his arms to make it easier for the Pole to wrap the cloth round his stomach. Lanski pulled tight and Jimmy yelled out again. He thought he was going to faint, the room and the woman and the Pole and Robert's dead body all seemed to shimmer. Then the room hardened up again.

"You won't bleed to death now boy," said the Pole. "No, you live now I think."

Marie Ferguson had started to crawl along the carpet towards her son's body. Jimmy and Lanski looked over at her.

"Come on," said Lanski.

He pulled Jimmy to his feet. The room threatened to swirl again. Lanski dragged Jimmy towards the living-room door. Jimmy looked back towards the crawling woman.

"Lanski. We've got to get her! Lanski! No!"

But Lanski had the boy in the hall now. Soon they were outside the front door of 72 Broomfield Road. Jimmy was shocked at the feeling of the cool night wind against the skin of his face. He had gone so far from life in so short a time. Now the Pole was dragging him back into the world. Jimmy saw the Subaru looming closer. He knew he couldn't have walked a step on his own, only the Pole's strength was holding him up. Surely it was better this way after all, to get away from that house after what had happened. But then it rose up again in Jimmy's soul, the pointlessness of it all if the woman was left alive to tell everyone.

"Lanski! Christ! Go back and get her! You work for my dad man! He won't want that woman left there!"

Lanski took an arm off Jimmy. He leaned the boy's weight against the passenger door of the Subaru. He got the door open and levered the boy into the car seat skilfully. Lanski slammed the passenger door and walked round the vehicle. He looked over the roof of the Subaru, at the house. He looked for the grey cat on the window-sill and saw it was gone. The living-room window was still rose-pink in the glow from the orange streetlights, like the stained-glass window of a religion yet to be conceived.

Lanski got into the Subaru driver's seat. He turned the key in the ignition. It felt better to be back in the car.

Lanski leaned across Jimmy and grabbed the passenger seatbelt. He pulled it across the boy's shirt-wrapped torso and clunked it into its housing. Lanski grinned at the boy.

"I don't work for anyone any more," he said.

Painstakingly, doggedly, Marie Ferguson pulled her hurting body across the surface of the living-room carpet she had chosen one rainy afternoon at Carpetworld. It had been difficult, choosing between the deeper twill weave of a more expensive carpet, or the compromised yet harder-wearing close-relation weave that she had finally got a better deal on. It was at those times that she missed her husband's presence most keenly. Her husband had been great at getting the best deals. Now Marie Ferguson was pulling herself towards the old, leather chair which her husband had gotten a fantastic deal on nearly twenty years ago. Even the gold cushion had been thrown in free and now her son's dead body was sprawled across that chair and cushion. Marie was half-aware that she was the only living thing left now in this house. She

The Survival of Thomas Ford

heard the Subaru's engine grunt into life beyond the double-glazed window. She heard it growl louder and move off down Broomfield Road. She knew that her son's murderer was being taken away into the night by some man who had come into her home like a ghost. She crawled now, just as her son had crawled earlier in the day, from the kitchen to the living-room, to watch The Rockford Files, after Jimmy had kicked his balls. She crawled until she was close enough to raise her hand and place it on her son's ankle. She tried to raise her head but could only get it high enough to hold it for a moment against the worn leather surface of her husband's chair before she passed out.

Chapter Forty-one

A soft rain began to drizzle down on the windscreen of the Subaru as Lanski drove to the end of Broomfield Road.

Jimmy felt light as he sat in the passenger seat and watched the raindrops fall individually down the glass in front of himself. Robert had come in from the kitchen with the knife. After that, there had seemed to be no choice left about what could be done. Jimmy blinked and looked out the window to his left. Robert had been his only friend.

"Where are we going?" said Jimmy.

Lanski sniffed.

"Maybe I drive somewhere far from anyone, Jimmy. I find you a nice ditch and leave you there maybe."

Jimmy looked down at the shirt tied round him. It was already dark with his blood. Lanski sniffed again.

"Maybe you die, Jimmy. Maybe you don't."

Jimmy looked over at the Pole and laughed.

"I always thought you guys were funny eh? Dark Bohemian sense of humour eh."

"I'm not Bohemian."

"Near enough," said Jimmy. "*Maybe you die, Jimmy. Maybe you don't*. Near e-fucking-nough man. Jesus, man, it's weird. I'm fucking hungry, man. All of a sudden. Got a Mars Bar or that?"

"You need sugar maybe. You're losing blood."

The Survival of Thomas Ford

Jimmy nodded.

"I've got nothing," said Lanski.

Jimmy laughed again.

"So tell me, Jimmy, what's it all been for? Maybe I take you to the hospital if you tell me. Or I get you a Mars Bar at a garage. It's not my business any more, but maybe you tell me anyway."

"I don't want to go to hospital. Fuck hospital," said Jimmy.

Lanski looked over at his ex-employer's son's face. The bird-like nose stood out starkly against the wet passenger window.

"Who was the man and the girl, from the house at Cromwell Drive?" said Lanski.

"That bitch," said Jimmy. "She was my girlfriend. She turned out to be just a grass. You know what a grass is eh Lanski? Like when someone tells on you for working illegally in a country or that eh?"

"I know what grass is."

Jimmy nodded.

"I trusted her like. I loved her. You should have seen the thighs on her man."

"I saw," said Lanski.

Jimmy looked up quickly.

"Aye? Fuck's sake. What did my dad do with her like?"

"She is on the hill."

"Aye. Right. That's what my dad says on the phone. The hill. Is Ford there too?"

Lanski nodded. He braked the Subaru suddenly and twisted hard on the steering wheel to bring the car into a tight parking place. Jimmy cried out as the seatbelt cut into his side.

"Stay there, Jimmy," said Lanski.

Lanski got out of the Subaru, the ignition keys in his palm. He walked across to the buzzer for the flats above. He pressed the button for 53. There was no answer. He pressed again.

"Yes?" said a sleepy metallic voice from the wall.

"Elena. Bring me down my phone here."

"What?"

"Phone Elena. Come down now with my phone."

"You come up."

"I can't."

There was silence.

Lanski walked over to the Subaru and sat in the driver's seat again. He left the door open wide. After a minute, Jimmy saw a young woman in a dressing gown appear behind the outer door of the building. She looked startled. Lanski waved his hand at her. She opened the door of the building. She had a mobile phone in her hand.

"What are you doing?" she said in a Polish accent.

"Nothing," said Lanski. "Working. I need the phone. Thanks."

"Come here for it then. I'm not going out there in slippers."

"Throw it," said Lanski.

The woman craned her thin neck forwards. She could see Jimmy in the passenger seat.

"Who is that there?" she said.

"It is no-one Elena. You have not seen him here, OK?"

"Who is it?"

"It is Jimmy, my boss' son. He is dying maybe. Someone put a knife in him. Throw me it."

She threw the phone awkwardly. It bounced off Lanski's palm when he tried to catch. Luckily it flew upward and Lanski caught it on the way back down.

The Survival of Thomas Ford

"Come in Lanski," said the woman. "Come home."

"I will be home soon Elena."

He looked at the woman and smiled sadly.

"Won't you risk your feet to come out and give me a kiss Elena?"

She looked at him. She opened the door of the building and hopped through the light rain like a huge rabbit. Jimmy heard her breathing loud in the Subaru as she gripped Lanski's shoulders and kissed him. She looked over Lanski's cheekbone as she kissed him, straight into Jimmy's eyes. Jimmy saw her eyes move down to the wet patch on his side.

"Now go in," said Lanski. "Get your feet dry. I'll be home soon."

The woman smiled. She did not look at Jimmy again. She turned and ran back to the building. Before she could get past the big glass door and back to the dry, she heard the Subaru engine come alive behind her. By the time she turned round to look, the car was gone.

Lanski started to punch buttons on the phone with his thumb, as he accelerated the Subaru along the broad road.

"Ah," he said, "stupid! They can trace it, no?"

Jimmy turned dazed eyes on the Pole.

"Eh?"

Lanski shook his head.

"Where a phone box, McCallum boy? This city still have some no?"

Jimmy shook his head.

Lanski started making random turns in the Subaru. It was a while before he saw a vertical metal box on a corner in the distance.

"You stay put boy. You're better in here sitting still anyway. Out on the street you bleed away in minutes I think."

"Who are you calling?"

Lanski slammed the door shut and went into the phone box. He picked up the receiver then swore. He walked back to the car, opened the driver door.

"You got change Jimmy?"

Jimmy sneered.

"Who are you calling?"

Lanski opened the glove compartment by the dashboard. He rifled through the boxes and CDs there. No money.

"You can phone my dad on the mobile no worries, Lanski. Give it to me. I'll phone him."

"I'll phone your dad soon boy. First, I'm getting ambulance for that woman you hurt."

Jimmy blew out air.

"You fucking dumb Pole. 999 calls are free here. This is a civilised nation."

Lanski looked at the boy's face. It looked very pale and thin. The black eyes and black hair made a surreal contrast with the white skin.

"You better be telling truth, boy," said Lanski.

Jimmy grinned and his teeth gleamed. He nodded as though to himself.

"Should just let that bitch go peacefully though, Pole. She'd be happier with her husband and boy anyway."

Lanski slammed the door. Jimmy watched him walk back to the phone-box. The Pole made the call. Jimmy saw the angular mouth talk into the phone. Jimmy saw the Pole's head shake. It occurred to Jimmy to open his door and walk out onto the pavement. But the Pole was right. It felt to Jimmy like his blood would all run away onto the concrete if he left the car.

Soon Lanski was back in the driver's seat. Jimmy felt better when the Subaru was moving again, as though

The Survival of Thomas Ford

centrifugal force and momentum were the only things keeping the blood inside him now.

Chapter Forty-two

Thomas Ford was moving slowly through the darkness. The moonlight wasn't powerful enough to penetrate all the way down to these spaces between the tight-packed birch trees. The girl could be anywhere. She could be dead by now. Polish. The man who had left as Thomas came up the hill and passed him, he had been Polish. He had not been the bird-faced driver, nor the square-jawed passenger. What was he doing here then? If he was involved at all, then why leave so easily?

Ford could call the girl's name, but then how many people could he be warning of his presence? At least there was something egalitarian in the darkness. Everyone at the same disadvantage.

Thomas stopped walking up through the trees. He stood quiet and listened. He could hear the water flowing, the stream, but it seemed to be in the middle-distance. There were occasional rustles and so far Thomas had moved towards them, but maybe that had been a mistake. They could be anything, animals, or just the wind in the branches.

As Jack McCallum dragged the girl through the trees, he heard the sounds all round himself of things moving in the forest. The moonlight illuminated big, sudden shapes that Jack took to be Thomas Ford, but they were never Thomas Ford. They were always trees.

The Survival of Thomas Ford

Lorna thrashed on the leaves as Jack pulled her along, like an eel. She had stopped screaming. Jack wondered why he was putting up with it, the hassle of her movements. He could knock her out with one boot. Then he realised, he must want her awake when she comes out of the blankets. But that would be stupid. He should get this done quick. She should go in the hole without ever leaving the blankets. It seemed hard though. All this work with no fun at all. There should be some fun involved, or why bother? A man had to live. Seek his amusements. Even with Ford loose out here somewhere, or down in the village telling his story maybe, even then there should be time for a little play. The girl writhed with renewed vigour as Jack dragged her over an unusually thick tree-root.

"That's it, girl," hissed Jack. "Never give up! Fight til the last fucking drop!"

Jack laughed in the diluted silver light. He looked up. The trees weren't so thick overhead. He looked down and around himself. It was the clearing. They were nearly at her grave now. Just another minute. Jack had chosen to put the girl down far from Shandlin's hole. It was an instinctive thing, the positioning of the holes. Jack had all the co-ordinates memorised, like a game of battleships. From Poppy the kitten onward.

Jack's mobile rang in his pocket. The sound filled the forest. The feral cats cringed and hunkered low to the leaves in dread.

Jack dropped the girl's feet. He put a boot on the middle of the blankets to pin her in place. She jerked and he stamped on her. He got the phone out of his pocket and its metallic scream filled the night air. Jack pressed the button.

"McCallum. It is me. I am with your boy. I have your boy. He is dying maybe. Someone put a knife in him."

"Eh? Lanski? Jimmy? What's happened to him?"

"I have your boy," said Lanski again. "He is maybe not dying. I bandage him. It is not certain."

"Let me talk to Jimmy," said McCallum.

In the Subaru, Lanski passed the phone to Jimmy.

"Dad," said Jimmy. "They put a knife in me man. Is this Pole working for you or not man eh? What's fucking going on eh?"

"Are you alright Jimmy?"

"I'm bleeding eh."

"Go to hospital boy!"

Jimmy laughed weakly.

"I don't think this fucking Pole wants to take me dad."

"Put that cunt on," said Jack.

Jimmy passed the phone back to Lanski.

"Hello McCallum."

"You get that boy to the fucking hospital now, Lanski!"

Lanski sniffed.

"I'm not taking your orders any more, McCallum. I don't care if your boy dies in your Subaru passenger seat here. I don't care if your houses crumble in the earth. You are an evil man. Your family is evil. My grandmother taught me better than to run with wolves. I only forgot what she said, that is all. Now I understand her."

Jack stood in the moonlit clearing. Lorna gave a muffled screech from under her blankets.

"Is that the girl?" said Lanski.

Jack kicked at the blankets.

"What do you want, Lanski?" shouted Jack into the phone.

"Maybe I take your boy to a hospital. Maybe he lives. What that worth to you, McCallum?"

Jack swallowed.

The Survival of Thomas Ford

"What do you want?" he said again, very quietly.

The feral cats were shifting among the trees like a strong wind. Their fur and feet rustled among the leaves and twigs.

"Maybe I want everything you have, McCallum. Maybe I take that home with me to Warsaw and I start building my own houses there eh? Or maybe I only need half of everything you have. Or maybe I only want you to let that woman go now. Let her go now and maybe I take your boy to the doctors now. What you think, McCallum? What you think it is I want from you now?"

Jack took a deep breath. A loud snapping sound came from the trees, beyond the moonlit clearing, from the darkness. Beneath the blankets, Lorna quivered. Jack could see the cloth vibrate where it touched her body. It was like electricity flowed through the girl.

"Don't hurt my boy, Lanski," Jack whispered.

"I'm not hurting him. He was already hurt when I got him. All I do is take him for a nice drive now. But he's bleeding on your car, McCallum. We all know you love this car."

"Please Lanski. Take him to the hospital. Money, aye, I'll get you all you want."

"You let that girl go."

"I can't. Not now."

"Then your son might die tonight."

Jack's mouth hung half-open in the moonlight. He thought of Cathy, in the house at Culloden, waiting for Jimmy and himself to come home. Jack felt lost suddenly on the hillside. He always knew what was best, for McCallum Homes and for the future, for himself, for his family. It had all been one thing in Jack's mind, one huge edifice. Now the foundations were crumbling, into the earth like Lanski had said. How could it all come apart so quickly? Jack stared at the blanket on the ground. It was because of her, that bitch there. Without her starting it all off this morning, coming to his office, trying it on, without her trying to blackmail his family none of the rest of it would have unravelled. Jack faced losing everything because of this woman on the ground beneath the blankets. His future, his business, his wife, his son, even his loyal foreman and his car.

Jack licked his lips.

"If I let her go, Lanski, I still lose everything. Either way now, I still lose everything."

"Not Jimmy. Not your son. He will be at the hospital. He will be alright."

Jack laughed into the phone.

Jimmy turned his face toward Lanski in the Subaru. He blinked and looked at the side of the Pole's left eye.

"Let me talk to the boy," said Jack.

Lanski passed the phone to Jimmy.

"Dad, I feel funny, I just..."

The phone felt heavy in Jimmy's hand. His eyelids felt strange too. It seemed like what he needed was to eat something sweet like a Mars Bar but he didn't have one.

"You can handle that fucking Pole, boy. I know you can do it. Do it for McCallum Homes. I'd love to help you boy but I've got to finish this job here. You do that fucking Pole son. Do him for me. Do him for your mum eh?"

"Dad..."

"I can't help you boy. I've got to put this bitch in the ground for what she's done to us. I'm putting her in the hill boy, beside Poppy the kitten. Good luck boy. I love you."

Jimmy heard the phone go dead.

"Dad."

The Survival of Thomas Ford

Jimmy's neck felt strange now, like someone had loosened the bolts in it that should have been tightly holding it to his head. His tongue felt thick.

"Lanski," said Jimmy. "Lanski…"

Jimmy turned his head towards the Pole. He felt Lanski's hand taking the phone from his palm. Jimmy saw Lanski's eyes beneath the moonlight that shone down on the parking place where the Subaru was resting. Lanski's eyes looked solid and honest to Jimmy, like Robert's eyes used to.

"You're dying boy," said Lanski. "I thought your father would let the girl go to save you but he is worse madman than I ever knew."

Lanski shook his head.

Jimmy blinked slowly.

"Aye, he is mental," said Jimmy. "You could still take me to the hospital eh?"

Lanski looked solemnly out the windscreen. They were parked above the loch, on the road between the city and the hill. The water sparkled with moonlight. It was just like sunlight glistening there except it was moonlight. Lanski hadn't expected McCallum to still be there to answer the phone. The Ford man had seemed an Angel of Death walking up the hill to the generator lights. Lanski had thought that maybe the girl would have been lost by now, if Ford was too late, but when he phoned McCallum's number he had not expected McCallum to have survived Ford's rage, the rage Lanski had felt in the air when he stared at Ford's eye on the hill. Lanski had expected a dead line, no answer. Then he would have left the boy at the hospital. Or was that true? If any of that was really true then why had he driven halfway to the hill with the bleeding boy before making the call?

It wasn't too late to turn away from it all. Lanski could open the passenger door now and push the boy onto the gravel. Then all he had to do was go back for his passport, then home. There was nothing difficult about it.

Lanski felt an intense and sudden sensation, in his stomach.

He swallowed and raised his hand to the ignition key.

Chapter Forty-three

Thomas Ford was standing in the darkness of the trees, staring out of his remaining eye at the moonlit features of the bird-faced man in the clearing. The man's nose was unmistakable. It was the nose of a parrot or cockatoo, not a human nose.

Thomas Ford could see the blanketed form at the man's feet. For moments, Thomas thought it was Lea under the blankets, then he remembered again that it was Lorna, the cleaner from the hospital, it was her there on the ground.

The molten, volcanic pain where Thomas Ford's eye had been would not let him concentrate. But he remained still and silent, watching.

The bird-faced man seemed older now, far older than he had been in that second of memorised life, the snapshot deposited in Thomas Ford's brain, the image of the face above the red bonnet in the sunlight by the loch that day.

The silver moonlight made the man's hair seem white, not black. It almost seemed to Thomas now that this could be a different man. He watched the man bend and take hold of one end of the blankets. The man started to drag the body through the silver-lit clearing. Thomas had no doubt that it was a body being dragged and that it was Lorna's body. The only doubt was about this man being the man from the car. But it had to be the boy from the car. He had imagined the age wrongly then, or was perceiving it wrongly now. No wonder the police had never found the driver, if that second of memory could be so mistaken. The man was dragging the body towards the next area of thick-branched darkness. They were going to vanish in a moment, the bird-faced man and the blanketed woman. Thomas Ford felt frozen, inert, as though he himself was captured now in a snapshot and being studied by some great eye far above. He felt himself the most unreal thing in the forest night. He looked up at the moon. It seemed real still, more real than himself, or the bird-faced man, or the blanketed woman. Thomas Ford let his eye blink as he gazed at the moon. When his eye rolled down again the bird-faced man and the blankets were gone, disappeared into the trees. Thomas Ford's lip began to quiver. He almost spoke aloud as though there was someone beside him to hear.

He lifted a foot and placed it on the dead leaves ahead.

Jack McCallum bumped and tugged the girl's body through the trees and darkness. He should never have trusted that fucking Pole. It had been a great error. Jack squeezed his fists tight around the blankets and pulled with renewed power. Maybe he could stand to lose the boy and Cathy. Maybe he was underestimating himself when he thought McCallum Homes would necessarily go down if Jimmy and Cathy went down. Certainly there was no room for weakness now. There were positives and negatives, after fifty years of life Jack knew that was all there was to it, more or less. You just had to emphasise the positives as long as possible. Take away the Pole, Jimmy, and Cathy, take all of them out of the equation, and maybe McCallum Homes and Jack McCallum himself could still prevail.

Jack laughed quietly. It was bullshit. He was going down and he knew it. You also had to be a realist. Well, Ok then, he'd take this little cunt with him.

The Survival of Thomas Ford

Jack pulled her blanketed body hard over the big, rough tree-knot that marked the edge of the next moonlit clearing where Poppy's grave and the girl's freshly-dug hole were waiting.

"Here you go then," said Jack. "It's a nice spot. Good drainage. You'll get the sun in the afternoon and nice nights like this. There's an old owl over there and the cats will come to play. You'll be fine here, lassie. Maybe I'll come to see you now and then. Depends how things work out. You've certainly churned things up, Lorna. No telling how all the pieces are going to land after what you did, I won't pretend it's not so."

Jack kicked the centre of the blankets hard.

"You awake Lorna?"

He kicked again. The girl gave forth a muffled cry.

"You think you can destroy lives and just walk away?" shouted Jack.

He kicked again.

"No! No! No! By fuck no!"

Jack kicked her four times, to punctuate his declamations. He paused and raised a thick hand. He swept the hand through his hair. In the silence Jack heard the light wind whistle. A rustle and crackling of twigs came from the trees nearby. Jack rubbed at the rough beard on his chin. There was no time to take her out of the blankets. He had to try to find Ford. Even if it was hopeless he had to try. He imagined his boy with a knife in him and blood coming out. Tears came to Jack's eyes. He bent his legs and crouched low by the tilled earth of the girl's grave. The wind mixed with the smell of the fresh ground. *Oh Christ help me oh Christ I'm sorry for it all please don't take my boy away.*

From inside the blankets, Lorna heard Jack McCallum moan like a whale torn from the ocean. She hadn't heard a sound like that since the day her mother had told her about the cancer. Her mother had told her very calmly. But then, after a silence, her mother had broken into pieces, like the remains of her tiny, thin body had been blown and scattered by a secret wind and, from her mother's mouth, Lorna had heard that same hopeless sound. Now she heard it through the blankets and, for a second, it nearly eclipsed her own terror.

Thomas Ford stood, staring, transfixed by the sight and sound of his enemy crouched by the hole in the earth. The sound the man was making was the sound Thomas Ford had been waiting to hear now for weeks from inside himself, the sound that had failed to materialise inside himself. His own agony had not welled up into anything so definite and powerful. Thomas' heart heard the call of Jack McCallum's low, plaintive moan and echo-ed it. Thomas almost nodded his head in agreement with the noise, all other details of these circumstances forgotten for a long moment. He walked out into the moonlit clearing and let himself be seen. Jack McCallum went silent instantly. Lorna heard the moan choke off suddenly. Jack McCallum stood slowly. He didn't recognise Ford. He saw a broken figure, almost naked in the moonlight. It could have been the ghost of any of them. Jack couldn't tell which. He had expected for a long time a visit from the ghost of one of those he had buried here on the hill. Jack nodded and grinned. Thomas Ford saw that this was not the boy who had driven the red car by the loch. So like him, and yet not him at all. Thomas Ford felt cheated in the silver light from overhead. His eye widened. On the ground, Lorna writhed suddenly. The blankets rippled and shifted like the surface of a stream.

"Which one are you?" said Jack.

The Survival of Thomas Ford

He had forgotten Thomas Ford completely now. The old ghosts were far more real to Jack. He hoped it was Shandlin. He had hated Shandlin.

"Shandlin?" said Jack. "Is it you, Shandlin?"

The wind was a cold pain against Thomas Ford's bare shoulders. Lorna heard Jack's muffled voice through the blankets. She stopped moving. She couldn't make out the words.

"*You bastard!*" she screamed from the blankets. "*You bastard!*"

Thomas winced at the scream. Jack McCallum stepped towards the blankets and kicked heavily at their centre. Lorna screamed again, wordlessly.

Jack watched the bare-chested figure in the moonlight, as though waiting to see what it would do about him kicking the girl.

"What are you here for?" Jack shouted at the figure. "Eh? Come on! You must have something to say! What's your business back here Shandlin eh? What are you going to do? What are you going to do?"

Jack spat on the blankets.

"You're *nothing*!" Jack screamed. "*Nothing*! *None of you*! *Nothing*!"

Jack breathed heavily. Thomas Ford listened to him pant. The wind seemed to blow harder for a moment. Thomas Ford remembered going through the windscreen of the Toyota, up into the loch's waters. He remembered knowing he was leaving his wife behind in the car to die. It felt like the ice of the loch was all round his skin again as he stood still and let the wind blow on his back.

"I knew I was leaving her," he said, quietly, through his broken teeth.

"Eh?" said Jack.
"I knew she would die."
Jack turned his head in the moonlight, like a dog listening to some strange signal.

Chapter Forty-four

The Subaru was coming up to the blind corner where Thomas and Lea Ford's car had left the road and gone into the water.

Even in the moonlight coming through the windscreen, Lanski could see how pale Jimmy's face had become now.

"Careful going round this bit," said Jimmy. "That's it there, where she went in the loch."

Lanski saw the badly repaired stone wall, the jagged irregular edge where the Toyota had ploughed through.

"She had a beautiful head, man," said Jimmy. "I saw her photos later, in the papers, but I remember her head like, above the blue bonnet, just for a second in the sunlight eh...that's how I remember her, man, and she was beautiful."

Lanski licked his upper lip. Jimmy said, "I'd have loved that eh, having a woman like that, that's the kind of woman I'd like man. You could see the quality man, the beauty, even just in a second when she was about to die eh?"

Jimmy whistled weakly and shook his head.

"Aye, Thomas Ford was a lucky man."

"And the girl?" said Lanski.

Jimmy turned to look at the Pole. Lanski waited, then turned to look back at Jimmy.

"The girl," said Lanski when he saw the boy's vague dreamy eyes. "The girl your father took from Ford's house tonight?"

Jimmy's eyes widened as though he was waking up slowly.

"Oh, that's Lorna, I told you, my girlfriend like. She's a cleaner, up at the hospital. She works with a lot of Polish lassies up there man."

Jimmy turned his head away. He faced the road again. The Subaru was approaching the edge of the village.

"It's two right turns here," said Jimmy.

"I know."

"I feel awful funny now, Lanski. Like I can't keep awake eh? Is that me dying you think?"

Jimmy laughed.

"Dying," he said again.

He blinked.

"I didn't want to do any of that eh? Back in the town. Robert was my friend. I always liked his mum too. But all the pressure like, it wouldn't stop building. And it was Robert like, who came in the living room with that big fuck-off knife. I knew he was going to open me up eh? But he was always a good lad. Then his mum went for me too eh? Fuck's sake. You know yourself. Sometimes there's no choices."

Lanski did indeed know. He took the second right turn off the main road. The Subaru entered the long straight stretch approaching the foot of the hill. For the second time that night, the Subaru headlights carved at the darkness like a blowtorch sculpting a path through hard, black ebony. The night's final shape was still unknown, undecided. Lanski felt the war going on right then, between light and darkness. It was in each twitch of the steering wheel as the four-wheel drive crunched against the rough road. It was a heat in his own spine, just above the tail-bone, where it met the driver's seat.

The Survival of Thomas Ford

"I think I am dying though," said Jimmy. "I've never felt like this before. It's like being really hungry and tired but I don't want food. It's like I'm hungry for something else."

Lanski barely heard Jimmy's voice as he swerved the Subaru far to the left, taking its nose through the parking place opposite the Chalet Reception building.

"You going for the hill eh?" said Jimmy. "Good luck man! It's more like going into space than driving eh?"

Jimmy laughed and put his fingertips up on the dashboard in front of himself as Lanski brought the car round in a broad curved sweep. The Subaru's wheels bit into the track. Its nose tilted upwards outrageously.

"*Whooooooooooooooooo!*" went Jimmy. "*I am the GANDOLFINI!*"

The Pole fought the hill with his wrists and his foot, while the boy screamed.

Thomas Ford and Jack McCallum craned and twisted their necks in synchronised reaction. They looked far downhill at the bobbing and jerking headlights. The vehicle's dull whine was distant, insect-like, not yet significant.

"Don't be thinking that's the police come to save you," said Jack quietly. "No, that's my man in my car. My boy will be there too."

Jack smiled.

"You'll wish you stayed dead when they get here," said Jack. "Whoever you are."

Thomas Ford kept his eye on the distant headlights.

"See that vehicle move?" said Jack. "People laughed at me, man, getting a Subaru. They expected Jack McCallum to get a nice four-wheel Merc for going round the building sites. But I knew what I was doing. That hill down there's littered with abandoned vehicles, but no that Subaru, it does its job. That's all that matters in the end eh?"

Jack waited for Thomas Ford to turn his neck and look at him with that swollen eye. Thomas Ford only watched the distant bouncing headlights coming up the hillside. Jack sniffed.

"We lived up here, for two years. I was going to build a house. But I never did. I should have. It's a wonderful place."

Except for the ghosts, thought Jack in the silence at the back of his eyes. *The ghosts like you.*

"There's cats all over here. I brought them," said Jack. "But you'll know about the cats. They're wild."

The blankets on the ground jerked and squirmed again. Jack grinned.

"She's wild too eh? She's come to the right place. Jimmy had good taste in that at least."

Thomas Ford turned to look at Jack McCallum.

"Jimmy," said Thomas Ford's broken mouth.

Jack looked at him strangely.

"Do you know my boy?"

Jack frowned.

"You're only Ford aren't you?"

Jack laughed.

"I must be going mad. I thought you were Shandlin or one of the others. I forgot to think about you there, Ford. You're Ford's ghost then. I see now."

Thomas Ford's eye stared in the moonlight.

"You're still just a fucking ghost, Ford," said Jack. "It doesn't make you any less a ghost, you just not having done the dying yet. What matters is like I said, how it all ends up. The order of the events won't change a thing. You can be a ghost now instead of later, I don't mind."

Jack kicked the blankets.

The Survival of Thomas Ford

"Like this bitch. I've dug her hole. Soon I'll plant her. But she's already dead. Like yourself."

Jack smiled.

"See Ford, you've been dead for weeks if you think about it right. Since the moment my boy's car sent you into the loch. That was you dead then. It's all just been confused until now. But I'll see you right."

Jack bent over and pulled Lorna's blankets in the direction of the hole in the ground.

"Want to give me a hand with her?" said Jack.

Thomas Ford watched the bird-faced man drag the girl's body across the earth. It was true that he had felt like a ghost since the day the car went into the water. The bird-faced man bent and embraced the long, blanketed form of the girl. Inside the blankets Lorna struggled, but her arms and legs were trapped too tightly by the folds of cloth. The bird-faced man lifted her off the ground. It looked to Thomas Ford like a weird dance. He felt an intruder, to be seeing it. He wished it would all stop without him having to do anything. He looked away from the man and the blankets. He looked down the hill at the vibrating headlights. They were doing a beautiful dance too. As Thomas Ford watched them out of his eye he heard a heavy thud behind himself. He didn't turn to look. He heard the unmistakable sound of a shovel being stamped into loose earth. He heard Jack McCallum breathe deeply and grunt as he turned his torso and dropped the first drizzly splash of loose earth on the blankets. It seemed such an old sound to Thomas Ford, as though he had heard it every day of his life. In reality he had only been to three funerals. *Ashes to ashes. Dust to dust. In the sure and certain hope...*

Thomas turned to watch Jack shovelling the earth onto the girl. Thomas had missed Lea's funeral. He had been asleep at the hospital. They called it a coma but it was just being asleep. It was only different to being asleep when you tried to wake up. Thomas had been trying to wake up ever since. He was still trying. The shovel bit into the earth with such a harsh sound.

"I thought I saw gas one day up here," said Thomas Ford. "It was the day Lea died. I saw a butterfly too, a white butterfly. I saw it again tonight. The gas and the butterfly."

Jack McCallum didn't appear to be listening. He shovelled earth steadily onto the blankets, taking care to distribute the first layer evenly, from the girl's head to the girl's toes.

"I knew I was leaving her in the car," said Thomas Ford.

He laughed bitterly and bent his neck. He looked down at his bare feet. He shook his head.

"We'd been arguing for months. Two years. It was no good I suppose. But I loved her. Except I swam through the windscreen and left her."

Thomas Ford raised his eye and stared at Jack McCallum's bent shoulders.

"If I really loved her I wouldn't have left her, would I?"

His single eye blinked. Jack McCallum paused in his shovelling. He looked up at Ford from where he stood in the girl's grave. He jabbed his shovel deep into the pile of ground that was level with his belly. He rested his forearms on the shovel handle and looked pensively at Ford out of dark, soft eyes.

"I love Cathy and my boy," said Jack McCallum. "But I've always had the feeling it would have shown I loved them better if I did leave them. I'm not good to them. I'm not good to anybody."

Jack shrugged and raised his eyebrows. Thomas Ford saw Jack lift his foot in the grave and place it on the thin layer of

The Survival of Thomas Ford

earth that ran the length of the girl's blankets. Jack's foot seemed to pressure down on where the girl's chest would be.

"Take this one here eh?" said Jack. "She turns up at my office this morning, telling me something's up. I'd have been happy to co-operate with her, you know that? I even offered her a job. I could understand she was fed up with that cleaning job up at the hospital so I says to her, hey, come and work for me Lorna! That was me trying to be good to someone, see?"

Jack spat on the earth beside his foot.

"And look how it's ended up. All because she was greedy. People think I'm a greedy man myself, but that's no it, no, I've just been working for the future, that's all it was."

Jack looked down.

"Aye, OK, that's maybe all this lassie was doing, trying to lay something down for her future, but…"

Jack looked up at Ford.

"The mistake she made was she tried to steal it from *my* future eh? That was the fucking mistake."

Jack wrapped his fists round the shovel handle again. He pulled it out of the mound of earth, shifted it to the side, then drove the blade deep into the pile. He pulled back the new scoop of dark earth and flung it across the now almost buried girl.

The buzz of the Subaru's engine was getting louder in the distance.

Jack twisted his torso to stare downhill at its tiny, bobbing headlights.

Chapter Forty-five

The Subaru was devouring the hillside. Jimmy was impressed. The Pole seemed to be pulling something terrible out of the vehicle's engine, something beyond the scope of metal, oil and fuel.

"I think you're going to beat the record," Jimmy's new, quiet voice said from the passenger seat. "Me and Robert got almost all the way to the caravan a few weeks ago. The day the woman went into the loch. The Volvo's a good car for a mission like this eh? Subaru's good too mind."

Lanski turned quickly to look at Jimmy. Saliva had seeped from the edge of Jimmy's mouth and shone in the reflected headlight glare. Lanski thought it was blood for a moment, then he turned to face the hill again. There was a surge of cleansing energy within the Pole's kidneys as he thrashed the Subaru's power out against the hill's gradient. The car's broad nose lurched in the air. On the right, the abandoned tractor and van were coming up fast. Jimmy looked past Lanski's long nose and out the driver's window. He saw the corroded wheel arch on the tractor's near-side.

"That's all like sculpture eh?" said Jimmy.

He laughed.

"All them vehicles like, it's no like an accident at all eh?"

The Subaru engine screamed.

"*Whoooo*," went Jimmy weakly.

The Survival of Thomas Ford

A grinding, horrible sound came from the engine. Jimmy shook his head.

"No, man, we got higher with the Volvo. No kidding. You'll see our tracks maybe. We parked up here all that night."

Jimmy remembered the cold air on his back as he'd danced here in Lorna's boots, the white butterfly dancing with him invisibly in the utter darkness before Robert had spoiled it, turning on the headlights. Jimmy had known the butterfly was there dancing with him by the brush of its wings against his naked body. He hadn't known it was a butterfly. It hadn't mattered to him if it was a butterfly or a ghostly mouth, the dance had been all that mattered. Now it seemed the dance was nearly done.

The Subaru lost all momentum and came to a stop. Lanski pulled the handbrake up hard. His long wrist reached up to the ignition key as Jimmy watched. It seemed to take years for the Pole's hand to turn the key. When the engine died there was not the pure silence that Jimmy had expected. The generator's roar penetrated the Subaru's shell. It was only then that Jimmy consciously noticed the area of light further up the hill, where the caravan was.

Jimmy frowned, then smiled.

"My dad's generator, I've not seen that going since I was wee! That's mad, man, that old thing still going."

Jimmy turned to look at Lanski. The front of the Pole's face was pale from the headlights, but the side of his ear was silver from the moon.

"We should have stayed here to live, you know that, Lanski? My dad was going to build a house for us up here. It's a strange place, man."

"Your father is crazy now boy. Like an old, white wolf." Lanski sniffed. "This place is like where I grew up, boy, in

Poland. My grandmother had an old house in the forest there."

Jimmy blinked, staring at Lanski's ear. It was easier to keep staring at the ear than he felt it would be to turn his head to face the front again.

"Were there wolves there?" said Jimmy.

Lanski nodded.

"What did you do with them?"

Lanski frowned.

"We left them alone, if they left us alone."

Lanski looked at the McCallum boy's face. It seemed one side of the boy's face had become slack, the mouth and eye had started to hang low on one side as though the boy's face had melted there.

"Can you walk, boy?" said Lanski.

Jimmy tried to shrug. He couldn't be sure whether his shoulders had actually moved or not. Lanski stepped out of the Subaru, onto the angled track. He walked uphill and across the beam of the headlights. He opened Jimmy's door and leaned over. He undid the seatbelt and placed a palm against the wet material wrapped around Jimmy's wound. His hand came away hot with Jimmy's blood.

"Come on," said Lanski.

He held one of Jimmy's hands and lifted the boy by the shoulder of his jacket, until Jimmy was standing shakily on the hillside path.

"I don't know man," said Jimmy in a whisper that Lanski only just caught over the wind. "I feel pretty funny, man. My feet feel funny. I can't feel my feet like."

Jimmy laughed breathily.

"I know I'm standing on them like, but I can't feel them."

"Walk on them anyway," said Lanski.

The Survival of Thomas Ford

He put an arm round the boy's waist, careful to keep his hand and arm off the wound. They moved slowly up the hillside, in the Subaru's headlight beam. Lanski was carrying most of the boy's weight. The roar of the generator grew louder and more insane with each awkward step the Lanski-Jimmy three-legged beast made up the hillside. They passed beyond the range of the Subaru's headlights and into a moonlit zone. Jimmy and Lanski both watched Jimmy's feet which made odd, floppy movements as the boy tried to keep walking on the hillside. Lanski's arm, supporting the boy's weight, felt leaden already. Dragging Thomas Ford had drained that arm's power for tonight. Jimmy looked up and saw the perimeter of the generator lights. Through the trees ahead he saw the shape of the aluminium caravan.

"There's our home man," said Jimmy.

Lanski couldn't hear him over the wind and the generator. He leaned his head closer to the boy's mouth.

Jimmy nodded and kept looking at the caravan.

"There were cats under us," he said. "It was warm in the winter man. No-one's thought of that yet eh? Only my dad. Cats under the floor."

Lanski looked at the boy's laughing, twisted face. The boy's weight seemed to have doubled. There was no way to get him much further. Lanski looked at the caravan's shell and headed them towards it.

The generator was screaming by the time Lanski leaned the boy's weight against the aluminium and let him go. Jimmy's body twisted as he slid down and landed on his side in the dead leaves by the caravan's base of raised brick. Lanski watched him look around for a few seconds, confused. Then Jimmy arched his back, dug into the ground with his feet, and levered himself until he was sitting up against the side of the caravan. The space in the bricks at the caravan's base, where the cats had gone in and out, was just by Jimmy's hand. Jimmy looked at the space as though he expected to see a cat come out. He shifted his hand jerkily and poked it into the dark hole.

Jimmy blinked and looked up at Lanski. He swallowed.

"There's nothing you can do," said Jimmy. "No-one could ever do anything about my dad."

Lanski couldn't hear over the generator. He squatted down beside the boy and looked at his mouth.

Jimmy shook his head.

"I danced naked in the pure darkness with a white butterfly, just down there man. I had Lorna's boots on. Robert saw me."

Lanski watched Jimmy's face as the boy laughed. Lanski looked away, and up, towards the moon. He stood abruptly and walked across to the generator. He pressed his thumb against the fat button and the engine came to a stop with a last, slow grinding whir.

"You stay here, boy," said Lanski. "I go and see then, if you're right, that nothing can be done about your father."

Jack McCallum stopped shovelling and stared down the hillside at the silence and darkness where the generator lights had been.

"There was enough petrol for hours," said McCallum to Ford. "Maybe the old thing gave up finally after all these years eh?"

Jack smiled and shrugged.

"I should get a new one anyway. All I have to do is steal one off one of my own sites."

Jack laughed in the moonlight.

The Survival of Thomas Ford

"You're a strange man, Ford. You left your wife to die in a car and you're still whining about it. But here you are watching me burying your new woman and you do nothing."

Thomas Ford's mouth opened and worked silently for a moment. Jack McCallum shook his head. He dug the shovel hard into the pile of earth at his shoulder.

"What do you do for a living, Ford, if you don't mind me asking?"

Ford did not answer.

"I don't think you work with your hands, Ford, do you? That's the trouble, there's too many folk around these days who don't ever make anything real with their own two hands. It makes you a baby your whole life, that sort of thing. You have to get a feel, like, for the earth and the stones and that. It makes you sleep better at night. I'll sleep well tonight, see, after this."

Jack sprayed a thin layer of loose soil across the girl from one end of her to the other. Thomas Ford stared. The blankets were gone now, hidden by the earth. Ground was being laid down on ground now, covering the girl. She was gone already.

Thomas Ford let out a low moan as he stared at Jack McCallum's face.

Jack looked back at Ford in the silver light and grinned.

Down the hillside, in the darkness among the tight-packed trees, Lanski stopped walking as Thomas Ford's low wail travelled through the air toward him. The sound seemed pitched at some perfect frequency that stole Lanski's energy and left him weak and shaking as he stood. Not far from him, the gang of feral cats sank their bellies to the earth and hissed as the sound reached their more sensitive ears and souls.

Lanski blinked in the darkness. Another sound came down the hillside. It seemed to Lanski like the sound of earth being broken by a shovel. He focused on the sound's direction and began walking again through the leaves. A clearing appeared ahead, moonlit and open. Lanski hesitated, then walked into the light there.

The cats saw him appear, from their hiding place in the trees, a tall, pale spirit he seemed to them, as he travelled through the open area.

Lanski stopped halfway across the clearing and stood to listen again. The wind picked up for a second, then Lanski nearly cried out at what felt like a kiss on his cheek. He flung up a hand wildly. He blinked and stared around the air above his head. The kiss came again and this time Lanski saw the butterfly. He put his hand down. The boy had said something about a butterfly. Lanski's grandmother had made him listen, again and again, telling him that she had believed his father had come back to her, often, as a white butterfly, following her and staying with her as she walked in the forest alone. Lanski had only half-listened to the old woman, but he remembered her words now. Lanski's eyebrows raised and his lips parted as he watched the butterfly dance in the moonlight above him. He began to take a step forward but the creature darted towards his face so suddenly that Lanski felt forced to move back. He could still hear the regular and unmistakable sound of earth being shovelled further up the hill. But the idea had come into Lanski's mind now that the butterfly was not only a butterfly and that it was warning him. Warning him not to go further. Lanski stood in the clearing, shaking his head, trying to get the idea out of his mind. It was not his own idea, it was an idea of his grandmother's. She was dead, like her cat, Ixor, both of them buried in another country, on another continent.

The Survival of Thomas Ford

Their bones should be silent now, not interfering with things so far away from themselves. But they did interfere. Lanski wasn't sure now. He remembered Ford telling him not to come back here.

He had probably killed McCallum's son, taking him here, instead of to a hospital.

If he kept on going, what else could happen?

The sound of the shovelling filled Lanski's ears as he stared at the white creature's floating, vibrant dance.

The shovel was starting to hurt Jack McCallum's hands now, at the palms and the area between thumb and forefinger. How long had it been since he'd done any real work? Maybe not since the last time he had to come out here and bury someone. Was it getting old or just getting soft that was making him like this? Jack couldn't tell. He had waited for Ford to do something, to stop him, but Ford was obviously broken, just like Shandlin had gone as he watched his own grave being dug. Jack could understand it better tonight than ever before, the thin membrane that existed between who you were and what you could crumble into. Jack knew it didn't take much and it didn't take long. Even before the trouble with Jimmy, Jack had felt something weakening at his centre. It had been the butterflies that started it, they had been getting to him gradually. The butterflies and the gas. When Ford talked about the butterfly and the gas a few minutes ago, Jack had ignored it and pretended not to care, but his gut had twisted. Someone else then had seen it. It wasn't just an illusion in Jack's brain. It was real. They were all over the hillside now, these white butterflies. It wasn't like the cats that might be out there. If the cats were out there, then Jack knew why they were there, he knew he had brought them. But the white butterflies were another matter. Jack knew there had been none here until he buried the first body.

The gas was even worse. The gas was coming up from the earth exactly where the bodies had been buried. Jack had seen it and gone to the library, then later on the computer, looking for information about bodies and gas, but everything he read told him that it was impossible for gas to be emitted this long after the burials.

Jack had seen hazing in the air over the grave of the Irish builder from twenty years ago, down by the abandoned tractor, he had seen that the last time he came out here. It was gas, like Ford said. And the butterflies seemed to be attracted to the gas.

McCallum paused, with a shovelful of earth held heavy and ready to throw on the girl's mound. He looked up at Ford. He could see tears on the man's cheek, under the eye that still worked.

"You shouldn't take it personally Ford. That's what I think I've learned after all these years. I mean, you didn't choose to drive your car into the loch eh? No, it was my boy that made you do that. I don't think we choose much eh? Not really. This is all..."

Jack stood straight and waved the shovelful of earth around in front of himself, in a gesture that seemed to include the grave, the girl, the moonlight, and the whole tree-laden hillside.

"It's all, sort of, impersonal eh? That's how it seems to me."

Jack shrugged. He smiled.

"My wife's probably waiting for me at home right now. Well, she will be. Cathy. She'll be awake and worrying about me, and about my boy."

The Survival of Thomas Ford

Jack felt tears in his own eyes suddenly. He realised he should probably not have spoken, not until he was finished burying the girl.

"I think my boy's dying, Ford. Someone put a knife in him tonight."

Jack swallowed.

"But there's nothing I can do. I've got my hands full here eh? With this. I don't think it's fair. I worked my whole life."

Jack shook his head.

"There's people who..." Jack started to say.

He sniffed.

"I don't know Ford eh? It's a hard world right enough."

Jack felt weak suddenly, at the knees. He let his legs bend until he sat on the shelf of earth that was the edge of the girl's grave. He looked down at the shovel in his hands. He tilted the handle until the soil ran off the blade in a dry cascade.

Thomas Ford looked up when he heard the grains sprinkle on the earth that already covered the girl. Both his eyes hurt. The one he could still see out of hurt the most. He watched Jack McCallum sitting slumped on the edge of the grave. He felt some sensation, a tingling warmth, come back into his hands which had been numb, as he watched McCallum.

"I do work with my hands," said Ford. "I draw."

There was a rustling in the trees nearby. A cat screeched. Jack grinned. He looked up at Ford.

"I knew they were still here," he said. "The cats. Little bastards eh? Must be hard as nails, living up here. Just shows you."

Jack looked down again, at the empty shovel blade.

"If I'd known it would all end like this," said Jack, "I don't think I'd have ever bothered starting. No, not just for this. I must have gone wrong somewhere along the way. Or maybe right at the start."

The leaves rustled again and Lanski stepped out into the moonlit clearing. He saw the open grave and McCallum sitting perched on its edge. He saw Thomas Ford crouched naked on the earth, like a long bird, not far from the grave. In the silver light, Thomas Ford looked to Lanski like a terrible, deformed angel that had had its wings ripped away.

McCallum raised his eyes from the shovel blade, turned his head and saw his foreman standing there. He looked to Lanski's side, and then stared at the area behind Lanski, the border of the trees. He waited for his son to appear in the clearing. He licked his lips and looked at Lanski's long face. He saw Lanski's moonlit eyes and looked down quickly, back at the empty shovel blade.

"Did you leave Jimmy at the car?" said Jack.

"I left him at the caravan," said Lanski.

Jack looked up, not at Lanski but at Ford.

"This is the man I trusted most in the world," said Jack. "This is my foreman, Lanski. I trusted him with all my houses and with the future. I trusted him with my family and tonight I trusted him with my boy. You've got to trust somebody. That's what I thought."

Somewhere in the trees a cat hissed.

"I thought…" said Jack.

He looked all round the moonlit clearing, as though at the spaces in between Ford and Lanski. He seemed to look everywhere now except at the two men who were with him.

"It can't all have been for nothing," said Jack.

He gave out an odd, short, barking laugh that echo-ed among the trees.

"That wouldn't make any sense," said Jack.

He stared hard at Ford now, as though willing him to disagree.

The Survival of Thomas Ford

"Would it?" growled Jack.

Lanski had his eyes on the layer of earth in the grave.

"Where is the girl?" he said.

Jack spun his head to look at Lanski sharply.

"Where is my *son*?" he shouted.

Lanski blinked.

"I told you. I left him at the caravan. You should go to him."

Ford's single eye was a frozen sphere in the moonlight. He rose from his crouch, stood straight, and walked across the clearing to the edge of the girl's grave. McCallum glared up at Ford's ruined face and naked, filthy chest. Lanski saw that McCallum's fists were tight and swollen where they gripped the wooden shovel handle. He could have been about to swing it at one of Ford's legs and bring him down like a tree. Jack's erect hairstyle looked like white grass in the moonlight. His eyes were loose and lost, already half of him had faded away now that he believed the future had been finally cancelled.

He turned to look at Lanski, as though to assure himself that Lanski was still there. A scream came from the grave, through the blankets and the earth. It filled the clearing. In the trees, cats jumped their whole bodies off the forest floor as though electrocuted, their paws twitching. Their fur stood stiff and hackled on their flesh at the sound. Jack looked down at the grave, his mouth quivering.

He stood quickly and raised the shovel high above his head. He screamed back at the grave, louder than the girl. Before he could bring the shovel down on her, Ford threw himself across the grave and grabbed McCallum around the chest. They landed together on the earth, as though in an embrace. McCallum's scream had ended, but the girl's continued. Lanski looked away from the entwined shape on the silver leaves that was Ford and McCallum. He went to the grave and kneeled at its edge. He leaned over and grabbed handfuls of earth, scooping away the ground that covered the girl. He threw them behind himself where they pelted against Thomas Ford's bare back and Jack McCallum's gaping mouth. Soon Lanski had exposed the shifting blankets. The girl's screams were louder now. Lanski got down into the grave with her. He picked away at the earth around the sides of the blankets. He tried to find an opening in the folds of cloth but the girl was sealed in. He moved more earth away from the blanket edges until he could get an arm down and underneath the girl's whole shape. He pulled up hard but there was still too much earth packing her in. He turned to look at McCallum and Ford. They seemed hardly to be moving. Lanski got his fists and clawed fingers dug further now into the soil around the far end of the blankets. He got both arms far under the girl and lifted her up and out of the earth. He laid her gently at the edge of the grave but she writhed and fought under the blankets.

"No!" shouted Lanski. "No, still girl! Still! You will fall yourself back in there! Still! It is alright now."

He tried to find a place to start unravelling her from. The cloth was thick and tangled.

"*That bitch is the one did all this!*" Lanski heard Jack McCallum scream.

McCallum let out a wail that cut across the clearing and into the ears of all the listening cats in the trees.

Lanski's long fingers had teased an opening in the blankets. He saw the girl's huge, bare breasts. He pulled at the material that surrounded her face until he saw wild, moonlit eyes staring back at him. The girl screamed again when she saw the Pole's face above her. Lanski nodded.

The Survival of Thomas Ford

"You alright," he said. "Not worry. It's safe now."

The girl's face and mouth were covered in snot and saliva, mixed with her tears and blood. Lanski knew she was recognising him as one of the men who had come into the house at Cromwell Drive and taken her away. She glared and pulled back from him, shuffling her blankets across the dead leaves. Lanski nodded and tried to put a smile on his face. He wanted to tell her that he understood she had been in the Valley of the Shadow alone for a long time and that he knew it would be very hard for her to return fully, perhaps ever. But even in Polish he would not have been able to say the words.

Jack McCallum screamed again into the night. Lanski stood and turned away from the girl. He walked towards the amalgamation of bare limbs and clothing that represented Thomas Ford and Jack McCallum's union on the earth. Thomas Ford seemed to have the builder and entrepreneur under control.

Lanski shouted, "*It's over!*"

Jack McCallum howled on the dead leaves. He lay with his cheek against the earth, Thomas Ford's weight pressing him there. He had meant to build a house and home for his family on this hill. Instead, all he had done was fill the ground with bodies. He had made the place barren except for gas emissions, butterflies and feral cats. Now the future was cancelled and his son was stabbed. Cathy would never forgive him. It was very likely he would never forgive himself. The Pole was right. McCallum Homes was over.

Lanski was never sure, later, if he knew the girl was coming from behind him or not. It might have been that he did know, somehow, that she was coming, but he allowed it to happen anyway. He certainly felt the wind off her as she came past his shoulder, naked, the shovel blade raised high. The blade came down and cut halfway through Jack McCallum's neck. Thomas Ford's single, glowing eye was blinded with a jet of silver blood. The girl gave forth a muted, shuddering groan when she saw what she had done. Lanski looked at her and saw that she wasn't going to move again. He walked to her side and put his hand around her hand. He took the shovel from her and looked down at his employer. McCallum was still trying to live on the leaves. The main thing Lanski and McCallum had always agreed on during their association on the city's sites was never to leave a job badly done or unfinished. They had an unspoken agreement that this was bad luck, bad karma, and simply bad business. Lanski blinked and raised the shovel. When he brought it down, Jack McCallum's white-haired head parted completely and cleanly from the rest of what he had been.

Chapter Forty-six

Lanski had put the pieces of Jack McCallum into the grave McCallum had meant for the girl. He was filling in the hole now, steadily. In the trees, the cats seemed to be moaning more regularly. Thomas Ford and Lorna were huddled together, sheltering from the wind, beneath the blankets that had been intended as her shroud.

Lorna listened to the shovel bite into the piled up soil. She watched the tall grave-digger working in the moonlight. She was trying to understand how she could have gone from visiting Jack McCallum's office this morning to blackmail him, to cutting his head off with that shovel the tall man was now using to fill in the grave. She turned to look at Thomas Ford's ruined face. His single eye seemed sightless as she looked at it.

"My grandmother's village had an old white wolf like this," said Lanski suddenly as he tilted the shovel to drop more ground on his employer. "For years it took the sheep and hens, the little that the people there had. When they kill it, my grandmother say they cut off the head and bury it in one place, and they bury the body in another place."

Lanski sniffed and pushed the shovel blade against the packed soil. He rested his weight on it and looked at Lorna and Thomas Ford over his long nose.

"So that the spirit wouldn't come back again," said Lanski. "In another wolf. You understand? It was only a superstition."

Lanski shrugged.

"But I not think of it when I bury him. Not worth digging him up again just for superstition. Let him lie whole."

"He was a fucking psycho," said Lorna, her voice shaking.

Lanski nodded.

"Yes. But he was a strong man, a big man, very big. In a country like this, and even in my own country now, these men are of the past, not needed. But there was great need for men like this, always before, even if they were crazy."

Lanski looked down at the grave.

"A man like he was, in another time," said Lanski, "he would be a great man. Here he could only make money and go mad I think."

Lanski raised the shovel again. He stepped out of the grave. He began to use the shovel to pat and slap at the earth. He scraped the ground with the metal edge, from east to west, from north to south. He picked up handfuls of leaves and twigs and scattered them across the site of Jack McCallum's grave. Soon there was no sign that anything had been done to the earth.

"There is still the boy at the caravan," said Lanski.

"Your head is bad," he said to Ford. "I take you to the hospital when I take the boy there."

"I'm not going back to hospital," said Thomas.

"You have to Thomas. Your eye…" said Lorna.

"I take you to the house or the hospital," said Lanski.

"Who is at the caravan? Is it the driver?" said Thomas.

"Aye, it's Jimmy," said Lorna.

She looked at the Pole.

"Just leave him here," she said. "Just get rid."

"Get rid?" said Lanski.

"Aye. Get rid of him."

The Survival of Thomas Ford

They walked down the hillside in the darkness between the trees. They could only see each other as shapes. They passed the pack of cats without knowing. Thomas Ford and Lorna supported each other's waists with their arms as they walked. Twigs and rough leaves scratched at the flesh of Lorna's bare, broken foot. For Lanski it was like being back in the forest near his grandmother's house, lost, at night, too frightened of what might be in the woods around him to shout for help from his grandmother at the house. Too frightened in case Ixor the cat might be at his shoulder waiting to steal the breath from his mouth if he dared to call out for help.

"I turned the generator off," said Lanski, "so I could hear where you were."

"Do you know which way we're going?" said Lorna.

Lanski sniffed.

"One of us will see the caravan," he said.

It was Lorna who saw its huge shadowed shape. As they got closer to the structure, Lanski saw that Jimmy's moonlit form was still there, leaning against the metal shell of the caravan.

Thomas Ford stared at the figure. He walked closer until he recognised the bird-like features that had filled his soul since the moment he had seen that face above the red bonnet of the Volvo by the loch, just before the crash.

Thomas Ford saw Jimmy's eyes blink weakly.

"Dad," said Jimmy. "That you, dad? I got them man. I got them eh? Robert, and his mum. They'll no tell anyone anything eh. Dad?"

Jimmy tried to focus his eyes on Thomas Ford's moonlit head.

"You alright dad?"

Jimmy realised there were other people standing over him. Even through the blanket he recognised Lorna's thick thighs.

"You fucking bitch! What were you doing holding his hand eh? *Eh?* Grass."

Jimmy looked away from her and back to Thomas Ford.

"You're no my dad. Who are you?"

Jimmy turned to look at Lanski. He recognised the Pole's tall silhouette.

"Where's my dad eh Lanski? What's going on man?"

"Your father's dead boy," said Lanski.

Jimmy shook his head.

"Uh uh," he said. "There's none of yous could kill my dad eh. Lorna eh? Help me eh?"

Lorna shook her head and looked down. Jimmy turned his eyes on Ford again.

"What kind of fucking scarecrow's this eh?" hissed Jimmy. "What are you doing sharing a blanket with the cunt eh?"

Jimmy's eyes seemed to harden in the moonlight. There was something familiar about the broken face and head poking over the top of the thick blanket. Jimmy shook his head slowly as he stared at the single silver-glistened eye that was watching him from above.

"Ford? No fucking way," said Jimmy. "Get your paws off her man eh? Fuck's sake, your own wife's in the loch no? So get your hands off my woman eh?"

Lorna watched as blood oozed suddenly and thinly from the edge of Jimmy's mouth. Jimmy seemed to gulp and hiccup. His face looked surprised for a second, before hate twisted his features again.

"Get your hands off her!" Jimmy screamed.

He pushed his head back against the side of the caravan and tried to lever his body from the earth. There was no power left in him. He looked up to the sky and screamed, "*Dad!*"

The Survival of Thomas Ford

Then Jimmy was silent and looked down suddenly, his gaze seemed to take in all of them, his witnesses.

He looked directly into Thomas Ford's eye.

"It was just an accident man. Atoms. Atoms and that. Chaos eh?"

Jimmy started to laugh on the forest floor. The wind blended with the boy's laughter and amplified it. The trees bent toward the boy's laughter, gathered it to themselves and echo-ed it. The listening cats quivered and twitched.

Thomas Ford felt a wet surge at the centre of himself as he looked down at the boy and the laughter rang in his mind like an acid bell. That black-eyed, laughing bird head. The head that had haunted him and changed the course of his life. Thomas Ford collapsed suddenly on the forest floor, kneeling near Jimmy's feet.

"Thomas!" cried Lorna.

The pain came into Thomas Ford's chest, the great beast chewing there. Thomas Ford let himself lie on the leaves, waves of pain coursing from his head to his chest, back and forth. Lorna crouched beside him and held his shoulder and neck in her hands. Lanski stood and waited, his eyes on their long shadow-shapes.

"Thomas," Lorna said again.

She turned to look at Lanski.

"I think it's the thing that happened to him at the house today. He gets pain in his chest. I don't think it's his heart. The doctors said it's in his head. I don't know. I waited today and he got better."

Lanski said nothing. He was thinking he could have had his passport and debit card and been on his way home by now. But then this girl would have been in his head for the rest of his life as a ghost. Better to only have her and the man as an inconvenience a while longer than have ghosts. Lanski was already thinking of the new problem that would come now. McCallum gone, and then Lanski gone. They would blame him. They would look for him. He had better take his wife and children far into the forests of his childhood when he did get home, and stay lost there forever. He could get hens and goats perhaps. Some people still lived like that and seemed alright. It would not be the life he had worked for or his mother had dreamed of for him, but it could still be alright. Especially after seeing, through the builder McCallum, the rich man's life up close.

Ford's breathing was beginning to steady on the forest floor. The regulation of the man's breath gave Lanski fresh hope. If this man Ford could survive, then so could he.

"It will be alright," said Lanski.

"He's better now," said Lorna.

Thomas Ford's dark shape sat up on the thick leaves.

"I'm alright," he said.

Thomas Ford looked at Jimmy's head again.

It was strange to see the head without the red car bonnet beneath it and the square-jawed passenger's head beside it.

They all turned to look at Jimmy's head as they realised his laughter had stopped.

They saw that the boy was dead.

To Thomas Ford, it seemed Jimmy's sightless eyes and frozen, grinning face regarded the moon as though in appreciation of some great joke.

Lanski started walking away immediately, on his way to get the shovel.

Thomas Ford and Lorna held each others hands tightly, as a cold wind found its way up the hill, through the trees, and into their ears.

The Survival of Thomas Ford

The wind shrieked like a roaming spirit, suddenly returned home to find these intruders on its peace.

After Lanski had buried Jimmy by the caravan's brick base, he drove Thomas Ford and Lorna down the hill in the Subaru. When they passed the corner where Lea had gone into the loch, Thomas Ford's single eye lingered on the surface of the rippling water as the moonlight sparkled.

Soon the Subaru had taken them all back to the city and the hill was only a ghost, full of its own ghosts. It couldn't reach them or hurt them any more.

Lorna turned to look at Thomas Ford.

His single eye glowed orange from the rays of a traffic light overhead.

Lanski let his foot up off the clutch and the Subaru spurted forward into the bands of traffic that girdled the city from the surrounding darkness.

Later that night, the cats came out of the forest and arranged themselves on Jack McCallum's grave like long-lost, abandoned rags.

They slept and purred through the night, a thick blanket of fur and flesh insulating Jack McCallum from the cold wind that whistled above.

The next morning a golden sun shone down on the hill, making the caravan's blue-and-white aluminium shell glisten.

Just beside the caravan's brick base, a white butterfly danced over the ground.

It soared and plummeted, dived and swerved, moving into, out of and around the shimmering, hallucinatory haze of strange gas that rose from the earth where Jimmy was buried.

John A. A. Logan

The butterfly hovered briefly, dipped once, became absolutely still for a long moment, then veered off fast to the east, a fluid blur of whiteness that vanished suddenly against the sun.

About John A. A. Logan

John A. A. Logan is the author of six novels.

His fiction has been published by Picador, Vintage, Edinburgh Review, Chapman, Northwords, Nomad, Secrets of a View, and Scratchings; with reviews and features of his work in the *Northern Times*, the *Inverness Courier*, the *Highland News, Northwords Now, Scottish Studies Review, Scotland on Sunday, The Spectator,* and *The Hindustan Times*.

His work has been published worldwide in paperback anthologies edited by A L Kennedy, John Fowles, Ali Smith, Toby Litt; and he has been invited to read his work at the Edinburgh International Book Festival.

He wrote monthly columns and film reviews for the magazine, 57 North, in Aberdeen, where he was also president of Aberdeen University's Creative Writing Society for three years, while attaining his MA (Hons) English degree there, which included study under the novelist, William McIlvanney.

You can follow John A. A. Logan on

www.johnaalogan.com

twitter.com/johnaalogan

authorselectric.blogspot.co.uk